# HOOFBEATS OF THE APOCALYPSE

Produced by Leo Arland

Author of: -

*'The Exit Machine'*

**Availability**

Paperback Version
http://www.lulu.com/spotlight/arland

Also available on Amazon and Amazon Kindle

# HOOFBEATS OF THE APOCALYPSE

**(Creative Works Exploring the Relationship between the Decay of Western Civilization, the Impact of Social Darwinism and the Growing Turmoil in the Middle East)**

Proverbs 29:18a
*"Where there is no vision people cast off all restraint"*

Thought Starter
*We have gone the way of Ancient Rome but now the barbarians are bred from within*

## Leo Arland

This document was: -

First compiled from June-August 2009

Released onto the Internet in December 2010

Re-titled January 2011

Revised February-March 2011

Prepared for publication in book form, April 2011

Further revised September-November 2011

Further revised October-December 2013

Released for International Distribution, May 2014

# Contents

# Dedication

*'Hoofbeats of the Apocalypse'* is a tribute to the memory of Malcolm Muggeridge (1903-1990) and Francis Schaeffer (1912-1984) who rightly predicted the collapse of western civilization. Both men saw what was coming. Also to Thomas Stearns Elliot (1888-1965) whose poem *'The Wasteland'* provided much inspiration and to Dr Samuel Johnson (1709-1784) who provided an example of creativity amidst great personal affliction.

It is dedicated to those who think for themselves and who stand apart from the crowd.

It's further dedicated to those future historians wishing to study the madness of the early twenty first century.

Also, to my own descendents so that they will understand the *'Age'* in which I lived.

However, most importantly of all, *'Hoofbeats of the Apocalypse'* is dedicated to *'the girl in the photograph'* who gave me the motive to complete this piece during what was a very difficult period.

## Preface

To read *'Hoofbeats of the Apocalypse'* is to encounter the growing madness and decadence of the early twenty-first century. It's a work that truly reflects *'the spirit of the age,'* clearly depicting the downward spiral of western society (and perhaps the whole of the world). It uses many literary forms to convey the experience of living in a *'culture of death,'* characterized by relationship breakdowns, a reduced capacity for rational thinking and the abandonment of all moral restraints. Chillingly portrayed is the type of mentality that could all too easily lead to the rise of a *'mass extermination'* society. Insight will have been gained into how this development could ever have come about in once civilized nations.

*'Hoofbeats of the Apocalypse'* is designed to provoke thought and to challenge the reader – with humorous intermissions to provide light relief. It offers a broad understanding of why things in this present day and age are turning out the way they are. Its aim is to better equip the reader to avoid the popular lies of our time; *e.g.* that people can break all moral boundaries and <u>not</u> expect to receive some very painful consequences in return. Ours is a *'live for today'* society where longer term consequences are rarely taken into consideration.

As a writer I aim to explore the mentalities and social pressures which could contribute to the rise of a *'mass extermination'* society. Where possible I write, not as a detached observer but as an active participant in some of the developments described here. I have no wish to pontificate from a distance about such vital issues as the death of Christian Britain, the rise of the New Age Movement or the growing madness in our society. In these matters, to be involved is to understand. I've also deliberately gone out of my way to explore subjects like anti-Semitism that most contemporary poets and writers would prefer to avoid. This is because I take the view that there is a need to explore such matters in a creative and original manner. I am not one of those writers who want their readers to drift into a magical fairy land. Instead, my emphasis is upon helping them to engage with some very grim realities. What may be termed a *'social realist'* approach is consistently followed.

Portrayed is a world in the throes of a cultural, techno-economic and spiritual revolution – all leading humanity into a *'New Age.'* This is totally different from *'the Aquarian Age'* anticipated in the 1960's musical *'Hair'* and also by a succession of esoteric writers and teachers from the late nineteenth to early twenty-first century.

A number of interwoven themes lie embedded within *'Hoofbeats,'* the most prominent of which is the fracturing and breakdown of Western Civilization. Such a negative cultural development has already impacted upon other major trends, including Globalization, the rise of religious fanaticism in the Middle East, the revival of virulent forms of anti-Semitism and the collapse of Christianity in its former heartlands of Europe and America. It has also emphasized the fact that the veneer of civilization is only ever skin deep and, with certain restraints removed, it becomes all too possible for psychologically normal people to commit (or acquiesce in) the worst types of atrocity. Becoming an accomplice to mass murder is easy.

Another important theme is the ongoing tension between the world views of Eastern Monism (represented in the religions of Hinduism, Buddhism and Taoism), Semitic Monotheism (represented in Judaism, Christianity and Islam) and Western Materialism (represented by the secular ideologies of free market capitalism, sexual libertarianism and Marxist-Leninism). Each world view is riddled with internal conflicts, so lessening the chance of any of them co-existing in relative harmony. Due to worsening economic and environmental conditions the conflicts between (and within) these worldviews will help create that lawlessness which in time, will fuel a demand for a New World Order (NWO). The enticing bait of peace and prosperity will be the NWO's main *'selling point.'* This *'order'* will eventually be headed by a hugely popular charismatic politico-religious leader who will embody all of its aspirations to build a better world. Carried to power on a wave of emotion he will wish to seduce the majority of the world's population into following him. They will be led on a path which will appear to be right but will end in the near-destruction of humanity.

'Hoofbeats of the Apocalypse' has drawn upon a variety of sources (listed in the Bibliography), the most notable of which have been The Books of Jeremiah and Revelation in the Bible, the works of Shakespeare, the Dictionary of Doctor Samuel Johnson, T. S. Elliot's 'The Wasteland' and the writings of Malcolm Muggeridge, Francis Schaeffer and Alexander Solzhenitsyn. Equally deserving of citation are the psychological studies of Stanley Milgram and Philip Zimbardo and also Laurence Rees's probing examination of mid-twentieth century totalitarianism. Another source of inspiration has been my own participation in different cultural venues which have provided opportunities to 'test out' some of this work. Mention must also be made of a visit two of my sons and I made to Auschwitz Birkenau, on Friday, 7th October 2011. During this heart-wrenching visit I concluded that those factors which had led to such a diabolical development <u>need to be challenged at an early stage;</u> by the time an 'Auschwitz' emerges it's far too late to remedy the situation; millions of lives will already have been lost. The times in which we now live are perilous in the extreme. Vaguely hoping that things will 'get better' all on their own will not suffice. Instead, raw courage, patient endurance and a willingness to deal with the obvious 'wrongs' in society will all be needed as the future we face will not be for the fainthearted.

**The Author, Thursday, 1st May 2014**

# THE SHATTERING

**(A Creative Exploration of the Death of Western Civilization – a Post Modern Sequel to T. S. Elliot's Poem *'The Waste Land'*)**

**Psalm 11:3**
*"If the foundations be destroyed what can the righteous do?"*

**Thought Starter**
*Sometimes it is the duty of the writer to challenge popular social trends*

# Introduction

'*The Shattering*' is published as an updated sequel to T. S. Elliot's poem, *The Wasteland'* (written from 1919-1922 in the aftermath of the First World War). Just as *The Wasteland'* reflected the mental fragmentation of the modern world following the First World War *The Shattering'* reflects the (not too dissimilar) fragmentation present in today's globalized Post-Modern World. As readers may guess, the shattered glass in the opening scene is a metaphor for the cultural and psychological disintegration of Western Civilization. This series of fragmented mental images began to be written on Sunday, 7$^{th}$ June 2009 following a fascinating BBC2 '*Arena'* documentary concerning the life and work of the poet T. S. Elliot. I'd been particularly gripped by a reading of his poem, *The Wasteland.'*

Further fragments were continually added to *The Shattering'* until March 2014. These reflected some of the momentous changes which have taken place since June 2009. Details of their composition have been placed as footnotes to the main body of this work. They show how *The Shattering'* was built up over the course of just over four years. Fragments deemed too large to be inserted into this present collection have been adapted and placed in the Section entitled *Broken Shards.'*

The author does <u>not</u> claim that his ability in poetry comes close to that of T. S. Elliot, but he does believe that *The Shattering'* provides an equally faithful reflection of the cultural/sociological period in which it was written. It does for the world of 2014 what *The Wasteland'* did for the world of 1922. To read *The Shattering'* is to gain some idea of what it was like to have lived amidst the growing madness and decadence of the Western World during the early twenty-first century. Vividly portrayed, is the increasing madness of a culture completely severed from its spiritual and moral Judeo-Christian roots.

## *Part A: Broken Fragments*

### <u>Prelude</u>

Smash! Splinter! Crash!
Hear the sound of shattering glass
As a stolen lorry lurches headlong
Into a fashion boutique window
Hear its discordant Stockhausan[1] music play
As shards of glass
Fly and spin in every direction
Hear the whoop and shout
Of triumphant thieves
As their quick-gloved fingers
Strip coats
From fallen mannequins
All to be sold
On a furtive black market
Watch them jump
Into the street
And dive into a waiting van
Which roars off into
A rain-sodden night

Ten thousand
Glistening, glittering shards
Pulsate a feeble orange
Dimly reflecting
The overhanging neon lights
A reek of petrol
Fills the air as it
Drains away into the gutter
The alarm bell rings

---

[1] Stockhausan was a German composer (1928-2007) deeply criticised for his musical experimentation. Hearing a Stockhausan album at a friend's house during the late 1970's convinced me that it simply wouldn't be worthwhile repeating the experience.

But who will listen?

A shattering has occurred
A shattering of decency
A shattering of dignity
A shattering of every boundary
A shattering caused by
Cultural and spiritual death
The alarm bell continues to ring
But still no one listens

### Fragment 1: Migraine Ballet

A winter of misunderstanding
Has now descended
Reason lies abandoned
Conscience silenced
Common sense has ebbed away
Leaving in its wake a violent stupidity
*'Dumb, dumb and dumber'*

The unity of language has been broken
LOL 4U☺!!! LOLA ROB
The art of honest speech has died
The spoken word has little value
And all that remains is moronic grunts
Or the deceitful sound bites
Of professional misleaders
And the endless tapping of a text message

Behold a people
Who delight in stupidity
They do not see
The way of light

Dancing images
Perform a migraine ballet

On a flat wide-screen TV
Children look on
Gawping, open mouthed
But nothing is learnt

The latest broadband width
Opens up vistas to bright new worlds
And helps to revive old forms of wickedness
Whole generations dwell in darkened rooms and risk
Becoming hermits who do nothing
But lurk in front of PC screens
Imbibing the image pollution
That results from corporate collusion

MP's line-up
Before a Telegraph Guillotine
Dreading the afternoon four o'clock phone call
Which announces
*'Your expenses will be published in tomorrow's edition of 'The Daily Telegraph''*
Members of the public look on with foaming rage, realizing that,
*"They are greedy dogs*
*Who never have enough*
*They are all false shepherds*
*Who cannot understand*
*Unwilling to care*
*They all look to their own way*
*Everyone for his own gain*
*From every quarter'*[2]

*'Spin'* has replaced communication
And all trust has died
Soon public anger
Will be replaced
By public apathy

---

[2] Isaiah 56:11, slightly amplified

## <u>Fragment 2: Crime Statistic</u>

A shot echoes in the night
A net curtain twitches
A heart beats faster
*"Och! It's only the backfiring of a van'"*
Sighs a delicate old lady
As, from a small china cup
She sips tea
A relic of a bygone, more genteel age
When people had values
And a sense of
*'What was right and proper'*

Suddenly, outside her window
Loud incoherent obscenities can be heard
*'Disrespect'* is shown
A scuffle
A cry
A gurgle of death
As a knife is thrust
Into the vitals of a fifteen year old boy
With a pinched childlike face
A flailing of arms
A look of glazed horror
A bloodied body
Thumps leaden onto the pavement
Just another *'knife crime'* statistic to tally

A homebred barbarism
Has crossed the threshold
The age of enlightened atheism
Has descended into a new Dark Age

*'Eat your heart out'*
Dawkins, Dennett and Grayling[3]
This is your society with no God
You are damned by seeing the realization
Of your dreams

Behind white lace curtains
The elderly quake with fear
Complaining, *'This is worse than the Blitz!'*
One ninety year old D-Day Veteran
Hides his medals inside a metal case
Shaking his hoary white head, he sighs
And quietly murmurs
*'Did my pals die for this?'*

Outside, young boyish eyes
Stare unseeing into a clear night sky
Only the far distant stars are witness to this young boy's death
The police will take twenty minutes to come
Something about overstretched resources
In the morning his mother will weep
Still, she has six other mouths to feed
(Each *'fathered'* by a different man)
Soon people will forget
His life will have no epitaph

---

[3] Dawkins, Dennett and Grayling were leading proponents of a militant atheism during the early twenty-first century.

### Fragment 3: The Hula Hoop Girl

Observe the attractive twenty-something girl
Twirling hula hoops
Around her slender, elf-like body
All to advertise some
Glossy new technological product
In an Industrial Exhibition Hall
Look into her narcotic-glazed eyes
See the sadness lurking behind her
Infectious laugh
Notice the white, long sleeved blouse
Covering the razor cuts on her arms

Within a week she'll be dead
Overdosed on her prescribed drugs
Her infectious laughter silenced forever

### Fragment 4: Sleazy Jack

Sleazy Jack,
With dissipated face and sunken, hollow eyes
Clutches a cigarette pack
In the sweltering Discount Store
A heavy gold chain
Hangs around his gaunt neck
Queuing in front of the drinks counter
He boasts to all who will listen
About the many girls he's got pregnant
He's got AIDS but hey – no matter to him,
*'Yer just don't know what tomorrow will bring
its best t' live fer the moment!'*
Yes, Jack,
*'Eat, drink and be merry
For tomorrow you die.'*

### Fragment 5: Much Too Old

Four middle aged ladies
Stand near the corner of a suburban street
In blazing hot weather
They gossip about the men
They hope to meet
And about the relationships
That never did seem to work out

A pretty teenage girl
With long brown hair
Stands slightly apart from the gossiping huddle
Thinking, in red-faced embarrassment
*'Oh mum, you and your friends are much too old*
*For this sort of thing!'*

### Fragment 6: Mild Delirium

As a scorching hot June brings
Long daylight hours and
A mucous torment to hay fever sufferers
Who wheeze and sneeze in response to any light breeze
A poet's words are scribbled down
In a mild delirium

### Fragment 7a: Clear the Pool

*'Clear the pool!*
*Clear the pool!*
*It's time please!'*
A young acne-faced attendant cries out
His face watching a poolside clock
To see if it really is the end of the session
In meek obedience swimmers
Leave their chlorinated waterhole

## Fragment 7b: Clear the Area

*'Clear the area!*
*Clear the area'!*
A burley London Policeman shouts
His slab-like face brooking no contradiction
Cross him
And you risk
Lying dead in the road
Felled by a savage blow
It doesn't matter
That you were just a bystander
Passing through a demonstration
The Metropolitan Police
Will try their utmost to slander your character
At the Inquest

## Fragment 8a: Silently Sinking

The tatty white tabby
Hobbles up the concrete steps
An unneutered Tom
His right forepaw twisted into an awkward *'L'* shape
Known by council tenants as
*'Poorly puss,' 'Skippy'*
Or *'that damned stray'*
He lives off food provided
By kindly people
Yet his only true friend
Is an elderly black cat
With a strange, strangulated, spooky *'meow'*
Approach this beleaguered animal
And with frightened face
He'll limp away
Silently sinking below the step-line

### Fragment 8b: Against the Odds

A failed Prime Minister growls
Paranoid, in a bunker
As surviving ministers feign a dissembling loyalty
Behaving like eunuch courtiers
Seeking to preserve their own lives
In the palace of a mad Chinese Emperor

Against all the odds he fights on
A lonely gladiator
Smiting down all of his enemies
Who brandish rubber knives
Yet despite his stand
The jeering crowd
Are already giving him a *'thumbs down'*

Nearby, in a rival court
Etonian eunuchs of the right
Gather around a foppish cavalier
Whom they hope will take the mad old Emperor's place

Yet they'd better beware
In the 24/7 media amphitheatre
Many a good name has been slain
By the jackals of journalism
Who relish picking to pieces
Once *'respectable'* reputations

But do not worry,
Retribution will come
Some of the jackals will be devoured
By the media monster
They helped to create

Merciless is the press
When one of their own falls

### Fragment 9a: A Post-Modern Wasteland

A post-modern wasteland
Has been created
A poet's predictions
Are being fulfilled
All meaning has vanished
And all that remains
Is the conflict of
Opposing viewpoints

### Fragment 9b: No Answer in the Wind

The
Wind
Outside is
Blowing hard
There is no answer in it my friend

### Fragment 10: Post-Ginsbergian Howl[4]

Howl! Dawkins, Dennett and Grayling
Howl! You unholy trinity of scoffers
Howl! You failed champions of humanity
Howl! Weep and wail because your dream
Of a *'progressive secular and moral social order'*
Melts before the fires of reality
It shrivels and blackens before your eyes
*'The God of battles'* is back
To inflict a terrible vengeance
Howl! You titans of mockery
Howl, as you see dark religious passion
Tear the world apart with a pitiless hatred
Howl, as you see

---

[4] This is a reference to *'Howl'* (1956) a Beat Poem written by Alan Ginsberg. It criticised the emptiness of the materialism of post-war America.

The ruthless champions of a merciless Deity
Rush into the moral vacuum
Which <u>you</u> helped create

Howl! Howl! Howl!
As this wrathful God
Returns to wage *'Holy War'*
Against the decadence
Your atheism initially spawned

Let *'failed to deliver'*
Be the epitaph
Of the Secular-Humanism
You represented

## **Fragment 11: Would Abortion?**

Within a stench-filled high-rise flat
An abused child whimpers
Cowering before the blows
Of an angrily swearing
Tattoo covered step-father
Empty beer cans and heroine needles
Lie carelessly flung about on the floor
Soon he will be another *'failure'* for
The *'Caring Services'* to register
Would abortion have been a mercy?

In the flat next door
An old lady lies dead on the floor
Beneath the neatly arrayed china knick-knacks on her mantelpiece
She's been lying there for two months now
And already the maggots have spewed out of her body
Unlike her neighbours
She will not make the front pages
Of national newspapers

### Fragment 12a: The lack of Money

In the recession
Many are learning that
*'If money can't buy happiness*
*The lack of money can purchase a huge amount of misery'*

### Fragment 12b: Nothing Left

The larder is empty and nothing is left for the people

### Fragment 12bc: National Characteristics

When an *'economic downturn'* takes place the Greeks have a riot, the Spanish demonstrate and the French go on strike, but the British organize a party.

### Fragment 13a: Social Darwinism

When bankruptcy looms the desperate take their own lives, the weak take to drink and the strong take action.

### Fragment 13b: Shared fate

*"I say! I say! I say! What will flamboyant homosexuals and fundamentalist Christians have in common in a future society?"*
*"What will they have in common?"*
*"Both groups will be marked down for elimination."*

### Fragment 14: A Foppish Cavalier

A foppish Cavalier entered *'Number Ten,'* joined by his gang of Etonian chums. In response, a wounded bear retired to brood in his den – but did anything really change under the coalition of the effete?

### Fragment 15a: Complicit

The *'Left'* have betrayed their ideals
With their posturing anti-Zionism
They have become complicit
In an ancient hatred

They now champion a Fascism
Which their forefathers fought against in Spain

All principles have been abandoned
Angry cynicism alone remains

### Fragment 15b: Intellectual Honesty

When *'leftist'* protesters
On an *'anti-Zionist'* demonstration
Hold aloft placards carrying the slogan
*'Free Palestine!'*
They would be more honest
If they added the words
*'And kill all the Jews'*

### Fragment 16: When I See

When I see Jewish and Muslim children
Playing in the yards of their separate schools I weep
For what I see is fodder for a future holocaust
Can my poems
Save even
One of their lives?

### Fragment 17a: The Death of Christian Britain

In Canterbury
A Druid Warlock
Busily weaved a well-crafted web of deception

Speaking in sweetly reasonable tones
He lured many into his sticky embrace
When he cast a spell
He turned into a mitred chameleon
Who was *'all things to all men'*
(And women too)
His was the kiss of Judas

A *'safe'* corporate man became his successor

## Fragment 17b: Huddled

Seven elderly ladies
Huddled in a damp and crumbling Methodist Church
Living on the warmth conveyed by happy memories
When Sunday services were well attended
The Sunday school thriving
And Charles Wesley Hymns were sung with gusto

Six elderly ladies
Huddled in a damp and crumbling Methodist Church
One has passed away and the rest await the end
Memories of past glories will soon fade

Christian Britain is dead
Welcome to the *'mass extermination'* society

## Fragment 18: Abandoned

When faith in God has been abandoned
There are those who sigh with relief
There are those who sigh with regret
There are those who sigh with remorse
A few may snort in rage
But others will calmly think
*"Aha! There's a spiritual vacuum for me to fill"*

### Fragment 19: Atheistic Delights

What has Atheism brought us?

In the East it brought us
Black Marias, secret police, torture chambers and Gulags
It gave the world
Lenin, Stalin, Mao and Pol Pot

In the West it brought us
Sub-prime mortgages, financial *'bubbles'* and the *'Big Brother House'*
It gave the world
Ian Brady and Fred *'the Shred'*

In both East and West it brought us
Uncontrolled State expansion, a culture of death and
Economic failure
It gave the world
Polluted lakes, a reinforced class division and
A debasement of decency

To observe such fruit is to become an atheist about Atheism

### Fragment 20: Progress

The narrow intolerance of Theism
Led to Atheism
The moral emptiness of Atheism
Led to Monism
The lawless spirituality of Monism
Led to Nihilism
The destructive amorality of Nihilism
Led to mass death

Call that *'progress'* if you like

### Fragment 21: Conditioned

Pavlov's dogs
Are to be found in the *Big Brother House'*
Displaying a conditioned stupidity
One believes he <u>is</u> a dog and the other pretends to be a cat

### Fragment 22: Totals

$$E = MC^2$$

Hiroshima Death Total: 90,000–166,000

Nagasaki Death Total: 60,000–80,000

Future Middle East War Death Total:

### Fragment 23: Losing Hold

A suction tube is applied
A fetus loses its hold in the womb
And is sucked out in bits
Another unwanted object to be discarded into a wastebin
Another unwanted *'product'* of our consumer society

Yet if the child had lived
It may have become feral

### Fragment 24: Locust Bankers

All around lies a
Decaying, deceptive decadence
As fungi grows on dead wood
So does the queue of the unemployed
Who shuffle into newly
Computerized Job Centres
Which offer every service

Except employment
As mortgages are foreclosed
Locust bankers
With legally secure pensions
Fly into a golden Cayman Island sunset
A smug smile on their faces

### Fragment 25: Overtaxed

A decent, hardworking
But overtaxed people
Fear for their jobs
Mortgage payments
Are in arrears
And debts cannot be paid

The Englishman's home
Is only a paper castle
The tentacles of
An all-embracing State have smothered enterprise
Squeezing the life out of a people
Whose only crime
Was a heartfelt desire to better themselves

Tight-lipped bailiffs
Hammer at the door
Another family
Sinks into the mire
Of poverty

Our society has tried to live without truth
And now many perish through
*The inhuman power of the lie* [5]

---

[5] A phrase attributed to the Soviet writer Boris Pasternak (1890-1960) who lived through the Stalinist era of Russian Communism

### Fragment 26: Assisted Suicide

**Step 1:** allow assisted suicide to be normalised in the media
**Step 2:** allow assisted suicide for the terminally ill
**Step 3:** allow assisted suicide for the permanently disabled
**Step 4:** allow assisted suicide for the clinically depressed
**Step 5:** allow assisted suicide for seriously ill or disabled children
**Step 6:** allow assisted suicide to reduce government expenditure
**Step 7:** make assisted suicide a universal obligation
**Voila!** We have the *'mass extermination'* society

### Fragment 27: The Thunder of Hoofs

In dingy, terraced red-brick houses
A cancerous hatred
Begins to spread
Merciless men plot
A skin-shredding apocalypse
In each of their communities lies
Despair, disintegration and
The death of hope

Hear the thunder of hooves
The four apocalyptic horsemen
Are galloping over the horizon

### Fragment 28a: Grim Expectations

When a mob calls for
The death of some person or *'Party'*
Expect blood to flow

### Fragment 28b: Ending-up

There are two ways for violent revolutionaries to end-up in
concentration camps
If defeated – as inmates, if victorious – as guards

### Fragment 29: Events

A wise father often said
*'We are morally and spiritually bankrupt as a nation'*

Events have proved him right

Another wise old gentleman observed
*'People today have become incapable of logical thinking'*

Events have also proved him right

### Fragment 30: Tossed

Moral bankruptcy
Has given way to material bankruptcy
Well known High Street Stores have closed
And those who'd loyally worked for them
Are now tossed onto the streets

### Fragment 31: Natural Boundaries

Ominous grey skies
Bode rain-filled depressions
Their tumultuous downpours
Allow only a fitful sunlight to flicker through

The boundaries of nature
Have been broken
And a filthy brown torrent
Gushes through the streets
Flooding cellars and
Ground floor premises
A stinking, heartbreaking end
To many a business dream

### Fragment 32: Glaring

Dingy charity shops
Begin to fill
With impoverished customers
All looking for *'affordable bargains'*
Under glaring neon lights

### Fragment 33: Torn Asunder

We are a nation
Having broken down
The (once healthy) division between right and wrong
Now the boundaries of nature
Are also being torn asunder
Cursed is the land
Where homes and livelihoods
Perish under a cascade
Of filthy foaming waters

But...
Doubly cursed
Is the land
Where homes and livelihoods
Also perish
Under a mountain
Of government paperwork and
Bureaucratic regulations

### Fragment 34: Going

Going, going gone...

### Fragment 35: Unchanged Views

*'What is life*
*But a miserable game*
*We all play*
*And never win!''*
So I used to say
As a boy of 14
To the amusement
Of my classmates

Little has happened since then to change my view

### Fragment 36: Secular Prison

Shut in a secular prison
Many indeed have found that –
In the words of Thomas Hobbes[6]
Life has proved to be
*'Solitary, poor, nasty, brutish and short'*

### Fragment 37: Fun Time

*'Clear the pool!*
*Clear the pool!'*
It's now the end of the session
*'Fun Time'* is over

---

[6] An English philosopher, chiefly remembered for his seminal political work *'Leviathan'* (published in 1651). He lived from 1588 until 1679.

### Fragment 38: PC Gamesters

PC gamesters
Play their fantasy lies
Virtual reality
Has become their actual reality

But their understanding of reality
Has been shredded into
A thousand little pieces

False identities
Are eagerly assumed
On a website dreamscape

For them
Reality is illusion
And illusion is reality

Reality and illusion are one

### Fragment 39: Existential Despair

Hope is lost
As reason has been slain
A dark existential[7] despair holds on tightly
As the dream of progressive secularism
Is no more
In Britain *'Faith'* has died
And only a cold inhumanity remains

---

[7] A reference to the philosophy of existentialism that stresses the absurd meaninglessness of life in a world where God doesn't appear to exist

### Fragment 40: Prophet Pundit

An economist's forecasts of financial doom
Were long ignored
But come the *'Crash'* of September 2008
He became a pundit
Honoured with many a media interview
He now foresees the collapse
Of the unsustainable State[8]

### Fragment 41: Feline Frailty

I am the old, old cat
Whose once sleek black fur
Is now bedraggled brown tat
My elderly mistress can't hear me purr

On a sun-drenched window sill
I carelessly flop
Lying ever so still
Being afraid to drop

My joints ache with rheumatic pain
Mice I no longer want to catch
As every shape looks just the same
A nap is all I want to snatch

I long to sleep and not wake up
My bladder I no longer control
It all makes me feel so fed-up
To even bother with a stroll
Look and see
Because...
One day, you'll be like me

---

[8] An excellent analysis of the *'unsustainable State'* is provided in David B Smith's book, entitled *'Living with Leviathan,'* (published by *'The Institute of Economic Affairs,'* 2006). Mr Smith is a leading expert on the effects Public Spending and Taxation have had upon Economic Performance.

## Fragment 42a: Bank Holiday Innocence

In Coryton Bay
Beneath the red cliffs of Dawlish
Where the Western Railway roars by
I watched happy holiday-makers
Playing their traditional beach games
Later I swam in the sea
Bobbing gently over tugging waves
All seemed normal
All seemed at peace
Everyone was in a mood of carefree cheer
Just as they were
During bank holiday August the third 1914
The last day of peace
For a martyred generation[9]

## Fragment 42b: Swept Away

Yawn!
August is a listless month
When nothing much appears to happen
Best go on the beach
And swim amongst the waves
Opposite the rail bridge
Carrying the West Country Line

Enjoy a good swim
And watch from afar
As three children
Build their elaborate sandcastles
Soon they will be washed away
Later, it will be the turn of the railway line
Metal rails will be left swinging in the air[10]

---

[9] A reference to the outbreak of World War One, in August 1914
[10] A reference to the destruction of the rail line at Coryton during the great storms of February 2014

### Fragment 43a: Withdrawing Roar

Faith has completed its
*'Melancholy, long withdrawing roar*'[11]
Leaving nothing behind but dirt and debris

Beside a broken pleasure pier
A secular man
Is floundering in the sea
His arms flailing the air
Within minutes he's gone

### Fragment 43b: Foaming Waters

Hark! What's that I can hear?
Moving from a far off sandy horizon
A well of foaming waters begin to advance
Then craaaash!
A Tsumani wave of deception
Sweeps over the wasteland of Humanism
Sweltering, sleeping sunbathers
Are engulfed in its watery maws
Nothing can halt its terrible course
Soon it will create a new landscape
In which birds of prey will pick out the eyes
Of the sightless dead

### Fragment 43c: Myriad

Decay, decay, rancid festering decay
Is all I see
Hope has been abandoned
Compassion is no more
Truth has been denied
And only a myriad of lies remains

---

[11] From Matthew Arnold's *'Dover Beach'* (1867)

### Fragment 44: Cyber Power

At the click of a switch I begin to flow
Through many a fibre optic cable I go
On innumerable screens I flash
To produce a wad of virtual cash
At the speed of light go I
In self-promotion I'm not shy
I'm here – yes *'twenty-four seven'*
To offer a pornographic heaven
Endless opportunities I produce
The gullible masses I love to seduce

Many a business I've caused to fall
Fail to use me and you'll *'go to the wall'*
I am the power that fills every land
Especially when operating on broadband
The best and worst of human nature I reflect
Negative criticism I find easy to deflect
Tremble at the dominance I have now won
Thanks to me your world will become as one
Under my guidance humanity <u>will</u> unite
In an age of blinding cyber light and rotting moral night

### Fragment 45: Siren Call

The evil of Mankind
Has assumed global proportions
The wickedness of humanity
Has spread across the globe
Through the vortex of time
A new sight appears
Vast, adoring, cheering crowds
Worshipping one man

A reverential hush descends
As he utters beautiful and seductive words

His image appears in many a public square
Rapt attention
Is paid to his every word
Surely this man
Will save humanity

But...
His promise of Utopia
Is a siren call
A shattering of society has taken place
And on this earth not one man – even this man –
Can put the pieces back together again

### Fragment 46: Cult of Fools

Capitalism is the cult of greed
Socialism is the cult of The State
Both derive from Atheism
Which is the cult of fools[12]

### Fragment 47: Don't Despair

A distraught woman
Lays out the tablets
On her bedside cabinet
Upon which stands a glass of water
And a note –
A few quick gulps and it should be over
*'Peace and quiet'*
From the accusatory thoughts
That torment her

But, my love, please
Don't despair
With you things

---

[12] Psalms 14 and 53

Are not beyond repair

You are needed
My love
So desperately needed

Come to yourself and listen
Do not betray our love
No one wants you more than I!
Come
Cease being at war with yourself
Look outwards
And realize
That there is
A way forward in your life
Don't be angry
At not keeping
The impossible standards of perfection
You set yourself

The voice of conscience has spoken
The woman stumbles to the bathroom
And flushes the tablets
Down a toilet bowel

### Fragment 48: Isara

The River Aire
(In Celtic *'Isara'* meaning *'strong river'*)
Flows past hollow manufacturing premises
Now skeletons of a former industrial age
On it flows
On it flows
Past neon city lights
And plush converted mill flats
That are the emblems
Of a post industrial age

Onward flows the River Aire
Onward past the looming towers
Of a liquid-modern cityscape
The night-darkened waters flow
Onward to the sea
And to some future point in time

### Fragment 49: Break-up

On a rattling London Tube
Between regimented rows of book-reading
And *'I-pod'* listening commuters
Stands a tall Cypriot-looking woman
Her long black hair
Swaying rhythmically from side to side
She yells down her mobile phone
To her ex lover
*'Dickhead!' 'Liar!' 'Tosser!'* and *'Arsehole!'*
*'Pay back the money you owe me!'*

Suddenly, like a silver metallic worm
The tube vanishes into a black tunnel
Her line goes dead
Yet still she continues to yell;
*'I'll get my lawyer onto you,*
*Don't give me any more of your lousy excuses*
*You pathetic poser*
*I've had enough of your lies*
*Don't pretend you can't hear me!'*

She wants the world to know
What a lying scumbag
Her ex-lover had been

### Fragment 50: Political Power

Political power may grow out of the barrel of the gun[13]
But at best the gun can only remove a lie
It can never propagate the truth

### Fragment 51a: The Last Milestone

The final milestone has been reached
A ninety year journey draws to an end
Many have been her adventures
But now her feet shuffle wearily along
She leans on her walking frame and
Slowly ambles toward the setting sun

### Fragment 51b: Time to Relinquish

The cup has been drained dry
All the moisture has gone
There's nothing to soothe cracked lips
Or the ravening thirst in the mouth
Things are drawing to an end
Soon it will be time to relinquish life and
Go in peace

Thank you for nurturing my talents
Even amidst the frailties of old age
You were my inspiration
Thank God we can part as friends

### Fragment 52a: Departure

The *Ruah Kadesh*[14] has departed and only the darkness remains

---

[13] This observation was made by the murderous twentieth century Chinese dictator, Mao Zedong
[14] *Ruah Kadesh* is Hebrew for *'Spirit of Holiness.'*

## Fragment 52b: Seduction

I look into his eyes
Deeply trusting, caring eyes
Eyes that soften the heart
Eyes that seduce the mind
Eyes that stir the will
Eyes that make <u>me</u> feel special
How good, gracious and godlike he is
How I long to follow his cause
How I yearn for his approval
How I long to devote my life to him

I cried to my God –
And the spell was broken!
Now all I see is a gloating, mocking malice
In disgust I turn away
And push through
The adoring crowd
All transfixed to a three-dimensional screen
Displaying his triumphal motorcade driving by

## Fragment 52c: Immolation

A New World Order he glibly promises
And behold, people from all nations chase after him
In a mood of religious fervour
Singing and chanting his praises
Weeping and laughing with joy
Looking to him for global salvation
Most fail to perceive that
What he offers is a cruel deception
For his is a way that will lead
To a near total immolation of humanity[15]
Do you not see?

---

[15] *'Immolation'* means destruction by fire

Do you not grasp?
Do you not comprehend?
The old is being interred
And the new is yet to come
The Christ-figure you worship
Is nothing but a cruel deceiver
Be one of the discerning
Be one of the wise
Be one of the faithful and
Do not take his mark

## Fragment 53: Radical Action

When the skeletal finger of financial ruin taps you on the shoulder it's
easy to take radical action that will change the course of one's life

## Fragment 54: The Last Candle

The last candle is blown out by a noxious wind
Gusting through a broken stained glass window
A weathered and rusted church door
Creaks and swings slightly wider
As more debris
Is blown about on the floor
No one is here
But the sleeping glue sniffer
Lying full length on a dust-laden pew
A box of matches at his feet
Outside
Dead human bones lie interred
Beneath moss covered monuments
Reflecting the social divisions of a bygone age
Where supposed piety had walked hand-in-hand with snobbery
The darkness inside mirrors the darkness outside

In England, Christianity has died and nobody cares

## Fragment 55: Becoming

The centre no longer holds and
The people fly to extremes

What have we become?
What have we become?

Ruin lies all around us
Society dissolves in terror

How can we go on?
How can we go on?

Compassion has died
And only a raw hatred remains

## Fragment 56: Lengthening Shadow

Death is a lengthening shadow

I leap back
It follows me
I jump to the side
It pursues me
I dash forward
It engulfs me
As my body crumbles
Into skeletal dust

Only the shadow remains
Waiting, waiting patiently
Another victim to claim

### Fragment 57: Dreams

Inside a Dawlish holiday flat
My wife, wearing a long red T-shirt
Sits on an armchair
Her naked legs resting on a square pouffée
She sighs, as with red pen
She corrects a large manuscript
Time ticks slowly by
Her pen falters and stops
Head drooping down onto her chest
Red pen and manuscript slip silently to the floor

Asleep, her lips slightly parted
She dreams of the life she could have had
Had she not married a poet

### Fragment 58: Forbidden Fruit

Beneath a monastery plum tree
A young visiting guest lies relaxed
Spread-eagled on the warm grass
Wearing a straw boater, striped blazer and glasses
His face creased in an enigmatic smile
With slow deliberation
He stands up
Stretching out his arm to pluck a ripe plum
Is it forbidden fruit he wishes to eat?

### Fragment 59: Metro-Class-Landscape

Chiltern countryside
Melts into wealthy country village
Where *'rock stars'*
In plush mansions live

Wealthy country village
Melts into prosperous outer suburb
Where wealthy stockbrokers
In detached houses live

Prosperous outer suburb
Melts into respectable inner suburb
Where retired professionals
In snug semi's live

Respectable inner suburb
Melts into modern housing estate
Where council workers
In cramped maisonettes live

Modern housing estate
Melts into slum *'sink'* estate
Where asylum seekers
In emergency accommodation cower

Slum, *'sink'* estate
Melts into prosperous commercial centre
Where self-made millionaires
In plush penthouses live

Prosperous commercial centre
Melts into a core governing centre
Where shady politicians
In deep corruption walk quickly to and fro

## <u>Fragment 60: On Waterloo Bridge</u>

On Waterloo Bridge I stand, feeling like a
Skin-coloured breakwater
Against an ocean of humanity.
I stare across a gravy brown Thames
My face flint-sharp with disapproval
Opposite a parliament full of festering corruption

That edifice epitomised the centre of a once mighty Empire
Now downgraded to a sleazy regional council
Nothing but a compliable puppet
To a burgeoning European Super-State

Named affectionately as the *Mother of Parliaments*
Now an assembly of the despised –
The recipients of fierce public contempt

The power and glory has gone
But still the world invades Westminster
In the form of camera-clicking tourists

*'Ah-ha-ma please excuse me
Would you please take a eh-ah-ha
A picture of ma and ma family?'*

A bespectacled Chinese man
Of slight build asks me;
In a black suit
He resembles
A minor bank clerk

Gladly I oblige
Taking two pictures of himself
His short-statured smiling wife
And their blank-faced daughter
A citizen of the sun-rising east

His family and himself recorded for posterity
By a citizen from the sun-setting west

At that moment
I understood where the future lay

## Fragment 61: Lost Vocation

If Dr Harold Shipman
Had procured *'patient consent'* before killing them
The terminally ill would now be rushing to his door

His real vocation lay with Dignitas or
Some other pro-euthanasia Association

## Fragment 62: The Difference

*"I say I say, I say – what's the difference between Dignitas and Dr Shipman?"*

*"What is the difference between Dignitas and Dr Shipman?"*

*"Legality!"*

## Fragment 63: Stray Dog

A stray dog howls into a rain-sodden night
It howls from the centre of a *'sink'* estate
It howls into the surrounding desolation

It howls for the death of decency
It howls for the death of innocence
It howls for the death of Western Civilization

Let it howl, for the end of Great Britain is nigh

### Fragment 64a: Acceptability

**First,** it became acceptable to kill the unborn
**Second,** it became acceptable to kill the terminally ill
**Third,** it became acceptable to kill the elderly
**Soon,** it will become acceptable to kill just about anyone

### Fragment 64b: Not Bothering

*"I don't bother to think, therefore I kill!"*

### Fragment 64c: A Deadly Formula

Legalised abortion + Assisted Suicide + Euthanasia =
The *'Mass Extermination'* Society

### Fragment 65: The Universal Terrorist

It matters not whether the cause is religious or secular
You've just got to kill somebody

It matters not whether you're of the *'left'* or the *'right'*
You've just got to kill somebody

It matters not whether you're black or white
You've just got to kill somebody

It matters not whether you're male or female
You've just got to kill somebody

It matters not whether you're rich or poor
You've just got to kill somebody

It matters not whether your cause is just or unjust
You've just got to kill somebody

It matters not whether your weapons are *'high'* or *'low'* tech

You've just got to kill somebody

For you are the universal terrorist
The wrecker of buildings, the dealer of death and
The creator of many hells

And still – you've just got to kill somebody – just anybody

## Fragment 66: Haunting Questions

Who will decide who's *'a burden upon society'* and what's to stop this
category from being extended to cover everyone?

## Fragment 67: Three Flags

In the early morning hours I lay in bed, restlessly dreaming
In my night vision
I saw the Union Jack being pulled down
And tossed into a muddy field
Then...
Out of this same soil
Three other flag poles appeared
Each with a new flag being hoisted up
They were the flags of
England, Wales and Scotland
All three beginning to flutter and flap
In an ice-cold wind

I awoke to mourn the break-up of the United Kingdom
Then realized it was just a dream
But would it become a reality?

## Fragment 68: The Banjo Player

The Banjo player strums
Inside a crowded theatre of his own imagination
Unable to stop

He strums faster and faster

Then... twang!!!

A string snaps, the strumming ceases
Silence fills the hall
A look of helplessness
Plays across his face
He awakens suddenly
In a cold sweat
Realising that his talents are dead

### Fragment 69: Feline Twilight

Twilight has fallen
A tiger hued tabby lies hidden
In a bed of tulips
Crouching, staring, waiting
For a bird to land nearby
Suddenly his ears prick up
His noses twitches
His eyes keenly scan
The copse ahead
A twig snaps
Cat is ready to pounce

Then laughter
A spotty teenage boy and his dishevelled girlfriend
Leave the woodland
Holding hands and exchanging knowing looks

Disappointed
Cat begins to yawn
Cat begins to doze
Cat begins to snore
Dreaming of an elusive prey

Next morning
A distressed house owner
Stares at his crushed tulip bed
Cursing the animal responsible
A broken, bloodied wing lies dead centre

Cat had found his prey
And he is satisfied – for now

### Fragment 70: Coastal Retreat

The starving, gulping sea
Nibbles away at the muddy, coastal edge
Splat! Another lump of sodden brown clay
Falls into its ravenous foaming mouth
Another slice of England is lost
Another retreat is made
Another piece of ground is given up
Can nothing halt this watery advance?
Can nothing reverse this invincible tide?
Can nothing save England's *green and pleasant land?"*

### Fragment 71: Looming

Oh, the evil
Oh, the cruelty
Oh, the wickedness
Can nothing stop the Middle East's march to war?

A nuclear mushroom cloud looms on the horizon
Will an ancient hatred lead to the incineration of millions?

## Fragment 72: Choices

Love God and you will love
Hate God and you will hate

Adore evil and you will accept the lie
Follow unrighteousness and you will be deceived

## Fragment 73: Saint Jim

Once upon a time
A BBC showbiz personality was hailed as an eccentric Saint
So many people loved him, both young and old
Knighthoods and many other awards came his way
He inspired joy and happiness wherever he went
With his wide playful grin
Trademark dyed-blond hair and inane yodels
Forever sporting his phallic cigar
It seemed as if he could *'fix'* everything

But following his death at the age of 84
He was found to have been a monster of child molesting depravity
Many an innocent childhood memory he'd wantonly violated
Hundreds of his *'Guys and Gals'*
Sacrificed on the altar of social permissiveness
For them the *'Age of liberation'* had been a sham
The result – mental disconnection all around

A BBC Director General squirms before a committee of MPs
Unable (or unwilling) to answer their pointed interrogation
All about *'cover ups'* and sexual abuse on BBC premises
He's a middle aged *'Billy Bunter'* [16] about to be caned
Blushing a deep red
He feels the trapdoor of public disgrace

---

[16] Billy Bunter was a comical, fictitious public school boy, invented by the magazine writer Charles Hamilton, (1876-1961). Billy was best known for his obesity and ability to cause trouble. The BBC ran several series of highly amusing Billy Bunter stories, from 1952 until 1961.

Opening beneath his feet
He's *'Piggy,'* about to be knocked over a cliff edge in
Golding's *'Lord of the Flies'*
The trap door opens and he's gone
Fallen deep into the memory hole of public forgetfulness

As horrific allegations of sexual abuse multiply it's time to ask
*'Was Mary Whitehouse*[17] *right after all?'*

## Fragment 74a: Nature's Brillo Pad

The sand blows in the desert
Ensuring that desolation covers desolation

The sand blows in the desert
Forming a howling wall of dust

The sand blows in the desert
Terrifying unwary travellers

The sand blows in the desert
A brillo pad scouring the wind-worn rocks

The sand blows in the desert
The second law of thermo-dynamics[18] is applied

---

[17] Mary Whitehouse (1910-2001) was a former school teacher and a vigorous campaigner against the permissive society during the 1960's and 70's. She often clashed with the BBC over the alleged obscenity, bad language and violence in some of their productions. The media response at the time was often one of mockery; there was even a pornographic magazine named after her.

[18] The Second Law of Thermo Dynamics (also known as the *'Increased Law of Entropy'*) suggests that, over time, complex structures collapse into simpler structures, so that in the end no coherent structure remains. In other words, matter deteriorates over time, if left to itself.

### Fragment 74b: Instruction

Look at your circumstances with a *'lantern jawed*[19] realism
Whatever you see, look and learn

### Fragment 75: First Impressions

On a cold misty night, near Christmas, a young man travels home following ten weeks of voluntary service in India. His first impression upon returning to a snow-bound England is *'How miserable everyone is!'*

### Fragment 76: No Respect

In a City Centre bus queue I hear an elderly woman (in a ginger wig) complaining to an old crookbacked lady (wearing a faded green headscarf and leaning on a walking stick); *"The flamin' bus driver let 'er pass two stops after the one she'd paid fer. 'E only did it because she 'ad a pretty face. 'E wouldn't 'a dun it fer me. Two stops 'e let 'er! There's no respect fer us senior citizens. I'm glad I don't 'ave another 70 years t' live over again in this lousy country. There's just no respect fer the elderly these days."'*

Her companion looked at her with barely comprehending sympathy; but what did she care? After all, both of their days were drawing to a close.

### Fragment 77: Cosmic Career

The universe is dying
The sun is dying
The earth is dying
And...
I'm not too well either

---

[19] Medically, a *'lantern jaw'* occurs when the lower jaw protrudes outward, beneath an upper jaw – often as a result of some genetic dysfunction. It afflicted the Habsburg royal dynasty of sixteenth to eighteenth century Europe. Here, it symbolises a strong-willed determination to resolve a particular problem.

## <u>Fragment 78: Separate Worlds</u>

**(Transcript of a dinner party where guests are using their mobile phones to send text messages, just as *'starters'* for a lavish meal are being served)**

Tap! Tap! Tap!
Tap! Tap! Tap!
Tap! Tap! Tap!

Tap! Tap! Tap!
Tap! Tap! Tap!
Tap! Tap! Tap!

The bejewelled and beautifully gowned hostess looks on with increasing agitation at her seated guests. Her sumptuous dining table is covered with her best linen cloth and candles flicker dancingly here and there – but no one notices.

*'Your soup is getting cold! I think it's time to eat now!'* she suddenly states.

In unison her several guests reply

Tap! Tap! Tap!
Tap! Tap! Tap!
Tap! Tap! Tap!

A look of despair crosses her face, so she takes out her mobile phone and sends a text message to a friend about these awful guests who won't communicate

Tap! Tap! Tap!
Tap! Tap! Tap!
Tap! Tap! Tap!

### Fragment 79: Slogan

*'Power to the people'*
Was a slogan
That turned out to be a *'con'*
It really meant
*'Power to the party bureaucrats*
*And their intellectual lap dogs'*

### Fragment 80: Resilience

During the last century
It survived Communism
It survived Nazism
It even survived its own horrendous corruption

So what makes today's generation of posturing Atheists
Think
They can destroy
A major World Faith like Christianity?

Present within it is a mysterious resilience
That they can't even begin to understand

### Fragment 81: Another Closure

Another church closes
Another light goes out
The darkness increases
No one cares
Only the howling silence of
An absent Deity remains

## Fragment 82: Good Riddance

I've just got to leave and say farewell
I need to escape this bitter, relational hell

My decision was difficult to make
Yet it was one I knew I had to take

No point in giving things *another try'*
Now's the time to say a final *'goodbye'*

Your negativity just made me sick
I wonder did we ever really *'click?'*

Outwardly I now take my leave
Inwardly my heart still does seethe

Now's the right time to wriggle away
Yes – I'm finished – I've had my say

I'm gonna take courage 'n' make a new start
But this can only be done <u>if we remain apart</u>

## Fragment 83a: Revolutionary Times

There's now a revolution
Erupting against every institution
Struggling to find a new constitution
Arab masses now awaken
Whole nations are being shaken
The Middle East is in uproar
Many hopes begin to soar
Abroad there's a cry for *'liberation!'*
This has provoked much celebration
The guns of tyrants noisily crack
A people's outlook now seems very black
Militant factions prepare for civil war

Ready to produce yet more blood and gore
*"A challenge it was in that dawn to be alive
But to be young could be very"* lethal[20]

Behind the scenes aspiring
Robespierre's and Lenin's busily plot
To steal the hard won liberties
Gained with a people's blood
Is it a *'terrible beauty'*[21] or a hideous ugliness
We see being born?

### Fragment 83b: Honesty

In disappointment lies honesty
But in happiness lies strength

### Fragment 84: The Excellent Counsellor

Don't come to me for counselling
For I am the world's worst counsellor –
I really am!
If you lie on my psychiatrist's couch
Divulging all of your many troubles
I will read a book
Look at my watch
Text a message
Even do some paperwork
Anything – rather than listen to your boring problems

Should you describe
A bitterly abused childhood
A history of depression
Or some other kind of trauma

---

[20] These are in contrast to the poet William Wordworth's words which greeted the French Revolution, *"Bliss in that dawn it was to be alive, but to be young was very heaven!"*
[21] A phrase coined by William Butler Yeats, commemorating the Easter Uprising of Irish Republicans against the British Government in 1916.

I will yawn
Even snatch *'forty winks'* if I can
If you go on too much I will chomp on an apple
Or even eat from a tub of delicious strawberry yoghurt

Should you threaten to *'end it all!'*
I will exclaim
*'Pay up first then do your dastardly deed!'*
Should you threaten an act of murder
I will be greatly concerned about
The sullying of my own professional reputation

No sympathy will you receive from me
(No, not even a cup of tea)
No emotional support will be provided
No soft word will come your way
Instead, I'll use your problems
As material for my next book
On effective counselling
Entitled *'The Art of Showing Compassion to Sad Losers'*
As you fall into that category
It's yours for only £13.99
A remarkably reasonable price
I'm sure you'll agree
Would you like me to reserve you a copy?

Now, run along my dear
I've far more important matters to attend to
Don't be in a hurry to come back unless you're willing to pay cash

What do you mean *'You've found me to be an excellent counsellor?'*
*'Very helpful'* you say – but how?
Oh, I see!
You're relieved to find that
There's someone with worse problems than yourself!
The cheek of it!
Now pay up and clear off!

## Fragment 85: The World's Most Hated Belief

Be challenged by the world's most hated belief

It provokes hatred from all nations and classes
It inspires derisory laughter from atheists and sceptics alike
It's loathed by members of every religious faith
It embarrasses many a church leader
It fuels mob violence and state persecution
It's viewed as *'being mad, bad and dangerous to follow'* [22]
Because it subverts all other beliefs

It is the belief that
Jesus Christ is *"the way, the truth and the life"* [23]
And that
*"There is no other name under heaven*[24] *given among men
By which we are saved."*[25]

To hold firmly to this belief
Is to risk rejection, persecution and martyrdom
Yet it's a belief that has survived for almost two thousand years

## Fragment 86: Above Accountability

*"I say, I say, I say; what do political and religious activists have in common?"*

*"What do they have in common?'"*

*"The desire to be above accountability and to shut down honest debate concerning the exact nature of their cause"*

---

[22] Based upon a phrase used by Lady Caroline Lamb to describe the poet George Byron (The final word was *'know'* rather than *'follow'*).
[23] John 14:6a
[24] Acts 4:12b
[25] *I.e.* being *'saved'* from our sins and their ruinous consequences

### Fragment 87: Desert Flower

A young balding Arab man
From Luxor in Egypt
Gropes with a sixty something English woman
Old enough to be his mother
He wears a yellow 'T' shirt and
Fashion-styled moss green jeans
She, a sky blue denim jacket in
1970's *'retro'* style and a plunging black top
Its neckline braided in a delicate floral print

Her hair is peroxide blonde and garish red lipstick
Pouts from her deeply lined face
She has the slightly tipsy look of a woman
Who's had one man too many
The train they're on approaches a dark tunnel
The lights flicker and fade

*"I love you my beautiful desert flower!"*
*"Eee – get off yer cheeky devil!"*
*"I can't get enough of you, my gorgeous, precious honeysuckle!"*
*"Put yer thing away – we're in a public place!"*
A sound of kissing, accompanied by girlish giggling follows
The lights flicker back on and
There they are – locked in a pseudo-passionate embrace
Sheepishly, he withdraws his long fingered hands

The train clatters out of the tunnel
A natural light returns

In the seat opposite, a bespectacled middle-aged passenger
Wearing a white shirt and grey tie, awakens from a fitful doze
His gaze fixes upon the couple as he ponders to himself;
*'An excellent subject for a poem, I'm glad I brought some paper'*
At once he begins to scrawl down his thoughts in a vivid red pen

Another tunnel is entered
Another round of kissing, groping and giggling
Another exchange of endearments
Then out once more into the light and the final destination –
A City Centre Rail Station

The train slows to a halt
Its doors open

And the mismatched couple leave
Walking hand-in-hand to the newly automated exit
She blissfully re-living the youth she enjoyed three divorces ago
And he calculating whether marriage to this *filthy whore'*
Would gain him permanent entry into the United Kingdom
And enough capital to set up his own business

### Fragment 88: Drip, Drip, Drip

Drip, drip, drip,
A hospital chaplain is made redundant due to budgetary cutbacks
A drop of discrimination quietly falls

Drip, drip, drip,
Local councils re-brand the Christmas Festival as *'Winterval'*
A trickle of intolerance begins

Drip, drip, drip,
A popular atheist scientist brands Christianity as *'an unreasoning evil'*
A pool of intolerance gradually forms

Drip, drip, drip,
A Christian employee is banned from wearing a cross at work
A stream of intolerance flows

Drip, drip, drip,
A Christian registrar is disciplined for her *'narrow'* stance on marriage
A surge of intolerance gathers force

Drip, drip, drip,
A Christian nurse is suspended for offering to pray for a patient
A river of intolerance rushes on

Drip, drip, drip,
A five year old girl who told another child about Jesus at school is
sent home in tears
A wide, pounding river of intolerance carries all before it

Drip, drip, drip,
Librarians don't stock Bibles to avoid offending religious minorities
A raging river of intolerance bursts its banks

Drip, drip, drip,
A church is sued for allegedly violating anti-discrimination legislation
An overflowing river of intolerance drowns adjacent fields

Drip, drip, drip,
Teenage lesbians snatch a bible from a mild-mannered street preacher
before police intervene to stop his meeting
Filthy flood waters begin to invade people's houses

Drip, drip, drip,
A Commission publish rules announcing that chaplains can be
refused employment because of their views on Gay marriage
A rising flood of intolerance devastates surrounding communities

Drip, drip, drip
New anti-hate legislation threatens to quell religious liberty and
freedom of speech
A mighty deluge of intolerance now overwhelms us all

## Fragment 89: Having a Good Time

When you visit an English Urban Centre
Late on a Friday or Saturday night
You'll see the flower of English youth milling around
Eager to enter pubs and clubs
In order to enjoy a good time
This will consist of
Shouting, screaming and swearing
Listening to deafening music
Having casual sexual encounters
Getting blind drunk
Snorting illegal substances
Brawling in the street
Urinating on alleyway walls
Vomiting into gutters
Staggering into over-priced taxis
Whilst being fully resolved to do exactly the same thing again next
weekend

Have a good time folks!

## Fragment 90: The Morning After

A young man awakens with a blinding headache
Bleary eyed – his hand gropes for the aspirin
Conveniently placed next to
The glass of water
On a stranger's bedside cabinet
*'It were a great time we 'ad last night*
*It's a pity Ah can't remember more abaht it*
*Oh! Ma flamin' 'ead!'*

*Who's that girl sleepin beside me?*
*I dorn't remember dancin' with 'er!*
*She looks a right slag*
*With 'er dyed blond 'air*

*An' long painted fingernails!*
*Still wearin' a black skimpy dress too*
*'er tights are lyin' crumpled on the floor*
*We must 'a done it after all!*
*Aaargh! Everthin' is so blurred*
*The room's spinnin' around me*
*Where am I?*
*It must be 'er flat*
*It's much too tidy t' be mine*
*Yeuk! I feel...'*


A quick stumbling to the bathroom
Followed by loud retching noises and
A glance at a pasty-faced reflection in a mirror
*'That's better*
*Pity about the mess on the floor*
*I'll leave it for 'er t' clear up*
*I better get dressed an' sneak out quietly – like*
*Before there's any trouble*
*The last one threw a kitchen knife at me*
*When I last created this sort o 'mess*
*Hope Ah've enough dosh left for mi fare 'ome.'*
A quick combing of hair
An even quicker fumbling on of beer-stained clothing
An anxious checking of a near empty wallet
*'I've just got enough!'*
A final glance at a now stirring form
*'Ta-Ta, was great fun bein' with you, 'ooever you are*
*Sorry about the mess in the bathroom*
*Oh, an' in the 'all too*
*Would give you a fiver t'pay fer cleanin' it up*
*But am out o' cash*
*Ah'm sure y'll understand*
*Must go!'*


A clumsy fumbling of a key
Followed by a quiet opening and closing of a door

The soon-to-be forgotten man has departed
Blissfully unaware of the other mess he's left
Germinating inside a strange girl's womb

### Fragment 91: Tame poet

A tame poet blindly follows the values of the society they live in –
Do not aspire to be a tame poet!

### Fragment 92a: Obelisk

The
Stone
Obelisk
Stands as an
Old boundary marker from yesteryear

### Fragment 92b: No Light

If there's no light in the Churches where can there be light?

### Fragment 93: Blame Game

If the world's condition is not the fault of the CIA
It's the fault of the FBI
If it's not the fault of the FBI
It's the fault of *the military-industrial complex*
If it's not the fault of *the military-industrial complex*
It's the fault of *the lame stream media*[26]
If it's not the fault of *the lame stream media*
It's the fault of the electronic media
If it's not the fault of the electronic media
It's the fault of the political right
If it's not the fault of the political right

---

[26] *'Lamestream media'* is a pejorative term used by Conspiracy Theorists to describe the *'mainstream media'* of major Newspapers and TV/Radio Channels.

It's the fault of the political left
If it's not the fault of the political left
It's the fault of the bankers
If it's not the fault of the bankers
It's the fault of the Bilderbergers
If it's not the fault of the Bilderbergers
It's the fault of the Tri-Lateral Commission
If it's not the fault of the Tri-Lateral Commission
It's the fault of the United Nations
If it's not the fault of the United Nations
It's the fault of the Vatican
If it's not the fault of the Vatican
It's the fault of the Jews
If it's not the fault of the Jews
It's the fault of the Muslims
If it's not the fault of the Muslims
It's the fault of the religious fundamentalists
If it's not the fault of the religious fundamentalists
It's the fault of the Atheists
If it's not the fault of the Atheists
It's the fault of the Freemasons
If it's not the fault of the Freemasons
It's the fault of the Illuminati
If it's not the fault of the Illuminati
It's the fault of *'the men in black'*
If it's not the fault of *'the men in black'*
It's the fault of Aliens from outer space
If it's not the fault of the Aliens from outer space
It's the fault of Chemical Trails in the air
If it's not the fault of Chemical Trails in the air
It's the fault of sun spots
... And so we could go on

But one thing we can be sure of
Everyone else is at fault
Except me

## Fragment 94: Broken Boundaries

All boundaries have been broken
All barriers have been swept away

Nature howls in fury
Rivers foam and rage

Impurity sweeps across the land
Polluted waters cover the people

Former customs are lightly discarded
Old standards are rudely brushed aside

A fresh set of values has been constructed
A terrible set of lies has been fabricated

The unacceptable has become accepted
Many do what is right in their own eyes

A terrible psychosis has gripped our culture
The *'Savilisation'* of society[27] proceeds apace

Stand for reason and be mocked
Stand for truth and be hated

Is this what our Grandfathers fought to produce?
Is this what their wartime comrades died for?

Pity the children who are yet to be corrupted
Weep for a generation yet to be exploited

---

[27] *'Savilisation'* – named after Jimmy Savile, the insidious process whereby a society normalises (and even views as *'fun'*) the financial and sexual exploitation of its weaker members; such a process happened in the entertainment division of the BBC during the long tenure of the popular entertainer Jimmy Savile. His predatory antics are mentioned in **Fragment 73.**

### Fragment 95a: Personal Entitlement

*"I say, I say, I say, what trait unites greedy bankers, corrupt politicians, bent policemen, unscrupulous journalists and rioters who plunder high street shops?"*
*"What trait do they have in common?"*
*"A sense of personal entitlement, borne from a greedy materialism and a secular world view"*

### Fragment 95b: Logical Conclusion

*"What is the difference between an atheist underclass rioter and an atheist like Richard Dawkins?"*
*"What is the difference between an atheist underclass rioter and an atheist like Richard Dawkins?"*
*"The former takes his atheism to its logical conclusion whilst the latter doesn't dare to – he has too much to lose!"*

### Fragment 96: Riot Scene

Smashed windows
Blazing shops
Overturned cars
Melted tarmac
Violent rioters
Voluble reporters
Complete anarchy

Welcome to England's broken society
Where decency has fled the streets
And greed is king

### Fragment 97: Rap Gospel

Hey man – I'm not your fan
Your gangsta rap is a load of pap
You find it cool to play the fool
An' *'Living off the State'* is your fate

Carry a hammer in that manner
An' you'll be in jail, without fail!
But if you wan' more go 'n' smash in a store
It ain't a bad habit just to wanna grab it
An' don't let the *'fed'* do in yer 'ead
But cross the *'local boss'* an' it's your own sad loss
Let bling be only <u>his</u> thing
Avoid his curse les' thin's gets worse
The rule of the gun ain't any fun
A slash of a knife can end yer life
It's so bad yer could go mad
There ain't any hope – yer just can't cope
But pop another pill 'n' you'll be ill
Don't be thick – society's sick
Wan' a new start then get a new heart
'n'
Find a Saviour t' change your behaviour

### Fragment 98: Best Days

My best days are behind me
All I can hope for is a peaceful death
Youthful ambitions have ended in disappointment
Youthful enthusiasm has resulted only in frustration
Youthful hope has crashed into a dead-end of sorrow
Youthful passions are long-since spent
And now only the empty exhaustion of late middle age remains

### Fragment 99: Last of the Variety Show Greats

See an 83 year old, smiling comedian perform a five and a half decade
long routine

Snigger at his tatty black hair and buck teeth
Participate in the laughter and loud applause
Relish an outpouring of unique comic genius
Be tickled by his tickling stick

Enjoy his *'titterfilarious'* patter until the early hours
For tonight in a North Wales theatre is the last of the variety show
greats – a reminder of a kinder, gentler Britain where comic giants
bestrode the stage and loved their audience[28]

## Fragment 100a: Alternative Comedy 1

The transcript of an alternative comedy routine, minus all rude and
abusive words

Hello, let me tell you about the------- Laugh you-------------There was
this----------------
Come on! Laugh you---------------- This one is -------funny – why
don't you laugh you----? This man and this woman spent an evening---
-------- each other and-----Goodnight and------off

## Fragment 100b: Alternative Comedy 2

*"Why did the alternative comedian hurry across a busy main road?"*

*"Why did the alternative comedian hurry across a busy main road?"*

*"Because he was being chased by an angry audience wanting their money back!"*

## Fragment 101: Orwell's Room

*'Room 101'* was a place of horror in George Orwell's novel *'1984'*
Located in *'The Ministry of Love'* it was the place where a political
prisoner's very worst nightmares were realized.

Our whole society has become a vast *'Room 101'*

---

[28] This fragment was inspired by watching the comedian Ken Dodd give a brilliant performance at Llandudno throughout the evening and early morning of 14th-15th August 2011. Aged 83 he'd been fifty-five years in show business and was still at the peak of his powers.

## Fragment 102: Swirling Words

Words swirl around
Words join together
A new poem forms

Words break apart
Words fade away
A new poem dissolves

## Fragment 103: Frustrated Seeker

I tried so much to enter a *'realm of light'*
But my search brought me nothing – no inner delight

I strived to follow a *'certain way'*
But alas, my bills it could never pay

A Guru's fees broke my account
He refused to offer any discount

Why it failed I still cannot tell
But it landed me in financial hell

My heart began to boil and seethe
But with a sense of relief I decided to leave

A bitter exit I was forced to make
No more nonsense was I willing to take

And now fresh hopes of freedom re-appear
As I've begun to relinquish all of that fear

### Fragment 104: Post Modern Freedom

What does *'freedom'* mean today?
Well, it's
The freedom to get sloshed
The freedom to get high
The freedom to have sex
The freedom to abdicate responsibility
But above all
It's the freedom to become a five minute celebrity
On reality TV

### Fragment 105: Free To Disagree

I do not hate you
I do not loathe you

I do not despise you
I do not dislike you

You do not repulse me
You do not revolt me

I even admire your achievements in certain areas[29]

But in all conscience, I cannot agree with your views[30]
But isn't part of freedom being able to disagree, without hatred?

### Fragment 106: Without True Faith

Without true faith there can be no mercy, hope or love; whole
societies slowly die, leaving only the enticing distraction of
entertainment.

---

[29] This line may be omitted by performers
[30] *'Your views,'* may be replaced with *'the path you've taken'* or *'the lifestyle you've adopted'* depending upon the needs of the audience

### Fragment 107a: Uprooted

The tree has been uprooted
It cannot be re-planted

The tower has collapsed
It cannot be rebuilt

The relationship is over
It cannot be restored

It's time to move on
And begin afresh

### Fragment 107b: Closed Doors

All of the doors are closed
They are tightly shut
Cease knocking
And walk away

### Fragment 107c: The Times

The times call for a prophet
But instead they select a diplomat to be their leader

### Fragment 108: Nothing

*'Nothing'* multiplied by *'nothing'* equals *'nothing'* but it suits atheists to say otherwise by pretending that *'nothing'* can give birth to *'everything.'*

## Fragment 109: Slaughterhouse Losers

In Woolwich
A British soldier is run down and hacked to death
By two slaughterhouse losers
Driven mad by the reality of their own insignificance
They spit out hatred
Whilst waving a bloodied machete
A crime performed in Islam's name

Elsewhere a Muslim mother weeps
Dreading retaliation and
Worrying about the future of her children
She prays in maternal solidarity
For the mother of that slain soldier
An act of compassion performed in Islam's name

Two sides to Islam; which one will prevail?

## Fragment 110: The New Normal

Welcome to the *'new normal'*

Today we have same-sex marriages
And media-led encouragement of assisted suicide

Tomorrow we shall have polygamous marriages
And State-imposed euthanasia

The day after that we shall have inter-species marriages
And the casual murder of millions

Welcome to the *'new normal'*
Enjoy yourselves!

### Fragment 111: Only a Miracle

Into the darkness we have fallen

A darkness lacking any chink of light
A darkness with little hope of release

A darkness where true faith is no more
A darkness where compassion has died

A darkness which rejoices in a gaudy lie
A darkness which will cost millions of lives

Into the darkness we have fallen
Only a miracle can rescue us from its terrifying power

## Interlude

Fragments of shattered glass
Lie amidst toppled mannequins
As an alarm bell rings dolefully
Into the muggy night air

From the distance sirens begin to wail
But once again the police
Will arrive too late
The thieves have gone and
Taken their loot

A shattering has taken place
But who will bother to replace the broken glass?

# PART B: BROKEN SHARDS

## Shard 1: Bankruptcy

Mouth parched
Stomach creased in knots
A choking feeling
Gagging the throat

Legs unsteady
Hands trembling slightly
Nightmare thoughts
Stalk a haunted mind

Unstable emotions
Paralysing frustration
Despairing sighs
Paroxysms of rage

Applications rejected
Optimism withered
Desires thwarted
Hopes endlessly deferred

Broken promises
Shrivelled expectations
Dead-end ambitions
Dreams fade and fall

Dawn worries
Daytime struggles
Nights spent riding
A carousel of anxiety

Work has collapsed
Money's dwindled

No offers come
A phone broods in silence

Every penny counted
Expenses rigidly controlled
Each Bank Statement
Monitored with fretful care

Completely forsaken
Utterly abandoned
Faith flees
A pitiless darkness remains

Nothing is left
Nothing to live for
Nothing and no-one to trust in
Oh death how welcome you are

Suicide entices
Release is yearned for
A final end
Is anxiously desired

Wake up!
Stir yourself!
Face up to your responsibilities!
For the sake of those you love –
LIVE AND FIGHT ON!
LIVE! I SAY! AND FIGHT ON!

### Shard 2: Blazing Cities

The Cities are ablaze
(The Cities are ablaze)

Shopping Centres are plundered
(Shopping Centres are plundered)

Department Stores are set on fire
(Department Stores are set on fire)

By barbarians using modern technology
(By barbarians using modern technology)

They roam from one crime scene to another
(They roam from one crime scene to another)

Laughing, jeering, sneering
(Laughing, jeering, sneering)

A demoralised police force has lost control
(A demoralised police force has lost control)

Ordinary citizens watch with helpless despair
(Ordinary citizens watch with helpless despair)

Angered by their loss of property and livelihood
(Angered by their loss of property and livelihood)

A silhouetted woman jumps from a torched building
(A silhouetted woman jumps from a torched building)

A man lies beaten to death in a London alleyway
(A man lies beaten to death in a London alleyway)

Three martyrs to decency are run down by a stolen car
(Three martyrs to decency are run down by a stolen car)

The cities are scorched by a desperate hatred
(The cities are scorched by a desperate hatred)

Coming from a rootless generation
(Coming from a rootless generation)

Psychopaths, living only for the moment
(Psychopaths, living only for the moment)

Having known only violence, poverty and crime
(Having known only violence, poverty and crime)

They hold a violent party of hatred
(They hold a violent party of hatred)

And plunder the property of others
(And plunder the property of others)

They are the harbingers of a new *'Age'*
(They are the harbingers of a new *'Age'*

A new *'Dark Age'* we have inflicted upon ourselves

## Shard 3: Contrasts

### Part 1: Crack!

Crack!

A sniper's bullet in Aleppo, Syria
Shatters a twelve year old boy's spine
As he dashes back home with a loaf of stale bread
From inside the open entrance of his poor shell-battered dwelling
His mother emits a feral howl of grief
As he rolls in agony on the dusty rubble-strewn alleyway
Crying out for…

Crack!

Another sniper's bullet
Turns his head into an exploding red rose of blood and gore
Mother stumbles forward to cradle her dear baby

Crack!

As she falls
Her younger boys stand rigid, staring open-mouthed
A cold, hate filled vengeance enters their souls
A new generation of Jihadists has been born
And another small step taken toward
A Middle Eastern Apocalypse that could
Consume the lives of millions

Crack!

Another corpse
Another legacy of hatred
Left by a brutalized regime

Crack!

## Part 2: Martian Rover

On the desolate surface of Mars
The *'Curiosity Rover'*
Trundles around
The red rubble-strewn surface of Gale Crater
Taking photos that astonish scientists the world over
It shoots laser beams into rocks to test their consistency
Will it succeed in its mission in finding traces of life?
Who knows?
But it's odd that so much can be achieved on another planet
Over one hundred million miles away
And so little back home on earth

## Part 3: The Fading Flame

The London Olympic flame flickers and fades
As it takes one final incandescent bow
The ceremony has closed
The cheers have ceased and
And the commentators are silent
A stadium tidy-up has begun
Medal-adorned athletes return home to a hero's welcome
Time enough to return to reality

## Part 4: Glory to Man

We can discover the *'Higgs Bosom'*[31]
And scan the furthest reaches of space

We can wrap the world around in information
And genetically engineer whole species

---

[31] The Higgs Bosom is a zero charged sub-atomic particle (or family of particles) whose field gives everything its mass. Its discovery (announced on Wednesday 4th July 2012) confirmed *The Standard Model of the Universe.'*

We can ascend to the heavens in our rockets
And explore the deepest fathoms of the sea
*"Glory to Man in the highest! For Man is the master of all things!"*[82]

Crack!

Another sniper's bullet in Syria
Another child slumps to the ground, dead
Another hole is punctured through Swinburne's vain-glorious hymn

Meanwhile, a viper's nest of hatred has being created
It consists of those who murder in the name of God
Their venom will spread terror across the world

Funny how Swinburne's proud boasting
Now seems utterly shameful and hollow
It's totally irrelevant to our time

Rather than celebrate the imagined *'glory of Man'*
We should instead be studying the *'contradictions'* of Man
In order to better understand ourselves

Crack!

---

[82] From Algernon' Charles Swinburne's (1837-1909) *'Hymn to Man.'* He was a poet (and atheist) who liked to shock his contemporaries by parodying Christian hymns.

### Shard 4: Innocence

**Innocence Violated**

Things are now at an end
You almost drove me round the bend for...

You were not the person I took you to be

You had so much charm
Yet did so much harm

You were not the person I took you to be

You boasted of your enormous wealth
Yet stole my money with such great stealth

You were not the person I took you to be

You told many a fantastical tale
About those yachts you used to sail

You were not the person I took you to be

Credit cards you'd proudly flash
Before hurrying away in a furtive dash

You were not the person I took you to be

Fancy cars you loved to drive
To visit the nearest Night Club dive

You were not the person I took you to be

Saville Row suits were the style you wore
Even when unpaid bills began to sore

You were not the person I took you to be

You always sought after the very best
And made off with <u>my</u> savings with malignant zest

You were not the person I took you to be

My finances you completely bled dry
Laughing and sneering at my every sigh

You were not the person I took you to be

Whoever crossed you faced menacing threats and shouts
This continued to fuel my nagging doubts

You were not the person I took you to be

In your intimidating efforts to make me keep silent
Your behaviour turned more and more violent

You were not the person I took you to be

All of my other assets you decided to strip
Then I heard of your mysterious *'Asian Trip'*

You were not the person I took you to be

**Innocence Lost**

I borrowed heavily to pay for your fare
Desperate to end this hideous nightmare

I was no longer the fool you took me to be

At the airport check-in I waved you goodbye
Hiding a smile behind a blatantly false sigh

I was no longer the fool you took me to be

Certain authorities I quickly alerted
And at Customs you were swiftly diverted

I was no longer the fool you took me to be

A strip-search found a haul of Class A drugs
You'd fallen in with some gangland thugs

I was no longer the fool you took me to be

I smiled when a life-long sentence was passed
Here was your judgement at long, long last!

I was no longer the fool you took me to be

I heard you weep, howl and wail
As they took you down to the jail

I was no longer the fool you took me to be

Heard a prisoner had made a gash in your throat
That stark item of news really did make me gloat for...

I was no longer the fool you took me to be

## Shard 5: Fanatic

My Yorkshire accent
Is a perfect disguise
A sign of integration
A sign of commendation
A sign of social recognition
A typical Leeds *'loiner'* I appear
All-the better to deceive YOU, the godless

Perfect!
Now for mah mission

By day I teach
By night I preach
Hatred – raw hatred
For YOU
Who dorn't share my struggle

Eee!
By 'eck a reckoning is due

Tomorrow I kill,
The blood of YOU, the godless
Will flow
In crimson torrents
It <u>will</u> flow

Mah soul is satisfied,
Mah place in paradise is assured
A martyr's reward fer me
And a respected place in 'istory
You mah own dear family
Will be greatly honoured,
Please share in mah bountiful delight!

## Shard 6: Japanese Sorrow

Sliding plates
Build up of pressure
One lurch forward

Mass shaking
Uplifted sea waters
Opening chasms

Swaying office
Tumbling cabinets
Swinging lights

Spilling coffee
Desk-bound shelter
Loud cries

City panic
An engulfing Tsunami
Merciless advance

Uplifted boats
Swirling whirlpools
Flooded coast

Churning waves
Thunderous roaring
Bank of water

Floating houses
Piled up vehicles
Deadly onrush

Fleeing people
Washed away trains
Mass drowning

Shouting men
Onlookers shrieking
Women praying

Photos taken
Webcam recording
Instant news

City destruction
Mud-caked fields
Thousands lost

Loud explosion
Blazing refinery
A firestorm

Wrecked Reactor
Melting fuel rods
Lost control

Increasing heat
Televised explosions
Toxic clouds

Hissing steam
Dangerous readings
Masked workers

Anxious *'tweeting'*
Reassuring experts
TV reporting

Stoic calm
Mass evacuation
Tidal corpses

Food scarcity
Further aftershocks
Swinging signs

Harassed rescuers
Thunderous rumbles
Falling debris

Chilling snows
Freezing conditions
Blocked roads

Thousands dead
Debris-strewn wasteland
Few survivors

Costly bills
Economic disruption
Insurance losses

Mounting costs
Falling stock market
Sliding shares

Human frailty
Nature's cruel might
Fearful flight

A nation mourns
Japanese sorrow
Horrified world

## Shard 7: Jilted

With you the still waters of love
Ran ever so deep
You choked your passion
In the things you left unsaid
By your pregnant silences
You expressed an unrequited love
That led you to dance
On a seesaw of hope and despair

From your youth
You loved a man
Who was stolen from you
By your best friend
At that Procol Harum Concert
Back in '68

For 42 years you waited and waited
Watching him rise in the corporate world
Watching him acquire ever larger properties
Watching him and his wife
Raise a family of five
All Public School Educated
Whilst within your own womb
Their remained a yawning emptiness

You scraped by with that provincial library job
Which you really hated
Your hard won savings
Went into providing nursing care
For your widowed mother
As first her brain and then her body
Became wasted by a cruel dementia
*'An early onset of Alzheimer's'*
The Consultant had said
As he'd stifled a yawn

At what was to him
A drearily routine case

For 42 years you waited and waited
Still trapped in that grotty library job
Within your hearing
The women you worked with
Would make snide comments
About your nondescript appearance
And your taste in second-hand clothes
They gossiped about you being
An *'unwanted wallflower'*
Forever doomed to remain *'on the shelf'*
Your increasingly peevish and petty spinsterish ways
Came to be a growing source of workforce irritation
You would have taken early retirement
Except there was *'mother'* to provide for

At home the radio was your only companion
You couldn't even keep a pet
Because of your asthma

For 42 years you waited and waited
Watching <u>his</u> children grow up
And graduate into respectable professions
Twice a year you visited
Once after Christmas and
Once in the summer
Each time buying lavish presents
To win a love that could never be yours
His wife proffered you a cold toleration
Whilst your shy and awkward mannerisms
Protected you from being regarded as a threat
Besides, she needed your help
During the holiday periods
When the children were at home
He'd be away at some important high level Conference

Of the Multi-National Company he then worked for
She even conceded a vague *'Auntie'* role to you
To help relieve her own domestic pressures
At one time she'd confided her worries to you
Telling of his increasing absences from home
And of a certain secretary with whom
He'd regularly attend Conferences
You did your best to reassure her
But she seemed unconvinced
By your mumbled explanations

For 42 years you waited and waited
Then *'mother's* death
Freed you from that library job
You could take early retirement, even if it meant a meagre pension
Only your boss and her deputy
Turned up at your retirement and half-heartedly
Wished you farewell

Shortly after, he too retired with a gold plated pension
He went on a celebratory world cruise
With his wife
But within a year she'd sickened with cancer
And was dead

You attended her funeral
Attired in a respectful but alluring black
Offering a fumbled, mumbled comfort
Trying at the reception
To commiserate for a loss
That could fulfil all of your dreams

As was your duty
You listened patiently
In phone call after phone call
To his deluge of
Guilt-ridden grief

Your visits became more frequent
You helped him with the shopping
And provided him with meals
Containing the delicacies he especially liked
Gradually, you glided into a quasi-wifely role
He even gave you an old PC of his
So you could remain in contact

But at night you gnawed your finger nails
Until they bled
Still waiting and hoping
That his love
Would at last be yours

Then one frosty and glistening winter's evening
You received an email from Hell
*"Thanks for your help, but I'm due to re-marry shortly — its best we don't meet
again. It would serve no good purpose. Goodbye and thanks for the homemade
lentils."*

You howl
You scream
You sob
Like the first time
He rejected you
42 years ago
You even smash a dish against the wall
But there are no neighbours to hear
The flat next door is empty

Eventually, with the aid of prescribed medication
You go back to waiting and waiting —
For a great big nothing

In time you receive a hastily scribbled note from one of his daughters
Divulging that
He'd married one of his old secretaries

The one his wife had been worried about
Apparently, this development had caused something of a family rift
With the daughter and two sons not attending the wedding
Out of respect for their late mother
The cruise had been a final attempt at saving a failing marriage
He was selling up his London properties
And moving across to Jersey
Where he could enjoy the golf
It was <u>her</u> idea apparently
After that
Nothing more was heard

In the crumbling Geriatric ward where you now eke out your days
You repeatedly call out his long-deceased name
In a dementia-raddled old age
Before plaintively pleading, *'Please find our children!'*
Your underpaid Care Assistants
Wink at each other
Before dropping you down on the commode, remarking
*"Surprised you 'ad anyone at all*
*You never seemed the marryin' type."*

## Shard 8: Lest I Offend

In this politically correct age
There are many things I dare not write about

I dare not write about faith or spirituality
Lest I offend people of faith and those with none

I dare not write about religious fanaticism
Lest I offend and lose my head (both metaphorically and literally)

I dare not write about the Middle East
Lest I offend Israelis and Arabs alike

I dare not write about politics or politicians
Lest I offend activists from every political party

I dare not write about judges or lawyers
Lest I offend those who would sue me

I dare not write about money and financial corruption
Lest I offend my Bank Manager

I dare not write about the Mass Media
Lest I offend those who could destroy my reputation

I dare not write about Culture or Class
Lest I offend the Equal Opportunities Commission

I dare not write about sinister global conspiracies
Lest I offend the Freemasons and members of the Illuminate

I dare not write about the Age of Aquarius
Lest I offend geriatric hippies

I dare not write about writers and poets
Lest I offend literary critics

I dare not write about love and romance
Lest I offend the readers of Mills and Boon

I dare not write about marriage
Lest I offend both *'Gays'* and *'Straights'*

I dare not write about Public Houses and the beer they serve
Lest I offend the Licensed Victuallers Association

I dare not write about Health and Medicine
Lest I offend Doctors and Nurses

I dare not write about Education and Teaching
Lest I offend the Teaching Unions

I dare not write about Science and Technology
Lest I offend by providing inaccurate data

I dare not write about the beauty of nature
Lest I offend Creationists and Evolutionists alike

I dare not write about the joys of gardening
Lest I offend hay fever sufferers everywhere

I dare not write about the seas and the oceans
Lest I offend some obscure EU fishery directive

I dare not write about Planets and Stars
Lest I offend practitioners of Astrology

I dare not write in either a prosaic or flamboyant style
Lest I offend The Plain English Campaign

So, in this politically correct age what dare I write about?
The answer is *'nothing'* I suppose

# Shard 9: Masters of Hate

## The Motive

Hail, you masters of hate
Whose actions I now contemplate

There are many you wish to annihilate
Whole nations you yearn to decimate

Your mind turns over many a scheme
But hatred is your constant theme

You lack any sense of moral shame
Plotting is your never-ending game

Dealers of death you certainly are
Those betraying you won't go far

Cold organizers of many a *'hit'*[33]
Any dissent gives you a maniacal fit

For you are the masters of hate
Seeking always to be *'ever so great'*

## The Means

Deceitful words you often deliver
Their content creates an icy shiver

In your rants you furiously rage
Poisoning those of a tender, young age

From your mouth harsh words erupt
Vulnerable minds you love to corrupt

---

[33] *'Hit'* is a colloquial term, meaning assassination

Death-carrying children are your tools
You've turned them into zombie fools

Glory and vengeance is what you lust for
As you exploit your power base amongst the poor

For you, endless plotting is exciting fun
*"Power grows from the barrel of a gun"*

With gleeful, gloating malice you use every ploy
In order to slay those you wish to destroy

Acts of mass homicide give you a thrill
You're indiscriminate in the ways that you kill

To you terror is one long, drama
You might even be interviewed on *Panorama*[84]

But you are the masters of hate
With you there can be no debate

**The Crime**

A fumbling female finger flicks
A hidden detonator clicks

One huge ear-splitting roar
A column of acrid smoke begins to soar

Shopping mall glass bursts and shatters
To you it's all a routine matter

Metal nails shoot into passers-by
Many of whom will die for your lie

---

[84] A BBC current affairs programme

Dead and injured are sprawled all about
One legless man gives a final shout

A blood-spattered child wails over his glass-shredded mother
So what! To you he's just another *'hostile other'*

Sirens pierce the air with a forlorn wail
Into your trap they proceed without fail

A child's clumsy finger flicks
Another detonator clicks

Another even louder blasting roar
Another column of smoke begins to soar

Others have been lured into your trap
Their will to resist must surely sap

Shop window dummies melt in the fire
Temples of commerce now a funeral pyre

Broken human mannequins lie in the street
Soon each will be covered in a body sheet

A smell of burning death fills the air
Some of your targets have now lost their hair

Blood anointed streets are hastily cleared
You've given people what they most really feared

Breathless reporters publicise your act
With you they've struck an unholy pact

## The Aftermath

Ranting videos you gleefully release
Promising a war that will never cease

More threats are delivered with a cold, dead man's look
But you're confident you'll never be *'brought to book'*

This exercise of destructive power is your delight
All governing authorities you love to slight

You want these acts of mass homicide
To precede an even greater genocide

In your words you have repeatedly lied
In your heart all humanity has died

Your cause may succeed or it may fail
But much blood will follow in its trail

You may end your days as a respected Head of State
Being driven through Buckingham Palace Gate

Or torture in a secret police cell
May yet become your fatal hell

But one thing I know for sure
Of ritual violence you'll want more

## Shard 10: Memorial Cities

### <u>STRICTLY CONFIDENTIAL</u>

THIS DOCUMENT IS FOR <u>LIMITED</u> CIRCULATION ONLY

NO UNAUTHORISED REPRODUCTION PERMITTED

ANY UNAUTHORISED REPRODUCTION WILL RESULT IN LEGAL ACTION BEING TAKEN ON THE BASIS OF CLAUSE 13.6 OF THE NEW 'GLOBAL COPYRIGHT ACT'

MAXIMUN PENALTY THIRTY YEARS IMPRISONMENT

### <u>DRAFT REPORT OUTLINE</u>

### (STRICTLY CONFIDENTIAL, NO UNAUTHORISED REPRODUCTION PERMITTED)

Containing Figures FAO the Senior Global Reconstruction Commission for the Middle Eastern, Central Asian and North African Region

Memorial City 1
(Former capital city of...)
Dead 6,000,000
(Margin of error 3%)[35]
No known survivors
Status: uninhabitable

Memorial City 2
(Former capital city of...)
Dead 2,000,000
(Margin of error 3%)

---

[35] A *'margin of error'* is a statistical term meaning that the figure could be 180,000 either way of 6,000,000. 180,000 being 3% of 6,000,000

No known survivors
Status: uninhabitable

Memorial City 3
(Former capital city of...)
Dead 13,000,000
(Margin of error 5%)
13 survived for two weeks
11 subsequently died from radiation sickness
Status: uninhabitable
.

.

.

Memorial City 101
(Formerly known as...)
Dead 1,600,000
(Margin of error 3%)
No known survivors
Status: uninhabitable

Memorial City 102
(Formerly known as...)
Dead 1,500,000
(Margin of error 5%)
2 survived
1 subsequently committed suicide
Status: uninhabitable

Memorial City 103
(Formerly known as...)
Dead 3,600,000
(Margin of error 4%)
150 survived
132 subsequently died from radiation sickness
Status: suburbs now partly inhabitable

**Estimated Totals**

Number of dead 600,000,000
(Margin of error 3.5%)

Number of survivors: under 100,000,000
(Precise figures as yet unavailable)

Estimated proportion of land rendered permanently uninhabitable 6%

Estimated proportion of land rendered currently uninhabitable 13%
(Severe risk of radiation sickness)

Estimated proportion of land rendered partly uninhabitable 20%
(Some risk of radiation sickness)

Proportion of land cleared of radiation 0.03%
(Mainly transport networks and natural resource centres)

Level of Biochemical Contamination: As yet unknown

Estimated loss of Gross Domestic Product 90%

Estimated loss of oil production 81%

Estimated loss of agricultural production 65%

Regional food and fuel reserves: Nil

Long term re-settlement prospects: poor

Long term oil extraction prospects: variable

Refugee problem: severe, but will reduce as the number of survivors declines through natural wastage caused by the effect of radiation and deprivation of basic necessities.

The above estimates may be revised as further data is obtained from both aerial and satellite observation. Land surveys are currently only possible within narrowly defined areas.

## Draft proposal

<u>The Commission should continue to give priority to restoring basic communication infrastructure and natural energy supplies.</u> Funding (if available) is to be confined to those survivors having the required skills to assist in the above priority. A provisional estimate would suggest between 700-900 known such survivors.

The geo-strategic location of Memorial Cities 1 and 2 would suggest that, in the long term, their outer suburbs could be visited by tourists as long as strict decontamination procedures were observed. Brief over-flight visits, spanning their central craters should further enhance commercial revenue (as would visits made by those with former family connections).

In the very long term, these sites may provide dramatic settings for film production or historical reconstructions. Should the level of contamination remain high then alternative sites must be considered.

Until extensive decontamination takes place the precise real estate values are impossible to estimate.

A Memorial Book is to be produced with subsequent profits used to cover administrative costs.

A Public Relations Firm must be hired to encourage public acceptance of controversial decisions, with priority given to avoiding an uncaring image.

Due to the sensitivities involved, further discussion of this draft proposal is strongly recommended. Current adverse economic conditions may hinder implementation.

## Shard11: Relative Freedom

At home the politicians have fiddled their expenses

Don't worry, everything is relative
We must celebrate cultural diversity
And affirm individual freedom
It's politically incorrect to think otherwise

At home the bankers have fiddled their interest rates

Don't worry, everything is relative
We must celebrate cultural diversity
And affirm individual freedom
It's politically incorrect to think otherwise

At home the rich have fiddled their tax claims

Don't worry, everything is relative
We must celebrate cultural diversity
And affirm individual freedom
It's politically incorrect to think otherwise

At home the young destroy themselves with drink and drugs

Don't worry, everything is relative
We must celebrate cultural diversity
And affirm individual freedom
It's politically incorrect to think otherwise

Abroad, the politicians practise mass murder

Don't worry, everything is relative
We must celebrate cultural diversity
And affirm individual freedom
It's politically incorrect to think otherwise

Abroad, the officials practice mass extortion

Don't worry, everything is relative
We must celebrate cultural diversity
And affirm individual freedom
It's politically incorrect to think otherwise

Abroad, the community leaders practice mass hatred

Don't worry, everything is relative
We must celebrate cultural diversity
And affirm individual freedom
It's politically incorrect to think otherwise

Abroad, custom demands mass female circumcision
And the ritual sacrifice of children

Don't worry, everything is relative
We must celebrate cultural diversity
And affirm individual freedom
It's politically incorrect to think otherwise

Here at home I want to blow you up

Don't worry, everything is relative
We must celebrate cultural diversity
And affirm individual freedom
It's politically incorrect to think otherwise

BOOM![36]

---

[36] Performers may repeat the chorus after *'Boom!'* in order to highlight the absurdity of the position it represents

## Shard 12: Settling for Decline

Settling for decline
Settling for decline

There's no more that I can do
It looks as though we're through
You're settling for decline

I did my very best
But you failed to pass the test
You're settling for decline

Though allowed to have my say
You still chose the easy way
You're settling for decline

The announcement is oh so sad
Things could go so very bad
You're settling for decline

Once a church of such distinction
Now you're heading for extinction
You're settling for decline

The old ways no longer work
My own duties I can't shirk
You're settling for decline

Our paths which once converged
Are now separate and diverged
You're settling for decline

It all has become a bind
A fresh direction I must find
You're settling for decline

My energies are depleted
Separation is now completed
You're settling for decline

My heart could easily break
This whole affair has made me shake
You're settling for decline

Things were given a real good try
Now it's time to say goodbye

'Cos you're settling for decline
Settling for decline
An avoidable, decline

## Shard 13: Spinster by the River

You stand there
Lonely and forlorn beside
A fast flowing river
Wearing a dowdy, old fashioned dress
And a wide brimmed straw hat
A lost look on your ageing face
Even now you crave, long and yearn
For children to call your own

With sorrow
You reflect on how marriage
Always passed you by
Like the fast flowing waters
Of the river you now stand beside
In quietness you recall
How the men you loved
Always found someone else

Spinster by the river
You never did any harm
Content to display
A quaint *'old world'* charm

You glance at a bird
Bringing food to its hungry fledglings
You listen to the bleat of newborn spring lambs
A bushy-tailed squirrel scampers from branch to branch
Enjoying a heady freedom
So far above the ground

With tear-filled eyes
You reflect upon
What might have been
And on a life of thwarted hopes
Where relationships never quite worked out

Spinster by the river
You never did any harm
Content to display
A quaint *'old world'* charm

You turn and head quickly back
Past a weir of foaming water
Next to which a newly married couple
Who are having their photographs taken
You move quickly on
As their photographer barks yet another command
The next picture is taken
... But not of you

You drift back to the luxury hotel
Where your niece's Reception is being held
No one ever disclosed
You were only invited as an afterthought
To provide lifts for more popular guests

Spinster by the river
You never did any harm
Content to display
A quaint *'old world'* charm

You fade into the well-dressed
Happily chatting crowd
But no one really speaks to you
Time to put your memories into a bag
And force yourself a smile

A friendly dog – a Bearded Collie
Jumps up and licks your face
Before being pulled back by a flustered Best Man
Time for another frozen smile
To hide the longing in your heart

Spinster by the river
You never did any harm
Content to display
A quaint *'old world'* charm

You saunter to the edge of the bustling throng
Last photos quickly taken
Final goodbyes made
You edge to your car
Leaving behind another wedding
That wasn't yours

# Shard 14: The Enlightened World of Atheism

## Part 1: Collective Marxist Atheism

### A) The Delusion

Welcome to the enlightened world of Atheism
Free from Faith's cold, clammy clasp
And the oppression it brings
Enjoy the New Age of reason
Where *'Man is the measure of all things'*
Science has all of the answers
And thanks to Darwin all *'gods'* have at last been dethroned
A Brave New World is here!
Humanity's paradise at last!

### B) Past Reality

A winter palace is stormed
A violent coup has taken place
Blood spatters across pavements,
Red streaks in the soft white snow
It is the communion wine of revolution

Savage dictators oppress the masses
Ukrainian children with swollen bellies
Cry for *'expropriated'* bread
Peasant mothers, driven by utter despair
Eat their newborn children
Casualties of a callous *'five year plan'*
Who'll nurture an ongoing hate

The night time arrests
The thud of rubber truncheons
On bruised, bloodied flesh
Screams from Secret Police torture cells

(Later they would be padded)
Siberian death camps
Cambodian killing fields
Besotted crowds chanting
*'Mao, Mao, Mao Tse Tung!"*
In Madam Mao's choreographed carnival of death

Guerrilla ambitions
Outbreaks of terrorism
Walls festooned with barbed wire
Peaceful demonstrators crushed by tanks
Whole populations massacred or deported
As revolution is exported
Across one third of the world

Dried up seas
Acid-eaten forests
Irradiated Steppes
Chaotic collapses into bankruptcy
Endless queues for food
Hard-earned pensions losing all value
Inflation ripping out of control
Once-proud empires fragmenting
Into a chaos of contending ethnic groups
Their loss not regretted by a subjected people

Things should <u>never</u> have turned out like this
The bold Atheist experiment has failed
But possessed by a godless fury
We atheists <u>will</u> try again!

## Part 2: Individualistic Hedonistic Atheism

### A) The Delusion Developed

Man is evolving into a *'higher being'*
Progress is assured

Technology's revolution is endlessly working
To undergird all economic growth
Bringing the greatest happiness to the greatest number!
(Never mind the resultant pollution)
The *'pill'* offers sex without responsibility
*'Don't be a square, be groovy and follow the trend man'*
Let people be *'true to themselves'*
(Please ignore the sickening murders on Saddleworth Moor and
The repeated High School shootings)
A *'liberation mission'* is the ideal aim
The permissive society is a <u>civilized</u> society
With people <u>forced</u> to be free
History will end as liberal democracy triumphs
Science will solve all of our problems!
Relax, there is no God
Nor any *'friend in the sky'*
Not even a *'flying spaghetti monster!'*
Belief in God is a delusion
Let atheist Churches offer a new sense of community

## B) Present Reality

Broken communities herded into high rise blocks
The phallic symbols of a bleak Modernism
Blind, blundering bureaucracy
Mind-numbing forms
Financial crashes
Queues of the unemployed
Punitive energy bills
Mindless acts of violence from those with shaven heads
Elderly war veterans routinely dishonoured
Their frail wives not daring to go out
Whole-scale devolution has taken place
Rioting mobs chant gorilla noises; *'Ugh!' 'Ugh!' 'Ugh!'*
Fearlessly charging against a wall of police riot shields
(When not busily looting a shopping mall)

On a stifling Friday night
City centres receive a baptism of vomit
(Even worse on a Saturday night)
Everyone is *'dumbing down, down, down'*
Unwanted babies are sucked from their mother's womb
Losing their grip on life
They are hoovered away like so much household rubbish
The 1967 Abortion Act marked their exclusion from the human race
No matter! They were but a social inconvenience
Now the disabled and the elderly are poised to join them
In this one-way euthanasia parade

The *'culture of death'* rages like a plague across the media
The *'Big Brother'* den is really a human pig pen
With ogling commentators jeering and sneering
The political parties casually *'lie, lie and lie again'*
Each wanting a huge slice of the *'parliamentary pie'*
Intellectuals languish in a cannabis daze
Groping in an endless Post Modernist maze
People have become passive zombies
Their minds *'zapped'* by too many computer games
Always desperate for the latest thrill
A cavernous vacuum has opened for anything to fill

Oh dear, things should <u>never</u> have turned out like this
The bold Atheist experiment has failed – yet again!
But possessed by a godless fury
We atheists <u>will</u> try again!

## Part 3: Inclusive Global Atheism

### A) The Delusion Goes Global

A New World Order we <u>shall</u> build
Peace, justice and equality
We <u>shall</u> bring
Freedom, Democracy and equality for all!

Religion <u>must</u> wither away
Into its well-deserved oblivion!
In centuries to come
We shall modify our own human DNA
We shall ascend to the heavens
To conquer planet after planet
And star system after star system
Humanity will be the new Lord of the Universe!
All *'gods'* will have been dethroned –
We will be king! We will be Lord!
We will be our own God!
A global paradise <u>shall</u> be built...
At broadband speed

## B) Future Reality

Our *'great emancipator,'* once the embodiment of all human dreams
Has become our *'great enslaver'*
Our New World Caesar is now hell-bent on becoming God!
His worldwide rule is nothing but an electronic tyranny!
Ideals betrayed, Messianic promises broken
Mass persecution of dissenters, opposition crushed
Nothing left but a howling desert landscape
Full of ruined cities, each strewn with decaying skeletal remains
Mute monuments to a once-proud humanism
That tried to do without God

Things should <u>never</u> have turned out like this
The bold Atheist experiment has failed yet again
But possessed by a godless fury
We atheists <u>will</u> try again
We <u>will</u> build our God-forsaken paradise
For ours is a history from which we will never, never learn![37]

---

[37] First written on Thursday, 20th March 2008, then word processed on Friday, 16th August 2013 after having been found mislaid amongst some Family History documents

# Shard 15: The Night They Burnt the Newlands Down

*"UH-UH-UH!"*

Hear the moronic ape-like chant
Expressing hatred of all authority
A manic masked mob
Gathering on a concrete concourse
Near a frail and flimsy back garden fence

Hark! The criminals have come out to play
*"Yeah, let's go 'n' smash it!"*
*"Let's burn the foogin place down!"*
*"Let's go an' 'trash it!"*
*"Let's kill the pigs!*[38] *"*
*"Let's batter some foogin students!"*

It's a sultry summer night
And darkness has long since fallen

*"UH-UH-UH!"*

A vortex of hatred
Swirls around the concourse
It gathers strength and
Petrol bombs are lit
A volcanic seething well of aggression
Is about to rip open

*"UH-UH-UH!"*

Tremble and watch as this fuel-lit procession
Surges out of the concourse
Its ape-like grunting reaching a fearful animalistic crescendo

---

[38] A slang term for *'police'*

*"UH-UH-UH!"*

*No, not that van*
*It belongs to the musician 'oo does our gigs!'*

*"UH-UH-UH!"*

BASH!
Stones dent the metal body work of a student's car

CRASH!
A brick smashes through its windscreen
Leaving an explosion of shattered glass in its wake

SMASH!
A car is turned over
Before erupting into a petrol-fed inferno

CRUMP!
Another car vehicle is turned over

POP!
Its full petrol tank exploding
Into a dense smoke-filled fire

ROAR!
The ejecting flames of parked vehicles
Soar high into the air
Baptising it
With a petroleum reek of destruction

*"HAH-HAY!"*

The mob cheer as
As yet another car is turned over

WHOOSH!

And this latest overturned vehicle
Joins in the pyrotechnic display

*"UH-UH-UH!"*

Like the engulfing waters of a Tsunami wave
This mob, called *'Legion'*
Surge up Hyde Park Road
Towards Woodhouse Moor
And target The Newlands Pub
Where a few days earlier
The landlord had been beaten with baseball bats
For *'grassing'* on local drug dealers

Listen! Their animalistic chant rises to an orgasmic frenzy

*"UH-UH-UH!"*

*"Emergency!"*
*"Fire, Police or Ambulance?"*
*"Get the Police!"*
*"Central Police Point, how can we help you?"*
A supercilious female voice answers
*"There's a riot going on in Hyde Park Road!"*
*"What's your name, Sir?"*
*"Jones"*
*"Can I have your real name?"*
*"Jones!"*
*"Your REAL name"*
*"JONES!"*
*"I'm sure – what's your REAL name?"*
*"JONES IS MY REAL NAME!!! Check it against my telephone number, if you like"*
*"Come off it! Your REAL name, please."*
*"Oh, to hell with this! There's a riot outside and you keep asking me for my name! This is stupid – I'm putting the phone down!"*
*"Can I have your real"*

SLAM!
*"Silly cow! You think we're all scum just 'cos we live on the Hyde Park Estate!"*

*"UH-UH-UH!"*

A mother's heartfelt prayer
An oasis of peace
Young children continue to slumber
Oblivious to the evil surrounding them

*"UH-UH-UH!"*

The kicking down of doors
Wild, excited cries

A loud WHOOSH and roar of flames
As more frenzied cheers herald
A myriad of mini-nova explosions
Storage rooms detonating
With a POP! POP! POP!

More senseless cheering
As petrol bombs blaze comet-like into the furnace
That once was The Newlands Pub

Greedy fingers of flame
Poke their way through the roof

A creaking sound, CRASH!

*"HAH-HAY!!!"*

Thick acrid smoke billows into the air
As more alcohol stores explode
With their tell-tale POP! POP! POP!

The Newlands Public House is now an incandescent mess

CRASH!

More of the roof crumbles and tumbles
Into an open maw of flame
Surging ever higher into the smoke blackened sky
This erupting volcano of hatred
Testifies to a new barbarism

Another loud crash!
A ritual sacrifice has been made
Civilized norms are no more
Only a cruel savagery remains
The Lord of the Flies is King

The mob dance and prance around
Like begrimed savages at a pagan feast

SCRAPE! SCRATCH! SCRAPE!

Thieving, grasping hands
Pull and drag at vending machines –
Scraping them along the road
Tossing them onto
A sloping grass verge

BANG! BANG! BANG!

Like vultures descending upon prey
Crow-bars prize them open
Their innards distributed
To women bystanders
Who gawp and gossip
Outside lit doorways
Standing in gaudy dressing gowns
Glad of this free handout of cigarettes
A posse of burley Jamaican men
Smoke their *joints'* nearby

A whiff of cannabis
Adding a bitter-sweet scent
To the choking air

A thuggish-faced Yorkshire lad
Cycles up and down
His slightly sneering expression
Now feigning a look of unconvincing innocence

At the top of Hyde Park Road
A multi-racial mob of hatred[39]
Cheer the Newlands immolation
The local underclass is in full revolt
And for one and a half hours
There's no law
The mob rules OK
Wailing sirens announce the Law's belated arrival
Helmeted policemen line-up
Behind a wall of transparent riot shields.
Moving down Hyde Park Road
From Woodhouse Moor
They're greeted with a meteor shower of stones
Petrol bombs and other projectiles

*"Kill the Pigs!"*
*"Let's do 'em!"*
*"Yeah, burn 'em alive!"*

BANG! CRASH! CRUMP!

---

[39] The morning after the riot I was interviewed by a petite female Asian reporter for a local Bradford newspaper. It took place at the top of Hyde Park Road. She kept insisting that it was a race riot, thinking it was a matter of underprivileged *'blacks'* opposing a white police force. When I kept insisting that *'it was an underclass riot – involving members from every ethnic minority'* she still persisted in asking me about *'the race riot,'* marking it down as such in her note book. I also believe that many of the newspaper reports exaggerated the numbers involved in the riot – though in such situations it's difficult to distinguish between perpetrators and bystanders.

A pelting of stones
A smashing of bottles
A whoosh of petrol bombs...
But the thin blue line holds
And begins a slow advance
Down a debris-strewn Hyde Park Road
Like an expelled flood the mob surges back onto the concourse

*"Let's torch the petrol station!"*
*"Yeah, let's get it goin!'"*

BANG! CRASH! CRUMP!

Slowly the forces of authority
Establish a tenuous control
On an insurrectionist housing estate
The slamming of doors
Marks the exit of both rioters and bystanders

Only the thuggish-faced boy
On the wobbling bicycle remains
Watching and spying, still feigning an unconvincing innocence
Waiting for pay from his quickly vanished masters

A father and his fifteen year old daughter survey the scene
Where cars burn like a metallic funeral pyre
Melting the tarmac beneath them
Into a bubbling, smouldering goo
Together they watch and observe
But draw different lessons from what they see;
Forever etched into each separate memory is
The night they burnt The Newlands Pub down

# Shard 16: Water Flow

The water flows
From a reed strewn bog

The water flows
Over moss covered rocks

The water flows
Past withered moorland heather

The water flows
To gouge out a narrow gulley

The water flows
Over a towering ridge

The water flows
Into underground drains

The water flows
Into a lush green valley

The water flows
Into a large meandering river

The water flows
To a coastline landscape

The water flows
Into a boundless sea
Leaving nothing but
The signature of
Bursting bubbles in its wake

# Shard 17: We Shall Live

We shall live in a mass extermination society
Where death as a right will become death as a duty[40]

The old, infirm and terminally ill
All targets for a mass-medical kill

Those a burden to the State
Will find euthanasia is their fate

The unwanted elderly with money in the bank
Now due to die, with relatives to thank

Patients tremble with helpless dread
Soon they'll be among the dead

White coated staff prepare a lethal injection
Their humanity is now in a state of subjection

Mini-Shipman's[41] they've all become
Heavy sedation makes their victims numb

Another useless life to finish
The unwanted will diminish

Drug administration is done by machine
Psychologically, that's much more clean

Termination targets to complete
If the disabled are to deplete

White coat brutality is the norm
No longer any conscience to be borne

---

[40] This first stanza may act as a chorus to be inserted between each verse.
[41] Dr Harold Shipman (1946-2004) was a General Practitioner, notorious for murdering up to 250 of his patients through lethal injections. He hanged himself in Wakefield prison on 13th January 2004.

Teams compete to terminate quicker
And ensure that life won't continue to flicker

Bored administrators complete the paperwork
Important duties they will not shirk

No Nuremburg trial will they have to face
With names as statistics on a secret data base

As hospital mortuaries fill up
Financial budgets must add up

Funds exist for a new freezer lorry
No need for staff to feel sorry

Spare body parts can be extracted
Helpful laws have been enacted

No worries about a compensation claim
There's no one around to take the blame

In this country compassion has fled
The *'mildly sick'* may soon join the dead

A government decree adds to the fatal list
Including political dissenters – they do insist

Cardboard coffins will be mandatory
Highly ecological and highly inflammatory

Each cardboard coffin will increase saving
Ensuring fewer bills will need paying

It's our evolutionary duty to eliminate the weak
Our species won't be propagated by the meek

Good and evil are part of the *'one'*
And into its blissful realm we shall all come

Once death was inflicted by stealth
Now it's <u>free</u> on the National health

*'Dignitas'* laid the groundwork
Painful duties it did not shirk

The unwanted dead go up in billowing smoke
Give crematoria furnaces a good old stoke!

Perhaps some use for them can be found
Otherwise let's scatter the ashes on the ground

Compassion has died
Politicians have lied

The future ain't gonna be much fun
'Cos' in the end, we'll all 'get done'

We're becoming a mass extermination society
Death as a right is now death as a duty[42]

We're becoming a mass extermination society

La-la-la[43]

---

[42] Performers may close the recital at this point or they may proceed to the next stanza.
[43] Performers may end with a mad twirl and an ironic bow and smirk in order to express the bland amorality that's conveyed in this poem.

## Shard 18: World Messiah

I can make you free, I can make you free!
So long as you give your lives to me!
I can make you free, I can make you free!
So long as you follow me
I <u>will</u> make you free, I <u>will</u> make you free!
So long as you worship me

We want to follow you! We want to follow you!

I shall bring social liberation
Freedom from poverty and injustice
Greedy exploiters I will slay
The humble I will exalt
All you need to display
Is a simple faith in <u>me</u>!

We are waiting to follow you! We are waiting to follow you!

All you need do is put aside every fear
And banish those doubts that trouble your mind
Let reason go –
Enter the realm of light!
If you adore my image
I will raise you higher and higher
Through many levels
You shall ascend
Until full Divinity is yours
*"You shall be like gods (and goddesses)*
*Knowing the difference between good and evil"*
*You will surely live!"*[44]

We long to follow you! We long to follow you!

---

[44] Genesis 3:4-5

World peace is what I shall assuredly bring
Troubled nations I shall calm and soothe
In me every Messianic promise is truly fulfilled
I am the realization of every human hope
Behold! I enter the Holy City
Riding on a white horse and
And accompanied by a splendid retinue!
Hear the crowds cheering
The whole world loves me!
Forget the crucified Saviour
Recognize me as your Lord and God!
Bow down before my image!

We do recognize you! We do recognize you!

I will make you free, I will make you free!
Now that you've given your lives to me!
I am the world teacher
Whose mission is to enlighten humanity
I am the World Messiah
Who offers peace and justice
I am the god of this world
Who bestows the *'gnosis'* that gives salvation

We are worshipping you! We are worshipping you!

You're free! You're free!
Relax and enjoy your new reality
Now come and follow me
Spread my message far and near
Other disciples you must make
*"This is a blessing you just have to give away"*[45]

We're free! We're free! Eagerly tasting a New Age reality

---

[45] A quote from church meetings that propagated the Toronto Experience from 1994-1997

You don't see now but I'm taking you into a realm of fantasy
Come and drink the coke that's laced with cyanide
Or burn with me in that Branch Davidian Ranch
Love death – not life
And put an end to all strife

Take the road that leads to Armageddon
I will be your sure and steadfast guide
Come and burn with me!
Yes! Come and burn with me!
Burn with me forever, Amen!

Our minds and hearts belong to you!
We will follow you! We will follow you –
No matter where you take us!

## Postlude

Shards of broken glass lie in the gutter
As an alarm bell rings dolefully
Into an oppressive late summer night

The sound of sirens echo louder
As police cars draw near
Suddenly they screech into view
But no one is to be seen

Car-bound officers observe the scene
With a blank faced helplessness
There's nothing more they can do
Crime has won another triumph
Darkness has descended
And who will preserve the light –

Unless it be Him
With the nailed pierced hands?

# Background Details for 'The Shattering'

## Part 1: Broken Fragments

All 'Fragments' not included in the following list were first drafted between June-July 2009.

**Fragment 8b:** Written on Monday 22nd April 2013 after being disturbed at 6.00AM with a silly text message on my mobile phone. The final line was provoked by the title of Bob Dylan's famous song 'Blowin' in the wind.'

**Fragment 12c:** This piece was initially told as a joke to a family friend on the occasion of Queen Elizabeth II's Diamond Jubilee Celebration, on Sunday, 3rd June 2012.

**Fragment 13a:** Written on Tuesday, 15th May 2012

**Fragment 13b:** Written on Thursday, 19th January 2012

**Fragment 14:** Written on Tuesday, 29th August 2011

**Fragment 17b:** Written on Sunday, 7th April 2013 outside Heptonstall Methodist Church in Calderdale

**Fragment 18:** Written on Monday, 27th February 2012

**Fragment 26:** Written on Monday 18th April 2011. It followed the reading of two newspaper articles, the first of which concerned a BBC documentary which allegedly provided favourable coverage of an assisted suicide. The second article revealed that a pro-euthanasia film was about to be shown in Secondary Schools

**Fragment 28b:** Written on Tuesday, 3rd December 2013

**Fragment 41:** This first arose after seeing an elderly cat lying fast asleep on a window sill at Shaldon, near South Devon on Tuesday, 18th August 2009.

**Fragment 44:** Written on Sunday, 30th September 2012

**Fragment 49:** Written on Sunday, 13th September 2009 following a visit to London to conduct some family history research

**Fragment 50:** Written on Thursday, 5th May 2011

**Fragment 51a-b:** Written on Wednesday, 29th May 2013 and dedicated to my elderly mother who was experiencing growing physical frailty. Thankfully, she lived to enjoy her ninetieth birthday in November of that year.

**Fragment 53:** Written on Wednesday, 23rd May 2012 following a huge decline in the writer's business.

**Fragment 56:** Written on Saturday, 5th September 2009

**Fragment 58:** Written on Saturday, 12th September 2009. It was inspired by the Dr Who Episode 'Silence in the Library,' first broadcast during May-June 2008.

**Fragment 59:** Written on Tuesday, 22nd September 2009, three days after I'd returned from a family history trip to London. The poem is loosely based upon my view from a train window when travelling from Ricksmanworth to London.

**Fragment 60:** Written on Tuesday, 22nd September 2009.

**Fragment 65:** Written on Friday, 19th February 2010

**Fragment 67:** This dream occurred during the early hours of Saturday, 27th March 2010 and was transcribed on the following Wednesday

**Fragment 68:** Written on Saturday, 27th March 2010

**Fragment 69:** Written Friday, 23rd February 2012

**Fragment 70:** Written on Sunday, 27th June 2010

**Fragment 71:** Written on Wednesday, 30th June 2010

**Fragment 73:** Written on Sunday, 28th October 2012

**Fragment 74a:** Written beside a moorland stream on Wednesday, 23rd May 2012.

**Fragment 75:** The comment in this fragment was made by my youngest son, in late December 2010

**Fragment 76:** This was based upon a conversation I overheard whilst waiting for a bus on Monday, 7th February 2011

**Fragment 77:** Written on Monday, 7th March 2011 whilst suffering from a head cold. During the previous evening I'd watched the BBC2 documentary *'Wonders of the Universe'* presented by Dr Brian Cox. It suggested that the Universe would eventually break down to absolutely nothing.

**Fragment 78:** Written on Monday, 14th February 2011. It was inspired by a news report which drew upon the research of Sherry Turkle (2011) warning that people were too wired up 'to *talk like a human.'* (John Harlow *'Too Wired To Talk Like A Human,'* Sunday Times News Review p. 5.6, 30th January 2011)

**Fragment 81:** Written on Friday, 8th April 2011 after encountering yet another church heading for closure

**Fragment 82:** Written on Friday, 23rd March 2012.

**Fragment 83:** Written on Thursday, 17th March 2011 in response to the revolutionary uprisings in the Arab World that had begun some weeks previously

**Fragment 84:** Written on Thursday, 21st April 2011 following a discussion (the previous evening) about counselling.

**Fragment 85:** Written on Friday, 22nd April 2011 (the final two lines being inserted on Wednesday, 18th May 2011)

**Fragment 86:** Written on Friday, 22nd April 2011

**Fragment 87:** Written on Tuesday, 3rd May 2011 (the writers' fifty-fifth birthday)

**Fragment 88:** Written on Thursday, 19th February 2009 and was suggested by a remark the writer's wife had made concerning the *'growing torrent'* of anti-Christian discrimination within the United Kingdom. The last three stanzas were modified on Tuesday, April 1st 2014 in response to a Sunday Times report about rules published by the *'The Equality and Human Rights Commission'* (Marie Wolf p.3 Sunday Times 30/3/2014). The incident involving the street preacher was personally witnessed following attendance at the Manchester Gay Pride March of Saturday, 24th August 2013. (The preacher who was working as part of a team had not been in the vicinity of that event.) After I picked up his bible (which had been hurled onto the pavement) I got mobbed by the teenage girls mentioned in the poem. I had to push my way through them as if I was in a rugby scrum in order to return it to him. After the meeting was closed by the police I retired with an aching neck to a nearby Waterstones Bookshop in order to recover from this incident.

**Fragments 89-90:** These were written on Tuesday, 24th May 2011 and were first recited at a poetry evening on Wednesday 8th June of that year.

**Fragment 91:** Written on Wednesday, 29th June 2011

**Fragments 92a:** Written on Thursday, 28th July 2011

**Fragments 92b:** Written on Monday 22nd April 2013

**Fragment 93:** Written on Thursday, 28th July 2011 whilst reviewing a book on Conspiracy Theory

**Fragment 94:** Written on Thursday, 6th June 2013, the sixty-ninth anniversary of the D-Day Landings in France

**Fragment 98:** Written whilst staying at the Liverpool Travel Lodge on Saturday, 20th August 2011

**Fragments 99-100:** Written on Tuesday, 16th August 2011

**Fragment 101:** Written on Thursday, 28th July 2011

**Fragment 102:** Written on Friday, 23rd February 2012

**Fragment 103:** Written on Wednesday, 20th June 2012

**Fragments 104-105:** Written on Thursday, 28th June 2012

**Fragment 106:** Written on Tuesday, 31st July 2012

**Fragment 107:** Written on Wednesday 26th March 2012. The final part was written on Friday, 9th November, the day the Church of England announced that Justin Welby would be the new Archbishop of Canterbury

**Fragment 108:** Written on Saturday 25thAugust 2012

**Fragment 109:** Written on Saturday, 9th June 2013 in response to the murder of Private Lee Rigby by two Nigerians on Wednesday, 22nd May 2013.

**Fragment 110:** Written on Sunday, 19th May 2013

**Fragment 111:** Written on Sunday, 19th May 2013

**Interlude:** Written on Monday, 8th June 2009 and redrafted Saturday, 9th June 2013

## Part 2: Broken Shards

**Shard 1:** This lament was written on Friday, 23rd March 2012 during an economic recession when a collapse in work brought me to the brink of bankruptcy. It confirms that I was very much affected by some of the negative socio-economic forces described in this book. Only in October 2012 did signs of a personal financial turnaround begin to emerge. When my wife and I celebrated New Years Eve at my mother's I loudly exclaimed, *"Thank God I've survived!"* This remark was made as Big Ben chimed in 2013. We then held hands and sang *'Auld Lang Syne'* with great gusto.

**Shard 2:** Written on Tuesday, 29th August 2011

**Shard 3:** Written on Thursday, 23rd August 2012

**Shard 4:** Written on Wednesday, 17th April 2013

**Shard 5:** This meditation was written on Tuesday, 19th July 2005 in response to the London Tube bombings of 7th July of that year. Its theme relates to the blindness of religious fanaticism. Lending poignancy to this meditation was the fact that during this event, I had been living only five minutes' walk away from where the London Suicide Tube Bombers had housed their bomb-making factory. I have vivid memories of how, in hot blazing summer weather, the surrounding area was swarming with police for days afterwards. I noticed that individual members of the police force had dabbed sun cream onto their noses.

**Shard 6:** This series of haikus was written on Wednesday, 16th March 2011 in response to the terrible Japanese Earthquake which began at 2.46pm (Japanese time) on Friday, 11th March 2011. This created a thirty metre high tsunami wave and the destruction of the nuclear power plant at Fukushima, located 150 miles North of Tokyo. At magnitude 9.0 it was the fifth highest recorded earthquake since 1900. It was caused by parts of the Pacific Plate slipping under the Island of Japan. An estimated 28,000 lives were lost. Whole towns on Japan's North Eastern coast were completely destroyed.

**Shard 7:** Written on Tuesday, 17th November 2010

**Shard 8:** Written on Thursday, 25th April 2013

**Shard 9:** This poem was written on Wednesday, 15th April 2009 after reading a copy of Bob Dylan's lyrics, (a fifty-third birthday gift from my brother-in-law). I was particularly inspired after reading his lyrics for *'Masters of War.'*)

**Shard 10:** This meditation was written on Monday, 15th October 2007. It expresses the likely destructive consequences of the hatreds currently raging in the Middle East.

**Shard 11:** Written on Wednesday, 18th July 2012 in preparation for a poetry recital on the theme of *'freedom,'* held that same evening.

**Shard 12:** Written on Friday, 15th April 2011. During its composition I kept hearing the Doors Hit, *'Riders on the Storm'* which reflected my depressed mood at the time.

**Shard 13:** Written on Monday, 20th February 2012 following a family wedding

**Shard 14:** First written on Thursday, 20th March 2008, then word processed on Friday, 16th August 2013 after having been found mislaid amongst some Family History documents

**Shard 15:** This poem was written on Thursday, 27th January 2011 and describes the Hyde Park riots in Leeds which took place on Tuesday-Wednesday, 11-12th July 1995. Its contents have been drawn from vivid personal memories of that night.

**Shard 16:** Written on the bank of a moorland stream Wednesday, 23rd May 2012

**Shard 17:** This poem was written during the early hours of Monday 3rd August 2009, when awake with indigestion caused by overeating the night before. It had been inspired by reading two press reports on the activities of the Swiss Euthanasia group, *'Dignitas.'* (The press reports were Brian Appleyard's *'Whose Life is it Anyway?'* and Dominic Lawson's *'Don't Book a Ticket to Dignitas Just Yet,'* published on p.1.11 and p.1.14 of the Sunday Times, 2nd August 2009.) It was first published in the writer's novella *'The Exit Machine.'*

**Shard 18:** The final parts of this fragment were written on Wednesday, 18th July 2012 in preparation for a poetry recital held that same evening. However, it assumed its completed form on Tuesday, 31st July 2012.

**Postlude:** Written on Monday, 8th June 2009 and redrafted Saturday, 9th June 2013

# INTERMISSION 1:
# EXTRACTS FROM A CYNIC'S DICTIONARY

(What the devout, learned and worthy scholar Dr Samuel Johnson Esq would have wished to have added to his inimitable Dictionary of the English Language should he have lived into the twenty-first century. These definitions will show the estimable reader the true and honest meaning of words used in this bawdy, doltish and knavish age)

# A CYNIC'S DICTIONARY

**Disclaimer:** *The following definitions are meant to closely reflect the (often strongly) held prejudices of Dr Johnson (1709-1784) the author of the first widely accepted English Dictionary. By today's standards many of the views expressed in them are offensive and highly prejudiced. They do not necessarily reflect my own views. This piece was inspired by a visit to Dr Johnson's House in London on Friday, 18th September 2009.*

**Abortion:** Getting rid of unwanted babies, usually for reasons of social and psychological convenience

**Agnostic:** An atheist who lacks the courage to openly admit to their atheism

**Anti-Zionism:** A new brand name for anti-Semitism

**'Any Questions:'** A harmless radio debate in which participants attempt to give sensible answers to often very contentious questions (despite ceaseless interruptions from the Chairman). The panel often consists of three politicians who won't answer the question and a cultural figure who can't answer the question.

**Appeal Procedure:** A time-wasting rigmarole, designed to thwart the implementation of justice

**Arab:** A large *'people grouping'* to whom most of the world grovels because of their rich oil supplies

**Assisted Suicide:** Encouraging family members (or close associates) to assist in the elimination of those regarded as a *'burden on society'*

**Atheism:** The belief that there is no God but Charles Darwin and that Richard Dawkins is his prophet

**Bank:** A place where money is deposited and rapidly lost

**Banker:** An overpaid fraudster, awarded generous bonuses for wrecking the national and global economy

**Blue Sky Thinking:** The type of thinking bankers and senior business people indulge in when snorting coke in high class brothels

**BBC:** An overmanned and underperforming Broadcasting Organization which claims a spurious objectivity in its journalism

**Bigot:** Someone holding strong views that one <u>doesn't</u> like

**British Religion:** Football and shopping

**British Hymn:** The ringing of a shopping till

**British Nationalist:** A scoundrel who likes to beat up members of ethnic minority communities

**British Prayer:** A chant on a football terrace

**Broadsheet:** A semi-respectable newspaper that presumes to pontificate on matters to do with politics and economics – often too cumbersome to read comfortably outside a public library

**Buddhist:** A harmless religious dreamer and practitioner of Buddhism who believes that nothing is real. This often leads to such activities as trying to clap with one hand

**Burden on Society:** Anyone the State and/or Public wish to get rid of because their presence is deemed to cost too much money

**Cartoonist:** A hapless victim of death threats should he or she choose to draw cartoons depicting certain sensitive religious subjects

**Cat:** A furry mammal who loves to colonise human households

**Casino:** A place where fools lose their money

**Chairman of Any Questions:** An overpaid, middle-ranking BBC functionary whose role is to prevent panellists from coming to blows. (Also has free reign to interrupt panellists, often with irrelevant comments.)

**Christian:** Someone claiming to follow Jesus Christ even when they don't

**Church of England:** A neo-pagan sect pretending to be a Christian State Religion

**Church of England Bishop:** A unbelieving hypocrite who's first priority is the safeguarding of his position and the maintenance of a non-existent institutional unity at the expense of truth

**Communism:** A confidence trick designed by intellectuals to gain power for themselves and to justify mass murder in the name of the class struggle. In practice similar to **Fascism.**

**Compassion:** A meaningless *'sound bite'* used by politicians for electoral gain

**Compensation Claim:** An often time-wasting claim for damages which helps lawyers accumulate large fees for themselves at the expense of the claimant (or the party the claimant wishes to sue)

**Conservative Party:** A Party that can't be attacked for its principles because it doesn't have any

**Death with Dignity:** A pleasant-sounding term, designed to gain public acceptance for the elimination of those deemed to be a burden upon society

**Deification:** The delusion that one can become a god (or goddess) through the application of mind-emptying spiritual techniques – leads to the view that one is *'above'* any form of law or moral constraint.

**Diplomat:** A bureaucrat paid by the government to tell lies in a foreign setting

**Doctor Who:** A popular BBC science fiction programme whose speciality is scaring young children

**Doctor Who Theme Tune:** The best part of every Dr Who episode

**Dog:** Another furry mammal who loves to colonise human households

**E-Mail:** A means of providing the illusion rather than the reality of communication

**Eastern Orthodoxy:** A branch of Christianity which promotes nationalist politics, ethnic cleansing and anti-Semitism. Its leaders often display an undue subservience to the State whilst having a liking for long beards.

**Economic Forecast:** An often inaccurate prediction of future economic activity that tends to be less reliable than tea leaf reading.

**Economic Forecasting:** Fortune telling by those with economic degrees

**Election:** A means of throwing out one set of scoundrels and replacing them with another set of scoundrels

**Embryocide:** The gratuitous killing of the unborn; a crime given official state sanction within the UK and the USA

**England:** A land with pleasant views – but unpleasant people – who live only for money and pleasure

**Englishman:** A boring male person who lives only for football and getting drunk

**Englishwoman:** A boring female person who lives only for shopping, *'clubbing'* and getting drunk

**Enlightened:** Someone holding strong views that one <u>does</u> like

**Equality:** Pretending all people are the same when they're not

**Evangelical:** A Christian who resorts to annoying childish gimmicks to promote (what they view as) the gospel message

**Euro:** A currency that has helped bring Europe to economic ruin

**European Union:** A *'cover name'* for an unworkable Federal Europe in which power lies in the hands of unaccountable and often corrupt bureaucrats

**European Court of Human Rights:** The Strasburg-based Court that passes inept rulings which benefit criminals and terrorists whilst oppressing ordinary, hardworking decent citizens

**Euphemism:** A nice word used to hide nasty realities.

**Existentialism:** A meaningless philosophy which attempts to find meaning in a meaningless world

**Fascism:** A confidence trick, designed by intellectuals to gain power for themselves and to justify mass murder in the name of race or ethnic purity

**Fair and Reasonable Offer:** A veiled threat meaning *'you'd better accept my offer – or else!'*

**Feminism:** A Movement designed to promote the rights of women at the expense of men. It often believes that the ills of the world result from a male conspiracy to oppress females under a system called *'patriarchy'*

**Feminist:** A troublesome women who refuses to see that *'patriarchy'* is the natural order of things.

**Fundamentalism:** A system used to support rigidly held religious views which sanction and justify murder in the name of God

**Fundamentalist:** A zealot who shows a blind commitment to a sacred text so long as it suits them and can be used to justify any murderous inclinations they may have.

**Gay Rights:** The legal right to criminalise and harass elderly Christian Guest House Owners who object to accommodating same-sex couples.

**Gay Theology:** An intellectual exercise designed to annoy fundamentalists and effect a reconciliation between Christianity and same sex relationships.

**Geordie:** A person from the North East of England who speaks with a pleasant accent but has highly unpleasant manners when drunk

**Government Assurance:** A misleading statement or promise (made by a government) that shouldn't to be taken too seriously

**Government Denial:** A official statement that only the foolish believe in

**Government Enquiry:** An often expensive government investigation, designed to produce no result and answer no questions

**Government Subsidy:** A bribe designed to *'buy off'* a pressure group at the expense of the wider public

**Happy Hour:** A slogan used by pubs and clubs to encourage fools to spend their money by getting roaring drunk

**Having a Good Time:** Getting drunk

**Having a Great Time:** Getting violently drunk

**Heaven:** For the English person Heaven is a good friendly pub where drinks are served at a reasonable price

**Hell:** Any place where the workforce consists entirely of women

**Homophobia:** A pejorative term designed to shut down any discussion on the nature of homosexuality

**Hospitality:** In some cultures it's an occasion to treat an honoured guest to a three course meal. In England it's shown when a guest is generously given a cup of weak tea with two biscuits instead of one.

**Human Rights:** A confidence trick devised by lawyers with a view to pocketing large fees from legal cases

**Humanist:** A cultured despiser of religion who imagines they are intellectually especially enlightened and *'progressive'* in their opinions

**Internal Enquiry:** An enquiry that's designed to conceal rather than earnestly look for the truth.

**Ireland:** A financially bankrupt, rain sodden island where the majority of its inhabitants dislike being reminded that they were once part of Britain

**Irishman:** A man from Ireland who tends to like literature and alcohol in equal measure

**Irish Woman:** A quick tempered woman from Ireland who endures a lifelong vocation of holding a dysfunctional family together

**Islamophobia:** A term of abuse, designed to shut down any discussion on the nature of Islam

**Islamic Terrorist:** The son of ambitious parents who failed to make it as a doctor or lawyer

**Islamism:** A militant branch of Islam, designed to make its adherents feel good about murdering others in the name of God. Both Muslims and non-Muslims may be indiscriminately targeted.

**Israel:** A Jewish Nation State marked for elimination by a combination of military, economic and diplomatic means.

**Israeli:** A citizen of a Jewish Nation State whom most of the world would like to eliminate for economic, political or religious reasons

**Israeli Settler:** A self-righteous Israeli citizen whose hatred can rival that seen in the Islamic World; tends to loathe both Palestinian Arabs and Jewish Christians in equal measure

**ITV:** The same as the BBC but has the right to raise advertising revenue in order to fund its organizational inefficiency

**Internet:** An electronic means of distributing sick fantasies across the globe

**Jesus Christ:** A Jewish Carpenter who's been forgotten by the Church and ignored by the world (except when used as a swear word or the object of ridicule by comedians whose scriptwriters are running out of ideas)

**Jew:** A member of a religious and ethnic minority whom most of the world would like to eliminate

**Journalist:** A meddler in people's lives who writes stories that are not to be believed

**Labour Party:** A Party that believes that high taxation and government spending is the solution to every socio-economic problem (even when this belief is repeatedly falsified by events)

**Lancashire:** A County whose only attraction is the M62 Motorway back into Yorkshire

**Lawyer:** A liar who dispenses injustice for exorbitant fees

**Legal Rights:** A term lawyers use when wishing to protect their criminal clients

**Liberal Democrats:** A Party without identity or principles

**Liberal Theologian:** Someone who likes to study religion without having to believe any of it

**Liberation:** The often violent political process whereby one set of tyrants replaces another set of tyrants

**Liberation Struggle:** The crimes tyrants commit when on their way to seizing power

**Life Imprisonment:** Tax funded accommodation for violent or dangerous criminals

**Liquid Church:** A Church that's too wet (cowardly) to believe in Jesus Christ or the teaching of the Bible. It is characterized by a desire to adapt to the wider society at any cost

**Liquid Modernity:** A pretentious term used to describe post modernism and to justify an amoral approach to human relations

**Love:** A word often mistakenly used in place of lust

**Madness:** A term describing the current condition of Western Civilization

**Marriage:** A prelude to divorce

**Marriage Vow:** A meaningless promise

**Mercy Killing:** A euphemism to describe the elimination of those deemed a *'burden on society'*

**Misery:** Waiting in a long bus queue on a wet Monday morning

**Modern Art:** Childish daubing masquerading as art in order to fool gullible millionaires and art galleries to part with lots of money

**Moron:** An abusive term used by those with no real argument to offer

**Neo-Patriarchy:** A term invented by feminists who's meaning remains obscure

**New Labour:** A confidence trick, designed by Labour Politicians to delude the electorate into believing that they won't (yet again) ruin the British Economy

**News Night:** A current affairs programme characterised by hectoring interviews with often evasive public figures.

**Newspaper:** A purveyor of inaccurate information in the form of objective news reports

**Nursing Home:** A geriatric *'Gulag,'* designed to facilitate the death of the elderly; a warehouse for the dying.

**Old Age:** In some cultures it's a time of life where old people are honoured and respected. In England it's a time of life when they're considered a nuisance and potential candidates for euthanasia.

**Pansexual:** A fashionable designation for someone who's sexuality is all over the place; they are reputedly open to any kind of sexual encounter regardless of gender or other considerations.

**People Trafficking:** Another name for the slave trade

**Poet:** A humble pedlar of words who's usually short of money

**Poetry:** A play on words, all seeking to amuse and provoke, whilst sometimes doing neither

**Police:** Justice Officials too busy filling in forms to protect the public

**Politician:** A fraudster who didn't make it into banking

**Political Correctness:** Being told by the government what to think

**Popular Music:** An unbearable sound trying to masquerade as music

**Post Modern Art:** A trashier version of modern art

**Post Modernism:** An incoherent system of philosophy which uses pretentious language to argue that there's no system of philosophy

**Post Modernist:** An intellectual who writes unreadable books in defence of Post Modernism – often with a view to establishing a bogus reputation as a profound thinker

**Progressive:** A *'label,'* adopted by politicians wishing to improve a tarnished public image.

**Protestant:** A Christian who hates Roman Catholicism for a mixture of good and bad reasons

**Quakerism:** A pacifist neo-Christian Sect, prone to admire mass murderers like Joseph Stalin

**Question Time:** The TV version of the BBC Radio 4 program Any Questions, with the added disadvantage that one can actually see the panellists

**Racist:** A taunt used to shut down any discussion on migration

**Reasons:** A polite name for excuses

**Revolution:** A major social and political upheaval that's often used to justify mass murder and the establishment of a police state

**Roman Catholic Hierarchy:** A religious mafia which provides sheltered employment for child molesters

**Royal Wedding:** A wedding between members of the English Royal Family, designed to improve public morale during times of economic hardship and widespread discontent

**Scientist:** a supposed expert who fiddles his data and hopes not to get found out

**Scotland:** A country with nice scenery whose inhabitants are good at getting drunk and *'fleecing'* gullible tourists

**Scotsman:** A male inhabitant of Scotland who's good with money but can't always handle his whiskey

**Scotswoman:** A lady with whom no wise Englishman would presume to argue with

**Scottish Nationalist:** Someone who wants independence from England so long as it's affordable

**Sapiosexual:** A pretentious term for a wise person who loves knowledge and enjoys witty, intelligent conversation

**Social Acceptability:** The view that anything a society says is right

**Social Worker:** A convenient scapegoat, one blamed when things go wrong in Care Provision

**Social Work Manager:** Someone who blames the social worker when things go wrong in Care Provision

**Socialism:** A secular religion, passionately believed in by those who have ceased to believe in God

**Spain:** A bankrupt Southern European country where English tourists love to visit and get drunk

**Spin Doctor:** A journalist paid by the government to lie to other journalists

**State Socialism:** An ideological justification, used by left wing elites to accumulate power and privileges for themselves at the expense of working people

**Suicide Bomber:** A lowly terrorist operative who mistakes murder for martyrdom; often the brainwashed victim of terrorist godfathers

**Tabloid Newspaper:** A nasty, small-sized and small-minded form of newspaper, specialising in the destruction of people's reputations

**Teacher:** An overworked social worker in education

**Terrorist:** Someone who justifies criminal acts in the name of a particular cause

**Terrorist Godfather:** A terrorist leader who arranges the martyrdom' of lowly operatives whilst being unwilling to embrace it themselves

**Text Messaging:** An activity that precludes the need for meaningful conversation

**Tiddlysexual:** A rather obsessive person with an inordinate love and infatuation for the game of tiddly winks.

**The Elimination Mentality:** The mental attitude that casually accepts or advocates the killing of those deemed *'a burden upon society'*

**The French:** The only people whom the English can make prejudiced comments about and not be accused of racism

**The Internet:** A worldwide collection of electronic pathways that transmits mainly trivial and useless information; a profitable outlet for purveyors of pornography

**The Pope:** A protector of paedophiles and official godfather of the Roman Catholic Church. He claims a spurious infallibility when speaking upon matters of faith and morals

**The Worldwide Web:** Interconnected, electronic depositaries of mainly trivial and useless information

**Total War:** A disagreement between feminists

**Thinking *'Out of the Box':*** Generating incoherent ideas, having little relation to reality or reason

**United Nations:** A corrupt international bureaucracy which claims to address global problems

**Vicar:** A social worker in a dog collar – one who may have a peripheral interest in Christianity

**Wales:** A mountainous region where the inhabitants dislike the English but sing nice hymns

**Welshman:** Someone who can sing and sulk in equal measure

**Welshwoman:** Someone who speaks in a sing-song accent designed to baffle outsiders

**Welsh Nationalist:** Someone who wants independence from England even when it's not affordable

**Yorkshire:** The best place on earth

**Yorkshire man:** A person whose bluntness is mistaken for rudeness by the rest of the world. Is second only to a Scotsman in his ability to handle money (with a tightly closed hand)

**Yorkshire man's Wife:** A long-suffering lady who has to endure living with a Yorkshire man and pretend that all of his strongly expressed opinions are infallibly correct (which they usually are)

**Zany:** A person (or object) who's mildly amusing in an unusual sort of way

**ZZZ!** A symbol for snoring, all too frequently the reaction of those misfortunates who have read this dictionary

# RESTLESS ASHES

## (Creative pieces exploring the horrors of Auschwitz-Birkenau and its connection with present day events)

### Psalm 102:9
*"For I have eaten ashes like bread and mingled my drink with weeping"*

### Thought Starter
Hatred can have a fatal attraction

# PROLOGUE:
## *'ALWAYS THE SAME'* PART 1:1948

**Semper Eadem:** *'Always the same' – a common motto employed by the Roman Catholic Church*

Well, what could you expect me to do? As Bishop of the one, true and Apostolic Church, my first duty was to safe-guard its social standing. No specific direction came from Rome – the Holy Father's silence on the matter of the Jews was an example I was duty-bound to follow. Independent initiative would have been frowned upon, although not exactly forbidden. You just don't seem to understand how difficult the situation was. A third of my priests had been active (or tacit) National Socialist sympathizers whilst others were informers. The Trade Unionists had been arrested, political parties banned and youngsters were flocking to join the Hitler Youth. We were really *'hard put'* to retain a measure of influence in the Catholic schools. I did make successful representation on behalf of one or two Catholic prisoners – they'd had connections with influential donors to the Cathedral – but I was firmly warned by the Government authorities to go no further.

There was the added complication that the late Fuhrer himself had been a Catholic. Oh yes, he'd made a most convincing show of piety whenever he'd wished. I too had experienced his *'petit bourgeoisie'* charm although I'd never felt completely convinced. In his negotiations with a succession of Papal representatives he would pose as a champion of Christian civilization. He convinced us all that he was sent by *'Providence'* to defend Europe against the hordes of atheist Bolsheviks in the East. Admittedly, he was a little too vehement in his denunciations of a Judaeo-Masonic, Communist Conspiracy, but his ideas were hardly original. It was the extreme way in which he expressed them that was a little disconcerting. You must understand that there was a real threat; the Bolsheviks – led by that Jew Trotsky – had murdered thousands of our priests! Added to that, another Jew, Eisener, had caused trouble in Bavaria whilst that insufferable Jewess woman Rosa Luxemburg had, with all of her damnable agitation, brought about absolute mayhem in Berlin. That's not to mention the Jewish bankers who'd caused the Wall Street Crash in 1929. In the climate of the early thirties it seemed as if no alternative remained for decent Christians but to take a firm stance against this pestilential people. Wouldn't you have felt the same if you'd had to organize soup kitchens for the unemployed or had seen good Catholic families reduced to destitution?

With millions out of work the people were justifiably angry and it was part of the Fuhrer's diabolical genius to tap into that anger, to express that anger and to make it acceptable. He also had that uncanny knack of driving public anger to its logical extreme. I of course had my doubts about the regime all along. Goering was excessively vulgar and there was that frightful Rohm character – justifiably disposed of in my opinion. However, Himmler seemed a regular sort of a fellow and there was no doubting the intelligence of Dr Goebbels, though he tended to be a trifle loud in his manner. You see – they were <u>all</u> popular and to have expressed my doubts (such as they were) would only have disturbed my congregation. Our elderly ladies would have got themselves into such an agitation. Some had lost husbands and sons in the Great War and needed the assurance that their sacrifice had not been in vain. Maybe I should have said something before the National Socialists had taken control of the Government. But you must understand my position – as a newly appointed Bishop I had so many other duties to attend to. Giving out warnings about the National Socialists was not on my agenda. Of course, after the Reichstag fire in March 1933 speaking out became impossible. Why should I endanger my position for the sake of a futile martyrdom? To have done that would have accomplished nothing. Moreover, the legal quarantine imposed upon the Yids, (oh sorry, I mean Germany's Jewish population) by the Nuremburg Laws seemed reasonable enough to me. If only things had stayed that way then there would have been no fuss. A moderate amount of exclusion would have been enough to have served everyone's interests. In these civilized times there was no need for the techniques of the Spanish Inquisition.

You ask whether we should have challenged matters when Germany still had a Democracy – before they got to the stage of embarrassing our good name. But you see the Catholic Church doesn't do democracy – never has, never will. There's too much Masonic Freethinking and Atheist Socialism about democracy. It really is much easier to work alongside a respectable Dictatorship like that of Franco or Mussolini. After all, a Dictatorship is far more predictable and stable – we know exactly where we stand and with whom we're negotiating. In contrast, democracies are so unpredictable, so open to immoral influences. No sooner do you reach an agreement that the Party you made it with are *'thrown out'* so you have to start all over again! The French have a term for it, *'revolving door government.'* You only had to live through the Weimar Republic to see how awful democracies could be. How wise it was of the Holy Father to discreetly prefer a more authoritarian approach. Democracies never suit the interests of the Church – their *'gutter press'* is always trying to rake up something or other to destroy our good name.

We initially thought that the Fuhrer was one of us! He certainly seemed so at first – being exactly what we needed to preserve Catholic order in Europe. We thought that, like Mussolini, here was a man with whom we could do business. True, there were certain regrettable aspects to his regime, but we were quietly confident that things would settle down and that the cares of government would have a sobering effect. We trusted that a leader with the Fuhrer's evident strength of personality would be able to control the more extreme elements of his Party. Following the removal of that boorish ruffian Ernest Rohm (back in June '34) Hitler certainly appeared to lead very well. At least the Fuhrer got things done; unemployment diminished, the autobahns were built, order was restored and abroad Germany was once more respected by other Nations. France and Britain wanted to court us at Munich, leaving Stalin to glower on the sidelines. Given what had gone on before, these seemed to be miraculous achievements and they silenced any doubts about whether the Fuhrer was a blessed saviour sent from heaven to redeem the German people. To many he was their Moses, leading them into the Promised Land; to some he was also their Christ! Of course, I didn't fall for that one – that really was a step too far! What I mean to say is – there was no need to question anything – the results spoke for themselves.

I was, of course, a little troubled when news was received of the harsh treatment given to Polish Priests. But by then we were at war and it would have been unpatriotic to have made any obvious stand. The Jews simply weren't my concern. The best policy was to bypass the problem and concern myself with more pressing matters. I didn't exactly like what happened at Crystal Night in November '38; it was <u>so</u> disorderly and things certainly did get a little out of hand. However, most of my congregation were convinced that the Jews had somehow deserved it. Also, as a loyal *'son of the Church'* I was well aware of how shamefully our Holy Father had been treated when serving as Papal Nuncio in Munich. He'd been robbed there by insolent Communist Jewish gunmen. This was after the First World War when everything was in chaos. They'd behaved in such a rude over-familiar fashion, showing not the slightest respect for his priestly office! Mind you – this shouldn't have surprised anyone, for they treated our Lord the same way, jeering at Him as He'd struggled under the weight of the cross! The Fathers of our Faith were so right to have branded them as a perfidious people, shut off from mercy and reason alike. They're just so very pushy too. Back in 1904, that Herzl chap had had the impertinent notion of visiting the Vatican and pressurising the then Pope to support his ridiculous notion of a Jewish State. It was hardly surprising that the answer was *'no'* unless they all agreed to accept baptism. This, of course, was something to which an atheist Jew like Herzl would never have agreed! So you see I regard the policy of silence followed by the Vatican as being the most appropriate – especially given the Jews' persistent rejection of our Lord. Who was I, a humble servant of the Church, to question the eminently wise policy of Rome?

Please understand the complexities involved in my position. Some of my priests heard frightful things during the confessional, especially about the *'carryings on'* in Poland and Russia. Some of them even took to drink and a few had to retire to a monastery with a nervous breakdown. But what else could we have done but to have pronounced absolution and reassurance to those troubled souls? A few *'Hail Marys'* and *'Our Fathers'* would surely go a long way to setting things right. *'Guilt'* is the one uncomfortable human emotion that our Church is able to manage with some degree of expertise.

Also, what were our esteemed American liberators doing to stoop so low as to make members of my congregation visit the nearby Concentration Camp? How could we have even begun to have guessed the full scale of the excesses being committed there? True, there'd been troubling rumours and these did seem to be backed-up by the awful stories heard in the confessional. However, rumours are rumours and war can have a strange effect upon soldiers – I speak as one who served as a military Chaplain on the Western Front. (I was awarded an Iron Cross you know.) There was no means to assess the information pouring, sorry, I mean *'trickling'* my way. What business of mine were the Jews – am I their keeper? The Americans were so melodramatic about what had happened – I suspect they'd been influenced by Hollywood. Yes Hollywood – its run by Jews you know. I wouldn't be surprised if they make an *'epic'* film about it all.

Thankfully, matters are now on a more satisfactory footing. Through their military presence the Americans have gladly assumed the role of our protector against Jewish-Bolshevik machinations. Diplomatic relations between Washington and the Vatican have improved, despite some earlier, unfortunate misunderstandings. Between you and me, senior Vatican diplomats are quietly confident that the Catholic presence within the American Democratic Party will ensure a Catholic President by 1960. That would indeed represent a most positive turn of events. Thanks to *'Marshall Aid'*, conditions for the German people have greatly improved; there's now even enough to eat after that dreadful winter of a year ago. Hopefully the Nuremburg trials will have drawn a decent veil over a rather regrettable past. However, it's deeply troubling the way Judaeo-Bolshevik tentacles are spreading in the Middle East. The latest scheme is to establish a Jewish State in the Holy land! How ridiculous! How blasphemous even to consider allowing that damnable people to return to the land where they'd crucified our Lord! We'll have to put our foot down just as we did with that Herzl chap! I trust that the Holy Father will persuade Washington to veto this absurd idea when it comes up for debate in the United Nations.

## 1. AGE OLD HORROR

The horror is a horror from of old
The horror is a horror from the recesses of Hell
A horror springing from corrupt human hearts
Many are its lies and deceits

It has brought
Distress and tribulation
Ruin and devastation
Darkness and gloom[46]

It will express itself in
The poisonous gas cloud
The nuclear blast and shock wave
The looming mushroom cloud

This horror cannot be contained
It cannot be appeased
It cannot be pacified
Its hatred is relentless

It seeks the annihilation of Israel
It plots the destruction of the Jews
It longs to make an end of Zion
As an evil it never sleeps

Anti-Semitism is its name

---

[46] Zephaniah 1:15-16

## 2. AUSCHWITZ

Auschwitz
A place of infamy and death
A place where cruelty went off the Richter scale
A place where over a million died in the most degrading of
circumstances
A place where the lucky ones were those who were shot outright
Now it's a place where even poetry sickens and dies
A place leaving busloads of tourists inwardly numb
And unable to comprehend the scale of such an evil

## 3. BEFORE

Before I become a statistic
I want to make an impact upon human affairs

Before I become a statistic
I want to create an enduring body of literature

Before I become a statistic
I want to witness to the Gospel of salvation

Before I become a statistic
I want to fulfill my literary vocation

Before I become a statistic
I want to make a major difference in people's lives

Before I become a statistic
I want to challenge the complacent

Before I become a statistic
I want to know that my mission on earth has been fully completed

## 4. BEGINNING

To begin with they allowed assisted suicide for the terminally ill
Then they allowed assisted suicide for the permanently disabled
Then they allowed assisted suicide for the clinically depressed
Then they allowed assisted suicide to be taught in schools
Then they published reports advocating infanticide and euthanasia

Now assisted suicide is an obligation
Placed upon those deemed *'a burden upon society'*

## 5. DEVOURED BY HATRED

Tramp, tramp, tramp, tramp

With perverse resolution you and fellow brothers of the Franciscan
Order had churned out anti-Semitic literature
In your in-house pamphlet, *'Maty Dziennik'* [47]

Tramp, tramp, tramp, tramp

You propagated the view that the Jews were a criminal mafia,
conspiring with Freemasons and Communists
To destroy Catholic Poland

Tramp, tramp, tramp, tramp

You credulously accepted that the *'The Protocols of Zion,'* was produced
By a cabal of satanically-inspired Jews meeting in a Prague cemetery

Tramp, tramp, tramp, tramp

You wrote anti-Semitic articles to release your pent-up aggression
And provide a break from the ritual monotony of religious life

---

[47] Meaning *'The Little Daily'*

Tramp, tramp, tramp, tramp

You felt most superior when writing about Zionist plots to take over
the world
This deflected any need to be troubled about your own sins and
God's apparent absence

Tramp, tramp, tramp, tramp

You fervently championed devotion to the Blessed Virgin
Bowing before her image whilst despising her kinsfolk

Tramp, tramp, tramp, tramp

You disdain the smirking cruelty on the faces of your military escort
Isn't Auschwitz is part of a Zionist plot to destroy Catholic Poland?

Tramp, tramp, tramp, tramp

You felt a cold dread as the camp gates opened to receive you
And your fellow Franciscans
Further proof that Auschwitz was part of a Jewish conspiracy
To take over the world

Tramp, tramp, tramp, tramp

You invoked a silent Virgin to prepare for martyrdom
Yet in your dead religiosity you couldn't see how you were being
consumed by a hatred you had legitimized

Tramp, tramp, tramp, tramp…

Soon your ashes will mingle with those of
A people you hated

## 6. EXCHANGE

A prisoner has escaped
Ten men are to be selected for death by starvation
In the much feared *'Block Eleven'*
A former Polish Army Sergeant
Franciszek Gajowniczek, pleads
*"My poor wife and children, they will be orphans!"*

An emaciated Franciscan Priest, Maximilian Kolbe
Reflects upon Christ's Passion
And how He had died for his sins
It's clear what should be done
In a weak but firm voice
*"Take me, I'm a priest and have no one."*

The guards look startled
*"Who is this holy fool?"* One thinks
Another shudders
Recalling the kind priest of his childhood
Who had provided his mother with basic necessities
When his drunken, violent father
Had, at last, deserted the family home
One nod from the Colonel
And, along with nine others
Kolbe is marched to his Block Eleven Calvary

Gone is any pride in his priestly office
Gone is any remaining Polish Nationalism
Gone is any lingering prejudice against the Jews
(After all, hadn't he seen them suffer too?)
Now only the simple bedrock of faith remains

A wan but serene smile
Passes over Kolbe's face
He's thinking how Jesus had died for his sin
And how, as a priest he must comfort his flock

During the agonizing days of slow starvation
This once prissy anti-Semite
Was now becoming a heroic martyr
Through a mysterious grace

## 7. GIRL IN THE PHOTOGRAPH

When I saw you in that photograph
Aged thirteen, wearing striped prison garb
A bewildered expression on your uncomprehending face
I wanted to lift you out of that picture
And take you home
I wanted to provide you with a good education
And encourage you to keep the customs of your people
I would have treated you as my own daughter

But alas that could never be
For as a twin
You were to perish on Doctor Mengele's dissection table
A victim of those who first made euthanasia acceptable

# 8. GOOD MEN

These were good men
Cultured, refined scholars
Meticulous, industrious administrators
Pillars of their communities and churches
Well respected by their peers
Devoted to their families
Fair in their dealings with outsiders

These were men of high standing
Who provided a positive role model
Not possessing any trace of impropriety
Nor any financial irregularity.
To their congregations
They were deeply spiritual men
Who prayed often
All were sound exemplars of morality
They'd comforted many a troubled soul

Yet, upon assuming high office
They presided over a great evil
Which consumed many a life

Yet – how could this be?

The answer is painfully simple
These *'good'* men
Drifted into iniquity when
They chose to
Place the wellbeing of their *'Institution'*
Above all else
Thereafter all manner of evil became possible

# 9. HAUNTING ANSWERS

**1)** What were the main cultural influences which leading to the creation of Auschwitz-Birkenau and other similar camps?

**Answer:** The main cultural influences were a combination of Neo-Paganism, Social Darwinism, corrupt forms of Christianity and a hate-filled anti-Semitism. Each influence had operated within the context of economic decline, mass unemployment, failing political leadership, social decadence and a worsening international situation.

**2)** Are these influences present today?

**Answer:** All are strongly present today

**3)** What is the best way to counter these influences?

**Answer:** The best way to counter these influences is to avoid a blind social conformity and to challenge the evils of society whenever and wherever the opportunity arises.

**4)** What would the Palestinians do if they succeeded in driving all of the Jews of Israel into the sea?

**Answer:** Have a noisy celebration before starting to kill each other (just as they did in Gaza).

# 10. NAIVITY

We believed it would all blow over
That the League of Nations
Would put a stop to it
That *'decent people'* would rise up in protest
After all, wasn't Europe a civilized Continent
With a rich liberal tradition
Containing the most advanced of Nations?

We were determined to integrate
To be good patriotic citizens
Losing twelve thousand of our sons during the Great War[48]
Contributing enormously to the development of
The Arts and Sciences
Some of us even grew Kaiser Wilhelm moustaches
And attended Wagner Operas
To show our proud affiliation with *'High German Culture'*

Petty prejudice?
We were long used to that
After all, things in Germany weren't as bad as in Poland or Russia
Besides, we could always build our own Clubs and Institutions
As an alternative to those from which we were excluded

Pogroms?
We'd ridden them out before
And there'd always been sympathetic countries to take us in

Threats of extermination?
The anti-Semites were always on about <u>that</u>
And no one ever took them seriously
After all, what real influence did they have?
Europe had long progressed beyond their medieval outlook – or so
we thought

---

[48] A reference to the First World War of 1914-1918

We tried so hard to assimilate
To be good citizens
To be respectable members of the bourgeoisie

In our business dealings
We'd always offer a fair price and a good service.
Unlike our less advanced forefathers
We strove <u>not</u> to be different
<u>Not</u> to be viewed as an alien presence
We were embarrassed by those
Who insisted upon wearing the side curls
And the garb of the ghetto
We smiled at their primitive and unenlightened ways

Where did it all go wrong?
Why were we never totally accepted?
Why didn't any of the Churches raise a voice in protest?
Were we naive in our understanding of human nature?
Were we foolish to have believed that our contribution to society
Could *'buy off'* an unrighteous prejudice?
Were we mistaken in believing that social progress
Was the key to dealing with hatred?

Now we and our hopes are flimsy ashes, blown about in the wind

## 11. NEVER SLEEPING

The aim of all militant anti-Semites is simple, <u>it is to kill every Jewish person – preferably in as cruel and degrading a manner as possible.</u> It is an evil that never sleeps.

## 12. ONE TIN CAN

One tin can full of pellets
Two thousand dead
Two thousand cremations
Many goods plundered
Many valuables looted
No one cared
No one spoke out
No one bothered to act
When there was still time

## 13. PERHAPS

*'Where was Christ in Auschwitz Birkenau?'*
Is a question no one can answer
Yet coming to mind is an image of
A bruised, bloodied Saviour hanging upon a cross
Desperately struggling for every breath and
Slowly suffocating
Whilst feeling abandoned by God
Most of those who died in the gas chambers
Also struggled for every breath and were
Slowly suffocated
Whilst feeling abandoned by God
Perhaps a connection does exist between these two events?

# 14. RECIPE FOR GENOCIDE

First take a bowl of existing resentment
Then gather together each ingredient
Pour in a generous portion of lies
Shake on some half-truths
(To lend flavor to the lies)

Place all inside a bureaucratic structure
Add a sizeable portion of fear
Include the bitter herbs of economic uncertainty and national humiliation
Give the mixture a good stir

Throw in a sprinkling of personal cruelty
Include a heap of deceitful propaganda

Stir again

Put on a tight-fitting lid
So none of the ingredients can escape
Place in a well-heated oven
And cook for twenty to thirty minutes
To over 1000 degrees centigrade

Voila! A tried and tested recipe for genocide –
Perfect for use in any Age

# 15. REMADE

The bearded Haredim[49]of Arad shout in a frenzied fury
Their self-righteous hatred knowing no bounds
A family of Messianic believers has moved into town
An alien presence that must be blotted out
A threatening demonstration takes place outside their home
Placards are raised and insults hurled
Angry men mill around the driveway
Paid by their Rabbis to intimidate
This Afro-American family

*Come here you stupid nigger!"*
*'Nigger bastard!"*
*"They took some bastard and they believe he rose from the grave,"*
*"Where is your bastard?"*

Oh foolish Haredim of Arad
Why do you betray the finest ethics of Judaism?
Why do you behave like *'extras'* in a Nazi propaganda film?
Insulting the memory of those who died in Auschwitz
By aping the manner of their killers?
Is it not foolish to give those who wish to destroy you reason to
gloat?
Is not your undergirding influence the same as that which drove
Rohm's SA?
Why allow yourself to be remade in the image of those who wish to
destroy you?
You are *'whitewashed tombs,'* far from the Lord
For if you really knew Torah[50] you would not *'oppress the stranger'*

In Texas a man with cold calculating features
Taps on a keyboard in a darkened room
An *'attachment'* is opened

---

[49] Sects in Orthodox Judaism who reject the modern world and are dominated by their Rabbis
[50] The teaching or law of Moses that's revealed in the first five books of the bible

Bearing useful information about the Gur Hassidim[51] demonstrations
in Arad
A look of satisfaction crosses this man's unshaven face
He downs a glass of bourbon
Before letting out a belch
References are quickly checked

An e-mail is sent

*"To my esteemed colleague Dr Balidali*
*My fellow comrade in the anti-Zionist struggle*

*I've dug up stuff on Haredim abusing some ~~Nigger~~ Negro Messianic Jewish guy*
*in Arad. I think it can be very useful for our cause. In this neck of the woods it*
*should lessen the support that our wealthy Protestant Churches give to the Zionist*
*Conspiracy. Those Gur Hassidim folk are real dumb arses. They certainly prove*
*that all the things we've been saying about the Yids are right. I'll git my son Jessie*
*to do some animation to get the message across. See if you can use it to increase*
*sympathy for the Palestinians.*

*We the warriors of the West salute the brave warriors of Arabia*

*Senior Klansman Lee Harvey James*

---

[51] Gur Hassidim is a particularly militant Haredim Sect. It uses intimidation against perceived threats to its beliefs.

# 16. STENCH

Plumes of smoke billow upward from Auschwitz Birkenau
Swirling and spiralling away from crematoria chimneys
Conveying a sickening stench of death
A sight to terrify all newcomers
And an ample confirmation of the reality of evil
The smoke spreads everywhere
Settling on the crops of a terrorized peasantry
Who mutely turn away and ask no questions
Blown through time
The smoke spreads far and wide
A warning to those who would listen
A rebuke to those demanding *'euthanasia now'*
An *'object lesson'* to succeeding generations of school children
But meanwhile the wicked complain
*'There's unfinished business yet to be done*
*Hitler didn't do a proper job*
*We must resolve the 'Jewish problem' once and for all*
Almost imperceptibly the smoke of Auschwitz
Rests upon the fermenting hatreds of the Middle East
Warning of a future where millions more
May yet be reduced to ashes

# 17. SWEET EMBRACE

Wife dead
Children dead
Parents dead
Every ambition dead
Every desire dead
Every hope dead
All has come to nothing
Why not give up and accept the sweet embrace of death

# 18. THE LAST THOUGHTS OF RUDOLF HOESS: (COMMANDANT OF AUSCHWITZ)

Be hard
Show no remorse
Remember you are a member of *'The Master Race'*
The programme you followed was completely right
Don't gratify the Yids by showing any weakness

Any regrets?
Only that you didn't finish the job
Or barely had enough time to spend with your wife
Remember the good times you had together
The times you played with the children
The horse riding you needed to clear your head
At the end of a hard day's work at the camp

Remember how, as a boy of seven
You would invite *'Hans'*
(Your favourite pony)
To sleep with you in your bedroom
When your parents were out
How the servants smiled at this boyish trick

Keep your military bearing
Be proud of the way
You ran the most efficient operation in the Reich
Better than that shambles at Treblinka
Where the Commandant took to drink

Recall the face of Reichsfuhrer Himmler
Satisfied and obviously appreciative
Recommending promotion
During a visit he made back in July '42
Arranging a private audience with the Fuhrer
Who warmly shook your hand!

There's nothing to be ashamed of
You were a loyal Party Member
A good organizer who'd almost killed himself with overwork
Always trying to be affable to those fools working under you
Even managing a smile during those tedious comrade meetings

You sacrificed everything for the cause of racial purity
Willingly obeying the orders given you
It's a pity they got you in the end
Their global conspiracy was too powerful
It had ensnared the Ivans and the Yanks
As well as the Free Masons and the Vatican

Look defiant
Show no regret
As the noose is placed around your neck
Be encouraged that
Others will complete your necessary work
They will finish off the Yids with other means
Leave them an example to follow
Don't show fear as the noose is tightened
After all you are a soldier of the Reich
And your cause was just
History will remember you as...

SNAP!

## 19. THE NINE CIRCLES OF HELL

**Circle 1:** Prejudice – Jews disliked
**Circle 2:** Propaganda – Jews maligned
**Circle 3:** Boycotts – Jews excluded
**Circle 4:** Violence – Jews beaten
**Circle 5:** Arrests – Jews imprisoned
**Circle 6:** Deportation – Jews transported
**Circle 7:** Stripping – Jews left naked
**Circle 8:** Extermination – Jews gassed, starved or worked to death
**Circle 9:** Flames – Jews consumed by the oldest hatred

## 20. TO THE CHILDREN

Shelter their souls in the shadow of your wings
Make known to them the path of life
In your presence is fullness of joy
At your right hand bliss forevermore

Bestow upon them abounding happiness
May they see that, even to this present day
There are those who cared about what happened to them
May their death mark the end of all anguish and tribulation

# 21. TOXIC INFLUENCES

*'Where was God in Auschwitz?'*
Is a question no one can answer
Except God Himself
But I do know what influences were present;
Social Darwinism
Atheistic Materialism and
Mystic Paganism
All were present to a very strong degree
As was an ancient (and modern) hatred of the Jews

Social Darwinism was present
Every time a stronger stole food from a weaker prisoner
Or the stronger were selected for work
Instead of being sent to the gas chambers

Atheistic Materialism was present
Whenever gold fillings were extracted
From the teeth of dead prisoners
And melted down into gold bars
To be safely deposited in Swiss Bank Accounts
For evil comes naturally to bankers

Mystic Paganism was present
In the arrogant *'god complex'* of the guards
Who thought they stood above any law
And wore the emblem of the death head skull
A symbol of their work

Together these toxic influences formed a perfect bedrock of hatred

Now they're resurfacing in our own time and are rapidly being made
Acceptable by a credulous media

Social Darwinism is present
In Oxford Philosophers who advocate the murder of
Both well and sick unwanted infants [52]

Atheistic Materialism is present
In the *loads of money* culture and the unpaid piles of
Government, Business and Personal debt

Mystic Paganism is present
In the Harry Potter Films and other forms of popular entertainment
Designed to entice the young

Now, these toxic influences are forming another hurricane of hatred

Is this why I'm beginning to smell burning flesh?

---

[52] See Giubilini Alberto and Minerva Francesca's (2012) chilling article *'After-birth abortion: why should the baby live?'* Relevant web site sources on the controversy it provoked will be found listed in the Bibliography

## 22. TREAD WARILY

Tread warily all you who visit Auschwitz Birkenau
With your well-fed features, clicking cameras
And listening to explanatory headphones

Tread warily, for under your feet
Lie the ashes of those who were cruelly murdered
It is not a tourist theme park you're in

What would they think
How would they feel
How would they react
As your well-shod feet bear down upon their remains?

Would they be outraged – seeing it as another form of degradation?
Would they see it as an object lesson – at least for those school
parties who visit?
Would they show that mute indifference which only suffering can
bring?

No matter what the answer could be
Tread warily you well-fed visitors of Auschwitz Birkenau:
A place where hatred reached its ultimate conclusion

## 23. TWO GRANDFATHERS

A Russian girl I once knew in Manchester during the autumn of 2001 told me about her two grandfathers.

Her paternal grandfather had trained tank regiments for the battle of Stalingrad. He divulged that nine out of the ten men he'd trained had never returned.

Her maternal grandfather was a Russian Prisoner of War in Auschwitz. How'd he survived she never knew but whenever sausages were being fried he had to leave the room.

## 24. VOW AT BIRKENAU

Dear God! There's nothing I can do about those who perished here years before I was born. But I know I can do something about the millions who may yet perish in similar conditions, should present trends of nihilistic destructiveness continue to gather strength in our society.

In God's name I vow to challenge them as long as I'm given the opportunity and the strength to do so. It's now time to speak out, regardless of the offense which may be caused, in Jesus name, Amen.

## 25. WAR

War is awful
War is cruel
War is hell
A nightmare feast of destruction
That serves up huge offerings of human blood

War is an atrocity
War is a crime
War is a mess
A dance of death
In which the innocent suffer

Who in their right mind wants war?
But visit Auschwitz and you learn that war
Can be a <u>lesser</u> evil
For what other language do the wicked understand
But war?

## 26. WE ARE ALL HEZBOLLAH NOW

Angry *'peace'* demonstrators
Hold placards aloft boasting
*'We are all Hezbollah now!'*
Twisted female-betraying feminists
Ally with bearded female-hating Islamo-Fascists
An old evil stirs
Like Dracula from his tomb
(Watch out luv, he may throw acid in your face)
The little Stalin's of the left are in full flow
Spitting out hate and vitriol
In boiling, self-righteous fury
*"Death to Israel! Death to the Jews!*
*Death to all who get in our way!*
*Death! Death! Death!"*
Jew hatred has become respectable again
The gas ovens of Treblinka
Have been stoked afresh
With the fuel of a cruelly militant anti-Zionist hatred

Government officials grovel
Before a pitiless evil,
Adopting a Vichy France mentality
To save their own skin
Plotting politicians plan
The downfall of a detested Prime Minister
Lost in his world of *'spin'*

An effete establishment is dismayed
It adopts expedient after expedient
In a futile attempt to appease evil
Time for a scheming Prelate to seduce
Rabbis and Mullahs into a
New World Order of death

Degenerate Britain,
A nation now complicit in a
Future genocide of the Jewish people
The tormented shade of Hitler
Must hope with a frenzied hate-filled passion
That the likes of Hezbollah
Will finish the work he <u>failed</u> to accomplish
Hitler and Hezbollah agree
*'A final solution must be found to the Jewish problem*
*They are a bacillus on the face of the Earth*
*A vermin which must be removed'*

Britain has become debauched, depraved and utterly disgraced.
Her decadent society is riding for a downfall
Her culture of death is in terminal decline
Her loss of dignity as a nation is total
She languishes under a rule of leaders
Who have become blind fools
Their folly means that
We are all targets now!

Sieg Heil, Sieg Heil, Sieg Heil...

## 27. WEEPING MEADOW

From weeping trees
Yellow leaves fall
Twisting and twirling
Coming to rest on ground
Thickly carpeted by dead vegetation

A sky full of tears
Sheds its load
From leaden grey clouds
Present is the sweet smell of autumnal decay
Rain drenched trees stand tall
Meekly shouldering a damp October chill

Hush!
Do not interrupt
This sodden, sinister silence
Haunted by ghosts of murderous past
Pause
Reflect
Another leaf quietly falls

Soon snow and howling winds will come
Announcing a wintry desolation
To hide autumn's woven tapestry
Underneath a white shroud of death
But for now all is peace
In this meadow of fading life
A scene of beauty – maybe
A scene for artists – possibly
A walkway for hikers – most definitely

But hush!
Nothing can be heard now
Except the gentle pitter-patter of rain drops
Another shower has begun

Otherwise all is calm
In a meadow
Where once stood queues of terrified people
Awaiting the gas chambers of Auschwitz Birkenau

## 28. WHO BROKE THAT DOLL?

Who broke that doll?

Was it the original owner, determined that no-one else should play
with it?

Who broke that doll?

Was it some leering guard, indulging in a gratuitous act of spiteful
cruelty?

Who broke that doll?

Was it a distressed parent, when being forcibly separated from her
child?

Who broke that doll?

Was it trampled underfoot by some terrified stranger being pushed
toward a gas chamber?

No matter what
It remains a memorial in Auschwitz Museum...
Mute testimony to a brutally terminated childhood
In which both life and innocence perished

# EPILOGUE:
## *'ALWAYS THE SAME,'* PART 2: 2008

Well, what could you expect me to do? As Bishop of the one True and Apostolic Church I needed to guard its standing in society. It was my bounden duty to maintain the deepest secrecy; a policy straight from the Vatican itself and who was I to demur? Under John Paul (1978-2005) a centralization of power had taken place, lifting the weight of responsibility from the shoulders of Bishops like myself. It was somewhat unfortunate that a number of Priests and a Seminary Professor in my diocese chose to establish irregular relationships with young boys. The suicides that resulted were a most distressing development. The charge against a particular Priest who'd assaulted a succession of boys in his Youth Group was especially regrettable. Even worse, it was a public embarrassment that brought the good name of the Holy Church into disrepute! Most perturbing of all was that it all came to light on <u>my</u> watch! What else could I do but move this Priest around whilst offering him some counselling. I was only doing what <u>every</u> other Bishop would have done in my situation. If I were to place every Priest who was subject to an allegation (or even several allegations) into a monastery then the whole system would collapse. Don't you see that the Church depends upon the Priesthood and without our hierarchy there would be no means to offer the mass to atone for our sins? In a very real sense our Lord <u>depends upon us</u> to propagate His kingdom – frail human vessels though we are. The Vatican was adamant about these matters, especially when Ratzinger's influence was in the ascendancy; *'silence'* and *'secrecy'* were the watchwords. You must understand that my duty was to obey – I had, after all, sworn a vow of obedience. As Saint Ignatius of Loyola (of blessed memory) once said, *"We may be altogether of the same mind and in conformity with the Church herself, if she shall have defined anything to be black which appears to our eyes to be white; we ought in like manner to pronounce it to be black."*[53] That sums up our approach entirely.

---

[53] Extracted from http://en.wikipedia.org/wiki/Ignatius_of_Loyola (Sunday, 27th November 2011)

No! This isn't a charter for child abuse! However, it does highlight the fact that our relationship to the hierarchy must be one of trust. There must be *'faith in the system'* otherwise nothing would be left. It appears that much of the media want the Catholic Church to collapse but their commentators fail to see that the only alternative is a godless secularism or a militant paganism of the kind that afflicted Europe in the last century. There is, of course, militant Islam – but I'm sceptical about its chances of winning whole-hearted support in the West. It places too many burdens upon its followers and lacks our skill in soothing away guilt through the Confessional or the Mass. *'Closing down'* the Vatican would never result in some new age of liberal enlightenment. All that would remain would be a host of *'little Popes,'* each running around to replace the *'big'* Pope in Rome. Just imagine it – an atheist like Dawkins or some Eastern Guru for Pope! Ha! The very thought has me reaching for a tumbler of whisky! Do you mind if I do?

The downfall of Catholicism would leave nothing to counterbalance the power of the State. We could well end up with another totalitarianism matching the horrors of atheist Communism or pagan Nazism. So, for all of its many human failings the hierarchy is a bulwark against something far worse. After all, it was the hierarchy who preserved learning and brought Europe out of the Dark Ages. It tamed a succession of despotic rulers, from Attila the Hun to the Communists of Poland. Yes, it was a shame that it displayed a certain naivety over that Hitler fellow but that was some time ago. Happily, lessons have been learnt since then.

So you see silence was necessary! It was this very same silence (or *'cult of secrecy'* as the media prefers to call it) which has preserved the Church throughout the Ages. How else could we have survived if every scandal involving a child had been brought to the public's attention? We wouldn't have survived the Reformation. Generally, I felt the policy of not responding to child abuse allegations to have been the right one. It was certainly a workable expedient until modern communications came along to spoil things.

I could have made private representations to the Vatican but what would that have achieved? Absolutely nothing! It would also have left me with the unfortunate reputation of being *'difficult'* and that would never do! After all, I had my reputation as a loyal Bishop to preserve. Under John Paul II it never paid to ask questions – or to raise objections. The Vatican quickly stamped on that sort of thing.

It is, of course, quite ridiculous to blame the *'celibacy rule'* on the grounds that it either creates or attracts those with deviant tastes. Celibacy is a supreme expression of sacrificial love. Unlike his Anglican counterpart, a Catholic Priest can give himself to the whole congregation. He is free from having a woman at home fussing for attention. Besides, the hierarchy find celibate Priests so much easier to control. As Bishop you can move them around at will unless there's the inconvenience of them being tied to a Religious Order. In such cases you may have to negotiate with some obstructive Superior who thinks a priest should serve the interests of his Order rather than the wider diocese. Over such matters their attitude can be wilfully schismatic.

I was a little *'put out'* when the mother of that ten year old boy had the audacity to quote our Lord's words in Matthew 18:6 at me. I was not going to tie a millstone around my neck and throw myself into any sea in order to gratify her regrettable desire for revenge. Fortunately, modern scholarly analysis renders the authenticity of that saying rather problematic and allows for a more compassionate interpretation. When I enlightened her on this point she wasn't having any of it and slammed the phone down when I gently chided her for adopting such a fundamentalist approach. She couldn't accept that she wasn't the only parent with a child who'd been the subject of Father Grub's rather perturbing attentions. Indeed, he'd been quite the master of deceit, with his plausible explanations and charming manner. He'd been one of our best spokespersons when it came to the local media – whenever the need had arisen he'd always been thoroughly robust in his defence of the Catholic cause. It suited everyone's interest to keep things quietly *'ticking over.'*

You just don't seem to understand my position. As <u>mere</u> secularists, the media simply fails to understand that no celibate priesthood means no Church and no Church means a vacuum into which a whole a legion of devils can fill. The media always loves to dig up the filthiest story and their reporting can be so inaccurate. There were only three (not four) suicides at the seminary and Father Grub assaulted only nine boys (not ten) and their average age was thirteen not twelve. Really! Such inaccuracies are <u>utterly</u> disgraceful! It wasn't as if we didn't try to arrange generous financial assistance. The only thing we asked for was some understanding and a little tactful discretion. There was no point to be served in *'washing our dirty linen'* in public. But the media were so intrusive, meddling in affairs which were best left well alone. They called me all hours of the day and night, ceaselessly ringing the doorbell and having the temerity to try and make <u>me</u> shoulder some of the blame! Even worse, the Police threatened to search the Diocesan Office unless co-operation was forthcoming. It was all so undignified, causing a great deal of personal stress. As a result, I had no alternative but to seek refuge in a Monastic Retreat House, where I at least had time to reflect and learn. I do of course regret the suicides and I pray for the repose of their poor benighted souls every day. However, I can't be held responsible for the actions of the likes of Father Grub – and it wasn't I who downloaded those beastly images from the Internet.

If only the proper authorities had been allowed to quietly resolve things in the time-honoured way – then a great deal of hurt could well have been prevented. Unlike the Anglicans we're not a *'free and easy'* Church. Homosexuals are strictly banned and rightly so. We do have standards. I remember how, as a young priest serving in England I used to joke with my Anglican counterpart over a glass of wine, saying, *"We may have all the drunkards but you have all the gays!"* He had such a large sherry cabinet! Ah – happy days they were! I used to gently admonish him for being a corrupting influence to which he would reply that I was very willing to be corrupted. What discussions we used to have! Its sad how things have changed and how the moral climate of our society has deteriorated.

Delegating responsibility to the laity may possibly have helped matters but they seem always to insist upon their own way and take an inordinate interest in matters that are really the Holy Father's domain. There have certainly been more than enough disturbances caused by that Liberation Movement in South America. To delegate any priestly authority would simply never do. Benedict is of the same mind as his illustrious predecessor, so things are unlikely to change. The Roman Catholic Church has always been proud of its continuity in matters of faith and pastoral practice. Not without reason our motto is Semper Eadem *'Always the same.'* This continuity is our strength.

Please accept that I find myself in quite a predicament, caught between the Vatican's requirement of silence and the media's endless demand for comments upon matters I know little about. The tabloid media especially are always keen to see another Catholic Bishop grovel in public. I'm sorry to disappoint the *'gentlemen of the press'* but I'm not the grovelling type. I do have the dignity of my Office to consider. It's sad to see how much of the media pay money to the parents of the youngest unfortunates to slander the good name of the Church. Their distress is understandable but do they have to parade their grief in such a public manner? It's all so unnecessary – especially when things could have been settled quietly and without fuss. Thankfully, I'll soon be out of it. Following the unjustified furore about my withdrawn resignation, I've agreed with Rome to retire on grounds of ill health. Unlike others in my position I've not taken to drink or lapsed into despair. Anyway, I'll just help myself to another glass of whisky. Ah... that's better.

# Background Details for *'Restless Ashes'*

**Prologue:** *'Always the Same'* **Part 1: 1948:** Written on Tuesday, 18th October 2011

**1. Age Old Horror:** Written on Friday 10th September 2010 whilst trying to practice Hebrew forms of poetry. It explores firstly the rise and then the final destruction of global anti-Semitism.

**2. Auschwitz:** Written on Tuesday, 18th October 2011

**3. Before:** Written on Wednesday, 19th October 2011

**4. Beginning:** Written on Monday 18th April 2011 after reading two newspaper reports about the growing pressure to legalise euthanasia

**5. Devoured by Hatred:** This piece was written on Tuesday, 18th October 2011, following a protracted internet debate with a deeply anti-Semitic member of the Franciscan Third Order (which consists of lay people). It had originally been inspired by seeing a photograph in the Auschwitz Museum of a party of Polish Franciscans being deported (under guard) to Auschwitz. Given the Order's history of anti-Semitism I was left wondering what may have been going through the minds of some of these men as they were being escorted.

**6. Exchange:** Written on Saturday, 29th October 2011 after seeing Kolbe's death cell. This led me to wonder what could have provoked such an act of heroic self-sacrifice. The man he rescued Franciszek Gajowniczek, survived the war, dying in 1995 at the age of 94

**7. Girl in the Photograph:** Written on Tuesday, 18th October 2011

**8. Good Men:** Written on Wednesday, 10th August 2011 whilst travelling on a Ferry from Douglas (on the Isle of Man) to Belfast in Northern Ireland; I had in mind the way the Protestant German Churches had collaborated with Nazism during the 1920s and 1930s.

**9. Haunting Answers:** Written on Saturday, 21st January 2012 with the last question and answer being inserted on Tuesday, 17th April 2012. It refers to Hamas' expulsion of the PLO from Gaza in 2007

**10. Naivety:** Written on Wednesday, 10th August 2011

**11. Never Sleeping:** Written on Tuesday, 13th November 2013. It assumes that more squeamish middle class anti-Semites may prefer to follow a more indirect approach by creating a climate of opinion in which the mass murder of Jews becomes acceptable. In such a scenario, the actual killing would be left to underclass thugs. Such an indirect approach appears to be the one followed by left-wing anti-Zionists and their media sympathisers.

**12. One Tin Can:** Written on Tuesday, 25th January 2012

**13. Perhaps:** Written on Tuesday, 18th October 2011

**14. Recipe for Genocide:** Written on Tuesday, 18th October 2011

**15. Remade:** Written on Thursday, 23rd June 2011 in response to watching some YouTube of Orthodox Jews harassing Messianic Believers in Arad. In earlier research, I'd come across a web site exchange between a White Supremacist and Fundamentalist Group. Their strained attempts to be nice to one another were almost amusing in a macabre sort of way.

**16. Stench:** Written during the early hours of 1st July 2012

**17. Sweet Embrace:** Written on Sunday, 27th November 2011

**18. The Last Thoughts of Rudolf Hoess: 19. The Nine Circles of Hell:**
Written on Wednesday, 10th August 2011 whilst on a Ferry from Douglas (on the
Isle of Man) to Belfast in Northern Ireland. Rudolf Hoess was hanged on the
Auschwitz Camp site on 16th April 1947. I saw where this had taken place on
Friday 7th October 2011.

**19. The Nine Circles of Hell:** Written on Wednesday, 10th August 2011

**20. To the Children:** This was adapted from p.323a & p.324 of the Jewish Prayer
Book, shortly after my visit to Auschwitz.

**21. Toxic Influences:** Written on Tuesday, 18th October 2011

**22. Tread Warily:** Date uncertain, but possibly written on Tuesday, 18th October
2011

**23. Two Grandfathers:** Written on Wednesday, 10th August 2011 whilst on a Ferry
from Douglas (on the Isle of Man) to Belfast in Northern Ireland.

**24. Vow at Birkenau:** Written on Tuesday, 18th October 2011. It was based closely
upon words I'd quietly uttered in the grove of trees behind the gas chambers at
Aushwitz-Birkenau I was visiting on Friday 7th October 2011.

**25. War:** Written on Tuesday, 31st January 2012

**26. We Are All Hezbollah Now:** This angry denunciation was written whilst
seated on a large grey rock near the top of Ilkley Moor during the afternoon of
Monday, 11th September 2006. It expresses the nauseous disgust the author felt at
the resurgence of anti-Semitism within the UK. This took place during the conflict
between Israel and Hezbollah during July and August 2006. Its angry tone is
designed to reflect the growing madness and moral disintegration of a society
careering down a dangerous anti-Semitic pathway. Final additions were inserted in
April 2014.

**27. Weeping Meadow:** Written on Tuesday 11th October 2011, the day after
returning from Poland.

**28. Who Broke that Doll?** Written on Sunday, 27th November 2011, whilst
reflecting upon a broken doll that I'd seen at the Auschwitz Museum

**Epilogue: *'Always the Same'* Part 2: 2008:** Written on Tuesday, 18th October
2012

# INTERMISSION 2:
# ON WOODHOUSE MOOR

**(Poems celebrating a particular inner city park)**

# MISTY MARCH MORNING

All the croci were blooming, yellow, white and purple
(All the croci were blooming, yellow, white and purple)[54]
And a damp mist hung over Woodhouse Moor
(And a damp mist hung over Woodhouse Moor)
I was walking to work, tightly wrapped in a winter's coat
(I was walking to work, tightly wrapped in a winter's coat)
A bulging red and black rucksack strapped to my back
(A bulging red and black rucksack strapped to my back)
A Sony Camera clasped in my hand
(A Sony Camera clasped in my hand)
As if holidaying on this late winter's day
(As if holidaying on this late winter's day)
Was wanting to write a poem
(Was wanting to write a poem)
About the croci on Woodhouse Moor
During this misty March morning

Got distracted by an old man's whistling
As I approached a long croci flower bed
That lay in front of the tennis court
Glanced to my side and saw a wrinkled face
With a silver beard and a beautiful smile
Pigeons flew all around
Feeding on the seed he'd scattered on the ground
A white dove fluttered onto his outstretched hand
Cooing in appreciation
As he pecked from a small offering of seed

---

[54] Ideally three performers should recite this piece. If possible they should consist of two female performers standing either side of a man. One lady reads the first line whilst the second the bracketed line. The narrative is read by the man. The very last line is best read by all three performers simultaneously. (It was first performed in front of an audience of 28 people on Wednesday, 20th July 2011.)

I turned aside
To kneel beside a croci bed
Snapped some close up photos
Got up and moved backwards to get a distant view
Seeking inspiration
About the croci on Woodhouse Moor
During this misty March morning

On the path beside me
Young students hurried by
Eager not to miss lectures
They'd paid hefty fees to attend
Breath steaming from their cold, wintry faces

Finished my photography and proceeded on my way
The old man's whistling fading into the background
I joined the hurrying throng
Heading towards the University
Beyond the statue of Wellington
With its garish red painted boots
Still seeking inspiration
About the croci on Woodhouse Moor
During this misty March morning

All the croci were blooming, yellow, white and purple
(All the croci were blooming, yellow, white and purple)
And a damp mist hung over Woodhouse Moor
(And a damp mist hung over Woodhouse Moor)
I was walking to work, tightly wrapped in a winter's coat
(I was walking to work, tightly wrapped in a winter's coat)
A bulging red and black rucksack strapped to my back
(A bulging red and black rucksack strapped to my back)
A Sony Camera clasped in my hand
(A Sony Camera clasped in my hand)
As if holidaying on this late winter's day
(As if holidaying on this late winter's day)

Was wanting to write a poem
(Was wanting to write a poem)
About the croci on Woodhouse Moor
During this misty March morning

All the blooming croci, all the blooming croci
Adorning this late winter's day, adorning this late winter's day[55]

---

[55] This poem was written on my fifty-fifth birthday, on Tuesday, 3rd May 2011. (It was inspired by a visit made to Woodhouse Moor (on Wednesday, 16th March) to take photographs of the croci flower beds. Also, I'd been humming the 1965 hit song *California Dreaming'* that same day.)

# SHOULD YOU VISIT

Should you visit Woodhouse Moor
On a warm April Sunday afternoon
You'll see the next generation gathered there
Wearing skimpy shorts and loose 'T' shirts
Base ball caps, sunglasses and the odd floral skirt or blouse
Dressed for a rare late April sunshine

Should you visit Woodhouse Moor
On a warm April Sunday afternoon
You'll see the next generation gathered there
Idly playing cricket, football and cards
Happily laughing and larking around
Conversing in almost every language

Should you visit Woodhouse Moor
On a warm April Sunday afternoon
You'll see the next generation gathered there
Athletic men chasing giggling young girls
Others lying beside their smiling conquests
Playfully placing pink or white blossom in their hair

Should you visit Woodhouse Moor
On a warm April Sunday afternoon
You'll see the next generation gathered there
Girls sitting gossiping in intimate groups
Hunky boyfriends struggling to light a forbidden barbecue[56]
And dropping smouldering matches onto tinder dry grass

Should you visit Woodhouse Moor
On a warm April Sunday afternoon
You'll see the next generation gathered there
A bespectacled lady reading a Jane Austen novel

---

[56] Local bye-laws prevent the lighting of fires on Woodhouse Moor; these are routinely ignored by students.

Unthinkingly biting into a scarlet red apple
Eagerly dreaming of finding her own Mr Darcy

Should you visit Woodhouse Moor
On a warm April Sunday afternoon
You'll see the next generation gathered there
A shout of *'It's a goal!'* reverberating from a football game
A loud *'Howzat!'* from its cricketing counterpart
And the distant *'thwacking'* sound of rackets hitting tennis balls

Should you visit Woodhouse Moor
On a warm April Sunday afternoon
You'll see the next generation gathered there
A column of smoke wafting up from an illicit barbecue
Conveying the smell of slowly sizzling sausages
Not quite masking the ugly stench of overflowing litter bins

Should you visit Woodhouse Moor
On a warm April Sunday afternoon
You'll see the next generation gathered there
Garish coloured ice cream vans plying a busy trade
Surrounded by unsupervised dogs of every size
Barking gleefully in celebration of their temporary freedom

Should you visit Woodhouse Moor
On a warm April Sunday afternoon
You'll see the next generation gathered there
Loud music blaring, mobile phones ringing
Young children laughing and screeching
As tired parents push on their heavy swings

Should you visit Woodhouse Moor
On a warm April Sunday afternoon
You'll see the next generation gathered there
Twenty *'somethings'* from every continent
Black, white, yellow and brown mixing in peace
A whole world squashed into a few acres of green

Should you visit Woodhouse Moor
On a warm April Sunday afternoon
You'll see the next generation gathered there
Loudly panting, vest-clad runners hurrying by
Eager to improve on their speed
Their ruddy cheeks covered in a layer of sweat

Should you visit Woodhouse Moor
On a warm April Sunday afternoon
You'll see the next generation gathered there
A spotty blank-faced teenager gliding by
Balanced precariously on a worn and noisy skateboard
Nearly knocking into a veiled lady, wearing a darker shade of black

Should you visit Woodhouse Moor
On a warm April Sunday afternoon
You'll see the next generation gathered there
Lolling casually amidst a sea of litter
Empty bottles, bags and takeaway boxes lying scattered on the grass
Lollipop wrappings and cigarette packets thoughtlessly discarded

Should you visit Woodhouse Moor
On a warm April Sunday afternoon
You'll see the next generation gathered there
At ease in their pleasant surroundings
Appearing to feel no need for revolution or demonstration
A generation *'ticking along,'* barely in motion

Should you visit Woodhouse Moor
On a warm April Sunday afternoon
You'll see the next generation gathered there
Symbolising *'old-style'* youthful rebellion
And *'new style'* mobile phone innovation
A collective harbinger of a world that's yet to be

Should you visit Woodhouse Moor
On a warm April Sunday afternoon
You'll see the next generation gathered there
Will their lives be dominated by success or failure?
Blessed with riches, blighted by poverty
Or characterized instead by a tedious mediocrity?
Who can really know?

But should you visit Woodhouse Moor
On a warm April Sunday afternoon
You will see the next generation gathered there[57]

---

[57] This poetical meditation was first drafted on Thursday, 12th May 2011 and was based upon memories of a visit made to Woodhouse Moor on Sunday April 24th. I also had just heard a recording of Scott Mackenzie singing the 1967 hit song *'San Francisco'* on *'YouTube'* and this acted as a *'trigger'* for *'Should You Visit.'*

# VICTORIAN PERSPECTIVES

## (Exploring the clash between Victorian Values and those of a Post-Modern Age)

Should I take my great Grandfather, Edmund
(Who lived from 1832 until 1915)
To revisit Woodhouse Moor
On a warm Spring Sunday afternoon
(Following an absence of almost one hundred years)
What would he find?
How would he react?
What would please or displease him?

Well, let's begin by placing him at the Hyde Park Road entrance, just
in front of Peel's Statue
*'Ah, Wood'ouse Moor.*
*I used t' bring my children 'ere*
*On a warm Sunday afternoon*
*Sometimes we'd ave an enormous picnic 'amper*
*Which the servants used to carry*

On looking around, standing stiff and straight, his hands clasped
behind his back, he would ponder at everything around him and
exclaim;
*'What 'ave we 'ere then?*
*They've still got the statue of Prime Minister Peel*
*Even though they 'ave moved it from outside the Town 'all*
*'e did a good job in abolishing those hated Corn Laws*
*But where's the Bandstand?*
*Hmmm, that's gone Ah see*
*But the air's good*
*There's no soot*
*Glad to note that the Moor*
*Is still 'the lungs of Leeds''*

On proceeding up the path towards the centre of the Moor he would
'tut' at the sight of scantily dressed female students enjoying a
barbecue with their boyfriends
*'The women of this age have become slatterns*[58]
*Their over-familiarity with the men*
*Lowers the tone of the place*
*Even worse, there's not a strapping Yorkshire lass among 'em*
*Perhaps they're visitors from a TB sanatorium on a day out –*
*The poor dears – but where are their nurses?*
*Oh! They must be the ladies*
*In those long black dresses and veils*
*At least they're modestly dressed*
*But the sanatorium appears to be run by a papist religious order!'*

Glowering at the men he would sigh;
*'Not a decent suit t' be seen amongst 'em*
*They look like seaside clowns or Irish navvies*
*They're so scruffy*
*The clothes they wear definitely belong to the lower orders*
*Yet they speak like the refined sort o' people*
*Are they gentry who've fallen on 'ard times?*
*Bet the demon drink 'as done for some of 'em!'*

On seeing two men walking hand in hand he would avert his head
and mutter;
*'Disgusting!*
*This country 'as sunk to the worst excesses of Ancient Rome*
*The end must be near!*
*Poor Britain*
*Ah never reckoned that 'the Italian vice' would be practised on Wood'ouse Moor!*

On seeing some students quietly reading paperback books he would
observe;
*'There's a lot o' folk readin' 'Penny Dreadfuls'*
*But no, no – on a closer look they're books with paper covers*

---

[58] An old term for untidy, slovenly dressed and immoral ladies – the modern equivalent is *'slut'*

*I bet that novelty won't catch on*
*Books should 'ave a proper bindin' as they did in my day*
*An' they should make a point of some Dickens!*
*What the Dickens! Some of em are reading Dickens!*
*'Hard Times' to be precise!*
*Still, ah bet they never knew what it were like*
*To lose a father in a mill accident and a mother through consumption a year later*
*Or to be threatened wi' the Work 'ouse*
*In the starvin' forties at the age o' twelve*
*These people seem to 'ave it too good*

*Good gracious! The indecently clad lady lying there*
*Appears to be reading from a mechanical scroll*
*What a remarkable contrivance!*

*Oh, Ah see Jane Austin is still popular*
*My daughters used to like readin' 'er*
*It filled their 'eads wi' giddy nonsense'*

Exciting strong feelings of disapproval would be some drunken,
chain-smoking youths, noisily passing by;
*'That lot deserve a good old fashioned floggin!'*
*The young o' this age 'ave no manners*
*An' they remind me o' the Chartist mob*
*Ah saw in Skipton when Ah were a lad.*
*Really frightening that were.*
*These young folk need to sign 'The Pledge' an' abstain from the devil's drink*
*I just 'ope 'Temperance' is doin' well!*
*It's a pity that smokin' seems confined t' the common type o' folk*
*Was told by t' druggist that a good smoke*
*Would clear yer lungs an' protect yer from the miasma*
*I often used to say*
*'What's a man without a cigar?'*
*Used to ply 'em t' mah customers*
*When sellin' cloth'*

On seeing another young lady download a picture on an *'I-pod'* he
would exclaim;
*What an incredible marvel —*
*The telegraph can send pictures now*
*An' play music too —*
*Exactly how — Ah dorn't know!*
*They must send somethin' through the ether!*
*Tiny typewriters with movin' pictures*
*That is progress*
*These contrivances are so small!*
*Yer need the fingers of a seamstress to work 'em!'*


Other things would both please and puzzle him;
*'The children look so 'ealthy*
*All of 'em 'ave shoes an'*
*Not a case o' rickets to be seen at all!*
*Yet how odd!*
*The women dress like prostitutes*
*The men like clowns or Irish navvies*
*But the children look as if they've been bred*
*By people of quality*
*What a strange time this is*
*The country 'as prospered in my absence*
*But the people are so continental in their lax ways*


*Just look at all at these people from the Colonies*
*Oh my! Hasn't the Empire done well*
*In spreadin' its civilizin' influence!*


*Thankfully, we must 'ave seen off that Kaiser*
*Never did like 'im or 'is struttin' ways*
*Always said 'e would cause trouble*
*Made a mistake in gettin' rid of old Bismarck*
*At least that chap knew when t' stop —*
*I wonder if he's still remembered?*
*What's that Ah can 'ear on those new fangled music boxes*
*— Summit about a Tsar Putin?*

*Odd name that*
*That mad monk Rasputin*
*Must 'ave married into the Royal Family after all*
*Bet that caused trouble*
*'e were causin' a stink near the end o' mah days*

*Hmmm – Ah can I see the Crimean cannon we used to 'ave 'as gone*
*Must 'ave removed 'em from the Moor*
*To keep in with the Russians*
*We must be real friends with 'em by now*
*'owever, I'd watch that Tsar Putin!'*
*'e could cause a lot of trouble*
*Especially in the Crimea*

As he approached the centre of the Moor he would notice more
members from different ethnic minorities;
*Those Indians with their turbans are splendid chaps*
*They 'ave longer beards than Ah do!*
*Must 'ave been soldiers –*
*I expect their kinsfolk at 'ome*
*Are still guardin' the North West Frontier*
*Against those troublesome Afghans*
*There'll still be trouble there – that's fer sure*

*Oh my! There's Chinese too!*
*They're 'ere in peace*
*We must 'ave solved 'The Yellow Peril' after all!*
*An' Africans also*
*I remember when America 'ad ter fight a Civil War*
*T' end slavery*
*That was an infernal institution*
*The war between the States ruined the cotton trade in Lancashire*
*Remember seein' 'ungry children beggin' on the streets*
*When visitin' mah brother at Staleybridge*
*'E 'ad to teach the poor mites –*
*Was always careful where 'e placed 'is hat*
*Whenever 'e visited them at 'ome*

*Lest 'e got 'eadlice in it!*
*But now*
*There's so many folk from the Colonie, all mixin' in peace*
*Bravo! British Empire, Bravo!*
*You've done a splendid job*
*In bringin' together the world's people*
*May the sun never set on yer!'*


On seeing an Orthodox Jewish man stroll by with his family, he'd remark;
*'Ah'd take a wager that*
*Ah sold cloth to yer Great Grandfather*
*Were always good fer business*
*Knew them 'ebrews would go far*
*'eard a preacher say that, one day*
*They'd get back to the 'oly land*
*'e went on about this new Zionist Movement*
*Founded by that Herzl chap*
*Personally, Ah think that was a bit o' fanciful speculation*
*The Turks would never allow it*
*Somethin' big would 'ave to 'appen to drive 'em there'*


After hearing a middle-aged Irish couple speak he'd grumble;
*'I expect they're still riddled with priests an' Fenian agitators*
*I'd wager they're still causin' brawls in East Leeds as well!*
*An Irishman with drink in 'im is the very devil!*
*Why our Frank 'ad to marry an Irish lass*
*(An' a guilt-ridden Papist at that) Ah' I never knah*
*Could see nowt but trouble from that marriage*
*Still, they made their own bed an' they can lie on it*
*At least they produced plenty o' grandchildren fer me*
*An' ensured that the family name would go on —*
*They didn't lose 'alf their children as I did!*
*Sad, sad days — laid too many of 'em to rest*
*As I did three wives'*

On picking up a Tabloid Sunday Newspaper left lying on a bench
He would exclaim;
*'Don't they make 'em small these days!*
*What's this about a Liberal-Tory Coalition?*
*Was always a Gladstone man mahself,*
*The speeches 'e gave moved me to tears*
*From what Ah remember 'e didn't like the Turks*
*'e wanted 'em out o' the Balkans*
*Couldn't ave imagined 'im in a coalition with Disraeli!*
*Not surprised to read that the Tories and Liberals still don't get on*
*They're obviously desperate to keep the Socialists out*
*That Cameron chap reminds me of Lord Salisbury'*
*Bet the Tory Party is still run by public school snobs*

As he left the centre of the Moor to approach Moorland Road, the
sight of passing cars would provoke him to say;
*'What a marvellous improvement*
*Every man with 'is own mechanical 'ansome cab*
*An' ladies too!*
*Humph! Ah'm not sure whether that should be allowed*
*The delicate sex are much too emotional to 'andle the roads*
*Mah first wife was always 'avin' the vapours*
*She never did appreciate bein' married ter me*
*'er passing away in child birth came as a relief*
*It was so different with the second and third 'uns."*

The sight of the old Grammar School would make him step back and
pause to take breath;
*'Upon my word, it's now a school for commerce!*
*What's 'appened to the old Greek and Latin?*
*Ah know my sons were never good at those subjects*
*And not one of 'em got to Cambridge*
*(As I would 'ave liked)*
*But in mah book, a Grammar School's a Grammar School*
*An' not a glorified Mechanics Institute!*
*What would the old masters 'ave said?*
*I suspect the rot set in when they 'ad those new fangled laboratories*

*Back in the nineteen 'undreds*
*The old school was always askin' parents fer extra money*
*If it's still around Ah bet that 'asn't changed!*

*But Ah suppose it's good that Leeds*
*Is still a centre o' manufacturing enterprise*
*Perhaps some big mill owner took over the school*
*Before sellin' it on to the University*

A rusting statue of the Duke of Wellington, having had his boots
painted a garish red would throw him into an apoplectic rage;
*'Outrageous! How dare they mock the dear old Duke*
*Who saved this country from Boney at Waterloo*
*I'd wager that socialists or suffragette harridans are to blame!*
*Aye, Ah bet we never saw 'is like again*
*Boney was mad t' try and unify the continentals*
*The Kaiser 'ad the same daft dream and that always leads to war*
*Wonder if Tsar Putin 'as the same idea?*
*The Russians were always wantin' to push their noses into other people's business*
*Ah remember 'ow they started the Crimean war*
*When I were a young man*
*Bet they're still meddling in that region'*

A glance at the vast expanse of Leeds University would slowly calm
his anger;
*'Oh my! The Yorkshire College' 'as done well!*
*It was gettin' big in my day*
*But now it's a vast temple to learni!'*
*There seem to be ladies there too*
*They can't all be domestics!*
*If they're students Ah jolly well 'ope they're properly chaperoned*
*They certainly could do wi' some other form of decent attire*
*Only the Indians appear to dress with a becoming modesty*
*They seem to be more Victorian than I am!'*

On turning back into the Moor and progressing towards the Queen
Victoria monument he could hear loud chanting from yellow robed
devotees of the Hari Krishna cult;
*'I see the Freemasons 'are makin' a public display o' their daft rituals*
*Never did like 'em an' now Ah know why*
*Cost me a lot o' business they did*
*But where's the Church on this warm an' pleasant afternoon?*
*There's not even the Sally Army to give people*
*A good old dose of 'ellfire an' Brimstone!*
*The churches must be asleep'*

On finding the heavily oxidised monument to Queen Victoria
He would sadly reflect;
*What an obscure place to put the dear Queen's monument!*
*How insulting!*
*I remember when it were unveiled outside the Town 'all back in 1905*
*The Lord Mayor gave a right pompous speech*

On gazing up at the statue's face he would ruefully declare;
*'My <u>dear</u> Majesty!*
*I've found the early twenty first century to be a most peculiar age*
*Yerr Empire is thrivin' and*
*Present are wonders exceeding the imagination of Mr Verne and Mr Wells!*
*But there are also indecent sights, recalling the worst excesses of Ancient Rome*
*The people of this country seem to 'ave gone mad*
*'as all the wealth our 'ard work 'elped to ter create been used wisely?*
*Ah don't know! But as your 'umble subject Ah can only ask*
*'What 'as become of the England we both knew and loved?'*[59]

---

[59] This piece was first drafted on Tuesday, 24th May 2011.

# SHORT STORIES

**(Exploring crimes old and new)**

# AN UNWELCOME DISCOVERY

## *S1: The Dog Walker*

An old man with a pinched, gaunt face was often to be seen taking a pack of up to four Alsatian dogs for regular walks on Woodhouse Moor. This was a huge diamond-shaped area of open parkland located next to Leeds University; it was a wonderful haven of green, nestled between the busy main road of Woodhouse Lane and the far quieter Moorland Road. The old Grammar School buildings occupied one end of Moorland Road, standing upright and solid in their mock Gothic splendour and now forming an integral part of the University itself. Right throughout the nineteen fifties, sixties and right on into the nineties this same man would be seen walking his dogs, always wearing his peaked Eastern European worker's cap. Even in summer he'd wear a long coat with a large collar which he'd pull high up his neck, giving the definite impression that he wanted to keep himself to himself. In winter he'd wear ear muffs as well as a peaked cap. His most noticeable feature was a deep scar down the right side of his face. It had always been there – from his first day in Leeds – somewhere in the late nineteen forties.

Over the decades his appearance changed little by little – his once fair hair becoming silvery grey; his face, at one time ruggedly handsome and (except for the scar) clean cut, now thick-set and wrinkled. By the mid-nineties his formerly erect military posture had lapsed into a slight stoop and his appearance had taken on a sallow and cadaverous look. Even with a cursory glance he looked malnourished. Yet he never slackened his pace and neither did he ever greet other dog owners whom he would silently pass by. Some of them were dog lovers themselves, wholly undeterred by his barking hounds; but a cheery *'good morning'* or *'hello'* was never to be heard from his lips. Should he have chosen to break his self-imposed silence then a distinct Eastern European accent would have resulted. Come rain or shine, snow or fog he'd be out walking his dogs on Woodhouse Moor – either early in the morning or late in the evening (when there were fewer people about). Fathers driving their sons to the Leeds

Grammar School would sometimes nod their heads in his direction and remark, 'His nerves must have been affected by the war.' Children would feel uneasy as he passed by – sensing there was something 'not quite right' about him. Suddenly, in mid January 2001, following all of his years of ordered dog-walking, the man and his Alsatians were no longer to be seen. They'd vanished as if into thin air.

### S2: An Open Door

It was a cold and dull late January afternoon, with more than a nip in the air. The red brick terraced house stood near to Woodhouse Moor, two streets away from Wrangthorne Parish Church. The key to its front door turned slowly as if resisting an entrance; finally the lock submitted and with a firm push it reluctantly opened. Father Thomas Lucre and his parishioner, the eighty one year old Joseph Wozniak, entered. Joseph was secretary to the local branch of the Legion of Pilsudski (a Catholic charity set up to look after the needs of ex Polish Servicemen). In appearance these men couldn't have been more different. Where Father Lucre was small, fat and balding, his companion was tall and slender, with the dignified bearing of a former soldier. Joseph's oval peasant face and large strong hands gave the impression of a life having been spent in hard manual toil. Despite his eighty one years, he looked far more vigorous and alert than his rather easy-going companion. Father Lucre's 'manual work' had only ever amounted to picking up a pen and writing a dissertation on 'Jesuit Casuistry' as part of his studies in the Gregorian University at Rome. Even their voices reflected their different backgrounds; Father Lucre spoke with an ingratiating Irish brogue (which either soothed or bored his parishioners) whereas his companion spoke in the loud sharp tone of a former Sergeant in the Polish National Army. However, over five and a half decades of living in Britain had eradicated all but the slightest traces of Joseph's Polish accent. Yet his emphatic manner remained – his speech and bearing almost shouting out his military credentials. A musty smell greeted this ill-matched pair as they entered the hallway. Fortunately, iron bars (protecting the ground floor windows) had prevented any intrusion or vandalism from the foulmouthed youths on the nearby Estate.

"Our friend had certainly made his house burglar proof – look at those bars – it's almost like a prison!" exclaimed Joseph. Father Lucre's reply was an absent-minded nod. He was here to honour the deceased's last wishes and he wanted to get started – small talk would just get in the way. He gave a short cough to clear his throat and stated, "His lawyer said the will would be hidden behind the picture of *'Our Lady'* which is in the living room. Now let's try this door... ah here we are!" He pushed open a faded cream door and proceeded to enter.

The living room continued the note of darkness and penny-pinching austerity, already obvious in the dull ancient paintwork of the hallway. As the remainder of the house would confirm, nothing had ever been renewed. The furniture consisted of an old TV, a battered leather sofa, a rickety wooden chair and a heavily stained rug of a dark but indeterminate colour. Indeed, the only real colour was provided by some well-chewed red balls which lay scattered all over the floorboards – obviously toys for the dogs. Looming above a simple gas heater was a large imitation painting of the Virgin Mary, holding baby Jesus. It seemed to have been based upon some old Renaissance piece – Father Lucre had often seen it before in other devout households. Unbidden, Joseph gently lifted the painting off the wall and placed it next to the now defunct heater. Revealed behind it was a small metal door, painted white like the walls in an attempt to make it less noticeable. Considerable trouble had been taken in the making of this homemade safe. Joseph struggled for some time to turn the key – once inside he found a long white envelope which stated in bold typed lettering, *'The Last Will and Testament of Marcin Nowak,'* a bulging brown envelope and a small black box. He left them in their narrow confinement, awaiting instructions from Father Lucre.

"According to his solicitor we're to open the white envelope containing the will and destroy all of the documents in the large brown envelope – which is <u>not,</u> under any circumstances, to be opened. The box is likewise to remain locked and we're to deposit it at the Oxfam shop in Headingley, where upon a receipt will be provided. Clothes are to be either destroyed or donated to the same shop. Further details will be given in the will. I gather you received the same instructions?" Father Lucre threw an enquiring look at Joseph who responded with a curt nod.

"His solicitor also stated that we're to sign and return a *'Declaration,'* stating that we've complied with these conditions. As you may gather he has copies of all of the relevant documentation. Our friend was obviously a man who left nothing to chance."

"Yes, yes... and to the destruction of things he'd wish others never to see."

"Possibly, possibly, but we still have a moral responsibility to honour the wishes of the deceased."

"Just look at all these bars on the windows! He certainly worried about his safety."

"Understandable – given the high crime rate in this area."

"No, no – he's been a worried man for a long time – they've been up for over fifty years! I used to see them when I walked to work."

"Possibly the effects of the war."

"Maybe."

"Anyway, let's deal with the will first. It'll be more comfortable to look at it in the kitchen. It should have a table and I certainly could do with a cup of tea."

"The gas and electricity are off Father."

The priest responded with a grimace before saying, "Well we'd better get on before it starts getting dark and it's certainly bitterly cold in this house."

"Polish winters are worse," was the gruff reply

### S3: A Conditional Legacy

"Hmm!– let's see what my former parishioner has to offer. Could you pass me a knife?" Joseph went over to the kitchen drawer, lying above two empty dog baskets. He found only one set of cutlery – the deceased had obviously never expected visitors. He returned to Lucre who took the knife and carefully opened the envelope.

"What is it Father?"

"Let me read it. Ah yes!"

A satisfied smile broke out on his face.

"I Marcin Nowak, being of sound mind etc bequeath the following legacies: -

To my old Parish Church of... I bequeath £50,000 for refurbishment of the new Parish Hall and to aid the Church Roof Fund.

To the Legion of Pilsudski I bequeath £40,000 for the care of ex Polish Servicemen and Prisoners of War.

To the Jewish Holocaust charity of... I bequeath £10,000.

To the Diocese of Leeds I bequeath this house to be used at the discretion of the Diocesan Authorities. Any tools found herein are to be distributed to Catholic Charity workshops.

As executors I appoint my local Parish Priest and the Leeds Secretary of the Legion of Pilsudski. These bequests will only be made if the aforesaid executors agree to accept responsibility for the disposing of all of my remaining effects. In particular, the terms of this will apply only if the aforesaid executors agree to: -

1. Burn <u>unopened</u> all of the contents in the brown envelope (containing personal papers and other documentation)
2. Anonymously hand the sealed box to the Oxfam Charity Shop in Headingley (who are to provide a receipt)

Clothing and minor household items are to be disposed of in any way the executors deem appropriate.

For this will to be valid the following Declaration Form is to be signed and deposited at the office of my Lawyer.

"What does that say?"

"Just this, "We N and N, the executors of this will, have fully complied with all of its Terms and Conditions and have disposed of all items in the way previously requested. We, the undersigned, fully understand that any failure to comply with the above terms and conditions will mean that all financial effects pertaining to Marcin Nowak will be left to the State.""

The two men looked at each other and smiled.

"Well, I thought there might be some form of legacy but I never thought we would have all of this!" opined Father Lucre, "He must have saved and saved!"
"He certainly didn't spend much on himself. Any spare money he had must have been lavished on those dogs of his."
"When he retired from the railways he did caretaking work for the Church. He was very thorough and even did some cleaning work on the side. Kept going until his eighty-first year."
"We Poles are hard workers."
"We know! You've all certainly helped to keep the Diocese going."
Again both men smiled at one another like two conspirators.
"What a blessed surprise! Our Lady must be smiling on us!" exclaimed Lucre with a smug expression on his face, "and what a good way to end my tenure as Priest and you to complete your final year as Secretary for the Legion!"
"Yes, yes – it certainly is good to know that things will be financially sound for the Legion. We're short of funds again. Well, the sooner we begin complying with the terms of the will the better."
"Indeed" enthused Father Lucre.
"I'll look downstairs and in the garage; you go upstairs and check the bedroom and bathroom. I don't think we'll find much – just another dog basket or two."
Both men laughed.
"He loved dogs although he only had two at the end."
"Shall we get on Father?"

### S4: Spillage

"Have you found anything?" shouted Joseph from the bottom of the stairs.
"Only some drab clothes, an Icon of Christ and an old radio. Oh – you were right about the dog baskets – they were beside his mattress. He didn't even have a bed – only some blankets and a sleeping bag."
"Have you finished?"
"Yes, what about you?"

"Nothing in the cellar – only a work bench with an old map of Eastern Europe on it. I was glad I brought a torch. His tools were in the cupboard at the bottom of the stairs. He doesn't seem to have used them for years. The kitchen cupboards were full of dog food and I found an old book about looking after Alsatians. Our man wasn't a big reader."

"Did you find anything outside?"

"Some petrol in the garage and some more old tools. Looks like he was building a large bonfire in the garden."

"Oh, didn't you know he was found there?"

"In the garden?"

"Yes, earlier this month – face down. He'd been carrying a large log and the effort had brought on a heart attack – was found a few hours later. His neighbours had been alerted by those hounds of his howling and barking non-stop; they've been 'put down' now of course."

"A lonely end to a lonely life."

"I'm afraid so" said Father Lucre with only a little feeling in his voice.

"At least it's been straightforward here. I've been to the houses of ex servicemen where it's taken days to clear everything. If they'd taken to drink you can imagine the mess. The worst we've had here has been dust."

"The Bishop will be most pleased to receive this property. He could turn it into a community house"

"I bet he will," was Joseph's slightly sarcastic reply.

"Have you dealt with all of the things from the safe?"

"Oh – you've just reminded me!" Joseph headed for the living room. Father Lucre called after him "I'm just going to pop into the bathroom and then I'll come down and help you with the garden fire. That's obviously the way he'd wanted to destroy it all!"

On returning to the kitchen Father Lucre found his companion shaking his head over a pile of papers and photographs lying strewn across the table top. Joseph's face had flushed a deep red before fading into a deathlike pallor, "I'm sorry Father! The envelope was old and split open when I brought it into the kitchen. Just look at all these photographs!"

## S5: A Question of Identity

Father Lucre looked at the black and white photographs of uniformed guards standing next to a barbed wire gate. One of the guards was smirking and dangling an obviously distressed white poodle by the collar. Another was struggling to hold back a snarling Alsatian by its leash – still managing to smile fondly at this fearsome animal. A further photo showed the same guard looking directly at the camera, half heartedly trying to turn his sneering grimace into a mock friendly smile. Names were scrawled on the back of the photos. One read *'Anton Dragon with Wolf.'* Joseph shook his head in despair.
"Father, do you know what this means?"
Creased worry lines appeared on Lucre's forehead. He knew what was coming and could *'see'* all of the legacies beginning to go up in a puff of crematoria smoke.
"Anton Dragon was one of the most feared guards in the Auschwitz Camp. He was always ready to use his whip and dogs to drive people into the gas chambers. The Ukrainians could be just as cruel as the Germans."
"Are-are you sure Joseph? D-don't you think that this could be a case of mistaken identity? Couldn't the photos have been kept by a prisoner following liberation?" Father Lucre was still reeling from this most unwelcome of discoveries. He'd quickly grasped the financial implications and was simply horrified. Nothing would be theirs, nothing. He knew he needed to resolve all of this. He would grasp at anything – any way out of this dilemma.
For Joseph it was all so obvious and straightforward. "Would a prisoner want to keep such photos for his own private use – even if he found them in the chaos of liberation? How would a prisoner normally get hold of such things?" He was convinced that these photos had been in the possession of a camp guard and never a prisoner. That was the only way this unwelcome discovery made any sense.
"Did you ever get to know him?" interrogated Joseph.
"We eh...we hardly saw him. Once mass was over he was gone!"
"I got a good look at him when he opened the Hall for the Legion's Annual Meeting. He seemed to want to hurry away without saying

anything. I always felt he had more of a Ukrainian than a Polish accent."

"That's just your impression."

"Take a closer look at the picture! Don't you see the resemblance, the broken nose, the high forehead, the stocky build? "

"It was taken a long time ago. Besides we'd need evidence that would stand up in a court of a law. A couple of old photos wouldn't suffice. They certainly don't show a man with a scar running down his face."

"Then look at this! These are receipts for jewellery sold in London during the late 1940's. There's also a receipt for private treatment to straighten his nose and deal with an old war injury. Anton was known to have had his nose broken in some brawl or other. It all fits in – don't you see Father?" Joseph's voice rose in anger – his face flushing a deep red.

"But Joseph! It's just possible that in the excitement of this very moment you're seeing a pattern which isn't really there! As I told you before – you'd need cast iron evidence for it all to stand up in a court of law! They would throw it out as it stands Joseph – you know they would!"

Joseph appeared not to listen, "Well – let's see what's in the box..."

"You can't! You must respect the wishes of the deceased..."

Too late – Joseph had forced it open and Father Lucre saw his companion's eyes almost pop out of his head. With slow deliberation he pulled out a long jewelled necklace, then a lock of dark hair and then out of an old white envelope (which had been placed at the bottom of the box) a faded photograph. This showed a young Jewish-looking girl who appeared to be in her early twenties. With raven, shoulder length hair she was clad in prison pyjamas. A slight plumpness in her features suggested that starvation had not yet set in. There was something in her defiant expression which suggested she'd come from a respectable family. Tattered edges around the photo gave the impression of having often been handled. Yet its storage in an envelope dated with a 1995 Polish Postmark suggested that in recent years it had been carefully looked after. All that now remained in the box were some rings and other trinkets of indefinite value.

"Hmmm! Seems Anton had had a love interest. Pity there's no name on the back. Look at this necklace! It must be worth a small fortune!"

"Really, this is going too far! It's showing disrespect for the deceased!"

"What respect did Anton show for <u>his</u> deceased? These are looted goods Father!" It's sickening – all of its sickening, I feel tainted holding these things. That poor girl..." Joseph's voice trailed off.

An awkward, emotionally charged silence followed before Father Lucre sighed and said, "All we have is supposition. I know from my experience as a witness in innumerable court cases that lawyers would pull such evidence to pieces. All we have is speculation."

"Alright, what do you really know about 'the deceased?'"

"He attended Sunday Mass regularly and of late the odd midweek service. He seemed to get more devout as he got older."

"A guilty conscience – needing to be quietened before he met his 'Maker.' Anything else?"

"He was a conscientious caretaker. Always punctual; took it badly when declining health forced him to retire three months ago. The Sunday before he died he came up to me and said he was troubled by re-occurring nightmares. Thought it could be something that happened in the war. I tried to arrange a pastoral visit but he kept putting me off."

"Hmm," Joseph said.

"When preparing for his funeral I contacted my predecessors and spoke to some elderly parishioners who'd been around since the early fifties. They could only tell me a few things. Apparently he'd worked a lot of overtime on the railways and many night shifts too. He'd begged one of my predecessors to offer him that caretaker's position about a week after he'd retired. Oh yes I remember something else now – he'd vanished one August about five years ago. Was absent for the whole month – had gone to attend to personal matters. He'd just lost two of his dogs in quick succession and I think that that had unsettled him."

"He seems to have been a restless soul."

"That could be due to any number of reasons."

"We should mention our little discovery to the Police. It would give his victims, some who are my ex servicemen, a sense of closure and peace. A ghost from the past will have been laid to rest."

Father Lucre involuntarily gave a start, "Really! Would that be wise?"

"It would be honest," replied Joseph quietly.

### S6: Money Talks

Father Lucre paused – he needed more time to think. He clasped his hands under his chin, as if in prayer. In a slightly wheedling tone he said, "Consider this; might not the deceased, assuming he <u>was</u> Anton Dragon, be trying to atone for his sins by bestowing generous legacies on those groups he'd most harmed?"

"Nothing could atone for what Dragon did!" replied Joseph, his voice rising again.

"But he was trying to! As good Catholics we must endeavour to adopt the most charitable explanation," Father Lucre said with great emphasis.

"You're thinking of the Church roof Father!"

"Oh nooo!!! That's the least of my considerations!"

Joseph just looked straight at him, his jaw firmly set.

"Look Joseph – I know it must be hard for you – but just think – what would be the lesser of evils?"

"Nothing could have been more evil than what he was caught up in," Joseph said very slowly and clearly.

"But think exactly what would happen if we did go to the Police?"

At this point Father Lucre felt it necessary to move Joseph's mind on to another, less emotive scenario.

"Eh – what do you mean by that?"

"Lawyers could tie everything up for months and it would all go to the State. Who would benefit from such a step? Not my parishioners, nor your needy ex servicemen and not even his former victims who would have their sufferings raked up to public exposure all over again. Would this <u>really</u> be a good thing?"

"But at least they'd receive closure and the satisfaction that Anton Dragon had led a miserable life."

"Would they? Surely the fact that he'd escaped justice and died with a fortune would serve only to add to their bitterness? It might even set off a crisis of faith in their declining years. Is it even morally right to trouble these unfortunates?"

"There was no morality in Auschwitz. You weren't there when Anton used to set *Wolf* onto prisoners or laugh when they were being herded into the gas chambers."

"Really Joseph! Does that sound like my quiet, retiring parishioner who, for decades, led a perfectly respectable, if rather sad life? You must be careful about libelling the dead." Lucre then checked himself, realizing that he risked patronizing his companion.

"Father you don't understand! People like that were cowards! It doesn't matter whether they killed in the name of National Socialism or Communism. What they wanted was to exercise power by making better people than themselves suffer. Dragon's name was notorious. One of my ex servicemen told me that when a certain prisoner was being taken to the torture centre at Block 11 he'd cursed Dragon, shouting that he'd forever bear the mark of Cain. Dragon's response was a smirk and an order to the guards to 'give him a good time boys.' Of course the prisoner was never seen again. The name *'Dragon'* is even now a curse on many lips. Only two weeks ago I heard it from one of my servicemen (suffering from dementia) who was dying in the Infirmary. They'd had to draw the curtains around and give him something to calm him. He was shouting Dragon's name over and over again. He was even then tormenting this man's last moments. What Dragon most feared was justice and vengeance. Just look at this house – its barred windows – it was his fortress! Just so long as people were kept out – that meant safety for him! That's the man whose money you wish to keep Father. It's <u>blood</u> money!" Joseph almost shrieked these last few words.

In response, the priest could only stand and stroke his chin. He suddenly felt very shallow and small. This unwelcome discovery had turned a blessing into a curse. But he still had a duty to his parishioners.

"Do you believe in the power of redemption Joseph? As a good Catholic don't you believe that inscrutable providence can bring at least a measure of good out of evil? Who are we to hinder God if He wants to do this? Should we compound Dragon's sins by ensuring that his legacy doesn't benefit those in most need of it?"

"Are you saying honesty is a form of robbery?"

"In this case – yes!"

"I never thought I'd hear these words from you Father – from a Priest of the Catholic Church! I feel ashamed!"

"But these are difficult circumstances Joseph!"

"In my home country *'difficult circumstances'* was used to justify the murder of millions and today it's used to justify the murder of the unborn and perhaps tomorrow the murder of the elderly and the seriously ill. The excuse of *'difficult circumstances'* has been used to justify many a crime. As a Priest you should know that!"

At this point Father Lucre fell silent – feeling smaller than ever. Yet he just couldn't get the prospect of a renovated Parish Hall and Church roof out of his mind. It dangled before him like bait in front of an open-mouthed fish.

"We're supposing that the deceased <u>was</u> Anton Dragon. In this *'difficult,'* I mean *'trying'* situation we should be prepared to give him the benefit of the doubt! It's only charitable to do so."

"Well, look at these other pictures."

Joseph pushed them contemptuously in front of Lucre. They were coloured, modern photographs of Eastern European landscapes.

"Now look at the back of them."

"They're place names – all dated August 1995."

"For your information the places he's named were where Dragon was active. Some of them are in the West Ukraine where he was first recruited. However, he hadn't the courage to revisit Auschwitz – he only took photographs from the outside. Perhaps he feared bumping into old ghosts. Was it there that he'd met his prisoner sweetheart?"

"The date does match his absence."

"You know the saying – a criminal always returns to the scene of his crimes."

"And so does a victim!"

"No victim would have survived being at all of the places where Dragon was stationed!"

"The evidence is telling but... but the lawyers..."

"The writing on the back – isn't it the same as in the old photographs? See for yourself."

"Oh dear! This is so... so disturbing."

"You bet it is Father! Anyway I think we'd better call the Police."

"No!"

"I can't believe you're saying that!"

"But listen," pleaded Lucre, struggling to regain some sort of composure.

"We're not responsible for what the deceased may or may not have done in the past. Let God be the judge of that. We're not even responsible for an unhappy discovery made by accident. But we <u>are</u> responsible for serving those whom the good Lord has placed into our care. This means that we <u>have a duty of care</u> to ensure that an act of charity (no matter what motivated it) <u>should</u> go ahead. Difficult though we may find it, our responsibility to those entrusted to our care should outweigh whatever feelings of distaste we may entertain for the deceased."

"Spoken like a true priest," Joseph replied with heavy sarcasm.

"We cannot bring back the dead or even heal the mental scars of the living. But I know that what we can do is to ensure that a legacy (which <u>may</u> have had murky origins) benefits your people, my people and the death camp survivors. It would be wrong to rob such people of this benefit, especially in the eventide of their years."

"It's still blood money."

"If we're wise and control our emotions it can be <u>redeemed</u> blood money!" Father Lucre exclaimed, thinking to himself 'Ah yes that sounded right – just right.'

Joseph responded with a deep sigh, "I find this... but never mind... it's almost as if Dragon is laughing at us from beyond the grave. He's got us exactly where he wants us. I bet he even made sure that the envelope was over-full and that that metal case was unlocked."

"That's speculation. It's best to view this matter as some form of trial sent by our Lord to test our faith."

"It's still blood money – trial or no trial of faith!"

"Now think of your own interests. You're 81, the same age as the deceased. Your health is remarkably robust for a man of your age but it could quickly change and you might find yourself in need of support." By this stage Lucre was speaking in a rather syrupy tone of voice which created a noticeable feeling of repugnance in Joseph.

"From Dragon!"

"From a man who <u>may</u> have had some connection with Dragon. Surely in your last months as Secretary of the Legion of Pilsudski you'd want to secure a sound future for your ex servicemen as well as for yourself! As you yourself have admitted funds are drying up and your Society can't live off *'Appeals'* forever. Besides, as you've often said to me, there's no one fit enough to step into your shoes. This is a *'now or never moment.'* Take hold of it for the sake of your old comrades!"

For the first time Joseph quietened, stroking his chin thoughtfully "Ah, but haven't you forgotten something – the little matter of the Declaration. If we sign it, we'll be telling a lie."
"Not quite – just a mere approximation to the truth. We've complied with the terms of the will as far as we've been able. As you've indicated, it was the deceased's carelessness that brought about this distressing incident. We aren't to blame – after all, we were just carrying out our duties with the best of intentions."
"They said that in Germany after the war. You're just giving me one excuse after another."
"A priest doesn't give excuses – he gives reasons!"
"Are you saying we should lie to a lawyer?"
"My dear Joseph, I should think that lawyers were the very <u>first</u> people you should lie to if necessity demanded it!"
"You think necessity demands it in this instance?"
"Most assuredly Joseph, most assuredly. Necessity outweighs all else in this instance."
"I wouldn't wish to agree with you on that. But what really angers me is why you've insisted on every other possible consideration except the obvious one that the deceased <u>really</u> was Anton Dragon!"
"I'm just doing my charitable duty as a priest in giving him the benefit of the doubt," replied Father Lucre, assuming a *'harmless as a dove'* tone of voice. "Once his remains have been released he'll be buried as the devout Catholic *'Marcin Nowak,'* who, despite a troubled background, left a generous legacy to the Church. I shall see to it that prayers are said for the repose of his soul. In such complex matters a policy of discreet silence is to be wholly recommended."
"I remember the Church following that policy toward the Jews when I was a young man. It didn't do them any good!"
"But times are different now!"

"Are they? Hasn't *'silence'* been the cloak used to cover a multitude of sins? Joseph felt dejected and somehow very alone. He clearly saw Father Lucre's logic but that was all. The money would benefit his servicemen but it would forever feel dirty and stained to him. He felt genuinely perplexed – Father Lucre – a man of the Church was willing to bury every single scruple in favour of monetary gain. Where were morals, where was the determination to *'do the right thing'* and hang the consequences? Joseph sighed "I feel sick in my soul" he muttered, half to himself.

On hearing the note of resignation in Joseph's voice Father Lucre briskly stated, "I think we should proceed now before it gets too dark to see."

"Alright Father, as you wish, but the responsibility lies with you. I'm only doing this for my servicemen. You can hand the jewellery over to Oxfam."

Father Lucre felt a sudden relief. Joseph looked away – down to the ground – anywhere except at Father Lucre. "Yes, I'll gladly do that Joseph."

Lucre looked on as Joseph signed his part of the Declaration. He then promptly added his own signature before folding it into the envelope provided by the Solicitor.

Another awkward silence followed. The darkness was drawing in and this seemed to stir the two grey figures.

"Joseph spoke first. "I'm going out to light the garden fire."

Father Lucre pushed his chair out as he stood up – it scraped across the floor, the noise piercing the gathering gloom. "Let's hurry" he said, suddenly keen to exit the house. "Let's get it over with – it's getting darker by the minute."

"I know" replied Joseph in bitter resignation. With that he sullenly turned away and left the room. Father Lucre stood a moment longer, his hands clasped under his chin. This surely was the best outcome – so many would benefit. Why rake up the past – what good had that ever done?

### *S7: Postscript*

In the end, the deceased was interred as Marcin Nowak – although no prayers were ever said for the repose of his soul. His house was sold at a good price to a *'Letting Landlord.'* To this day its student tenants often remark upon its cold atmosphere and rarely stay for more than a term. Rumour has it that it's haunted by the ghost of a young woman in striped pyjamas. Shortly afterwards Joseph Wozniak retired from his post as Legion Secretary and ceased attending mass at Father Lucre's Church – preferring instead to attend Saint Anne's Cathedral in Leeds City Centre. He lived for another six months and death, when it came was something of a sad surprise for those who'd known him for he'd been such a robust man for his age. The Oxfam Charity shop in Headingley did receive a box containing some trinkets of jewellery. A young, smiling female assistant had cheerfully agreed to produce a signed receipt for the Priest to return to the deceased's Solicitor. It didn't, however, mention any necklace.

Shortly afterward Father Lucre could be seen driving around Headingley in a new car, wearing a satisfied smile on his face. He attributed this vehicle to *"an unexpected legacy."* Whether any connection existed between the missing necklace and the new car could only ever be speculation. On such matters, a charitable explanation is <u>always</u> to be preferred.

# THE RELUCTANT DEFECTOR

## *S1: The Airport*

He knew his orders, he knew his brief and he knew the methods his Government used to extract confessions from unwilling prisoners. Indeed, he knew everything about the Government's dirty secrets and its singular way of running a turbulent State. He placed his copy of Dickens' *'A Tale of Two Cities'* into his briefcase and resumed scanning his instructions. Dickens made satisfactory reading on an air trip, but now there was business to be done. The fact that Habib Al Nubbai was the only passenger on one of the General's six private jets underlined the urgent nature of his task. He frowned as he read, and this accentuated the many lines running across his forehead like dried up waterways. He was silver haired, in his early sixties and of slender build. A recent diet ordered by the General had caused his expensive white suit to hang slightly loosely upon him. He adjusted his gold-rimmed glasses as his ice cold eyes scanned the document in front of him. Habib looked every part the *'hanging judge,'* which had indeed at one time been one of his roles.

*'Yes, all very simple,'* he would fly to Toghazi and liaise with the local Security Chief there. They'd decide which prisoners to be *'fitted up'* for a *'show trial'* and which consigned to the growing number of mass graves which littered the *'glorious Republic'* of Dayria. A few of the less important prisoners could, after *'due process,'* be released as *'broken sticks'* – acting as a warning to their neighbours – deterring them from causing further trouble. As Assistant Prosecutor to the General, with special responsibility for the region, Habib's role was to help draw up death lists, participate in the interrogation (torture) of the more prominent prisoners and to construct watertight cases against them. As media attention was now keenly focused upon the upheavals in Dayria the charges against this present batch would require a definite basis in reality. To accuse them of such fanciful things as poisoning the General's swimming pool or placing anthrax powder in one of his first wife's fanciful wigs would no longer do. *'The guilty'* (they were always *'the guilty'* – never mere *'suspects'* to be

released after a routine beating) would need to be linked to terrorist organizations, feared by Dayria's Western backers. This would give a more plausible reason for getting rid of them. Admittedly, all of this would entail a great deal more work on his part, but no matter, the job would get done. A partially true case could be constructed, the inevitable *'guilty verdict'* passed and ensuing death sentence handed down. All very orderly and predictable, nothing could go wrong.

The lawyer – or to give him his full title, *'Assistant Prosecutor with Special Plenipotentiary Powers for the Eastern Province of the Glorious Democratic Republic of Dayria'* fussily adjusted his garish green bow tie. If he could somehow arrange to get *'the guilty'* to appear at a national (rather than a mere regional) show trial he'd be next in line to become *'Chief Prosecutor with Supreme Plenipotentiary Powers for the United Provinces of the Glorious Democratic Republic of Dayria.'* That would indeed be the summit of his career. The Present Chief Prosecutor was due to retire in a year and Habib knew he would be in line for this post, so long as he handled his brief carefully. His rival *'Assistant Prosecutor etc, etc. etc for the Western Province of the etc'* had antagonised the General's son and heir *'Psycho Ali'* by mishandling some delicate business involving *'The Mountain Men'* who'd lived in the rugged interior. Habib had always taken meticulous care to court *'Psycho Ali's'* favour.

Suddenly, a slight shudder and the plane began to sway from side to side; it had hit turbulence – a sure sign that a descent had begun. This was confirmed by a male voice announcing *'Will our illustrious and eminent guest, whom we are greatly privileged to have on board this humble airline, kindly fasten his safety belt in order to secure the health and safety of his excellent person."* With an expressionless face Habib complied with this fawning request and then neatly folded his papers before placing them into his briefcase. It was a sign of difficult times that no refreshments had been provided for him. The journey from the Capital, Miseria, had been easy but now the turbulence in the air seemed to reflect the political turbulence on the ground below. Habib Al Nubbai's job was to help quell the unrest by arranging *'show trials,'* designed to terrify the people back into their usual state of abject submission.

As the plane continued its bumpy descent, a smudge of white cloud parted to reveal a desert landscape. Here, dunes gave way to barren rocky vistas, dotted with patches of green, denoting an oasis or a sizeable strip of irrigated crop cultivation. Soon the straight coastal road came into view, running parallel with an endless stretch of dark blue sea, lightly concealed in a misty haze. The large number of fishing boats suggested there'd been only a limited disruption to general economic activity. This was a good sign – the well-armed government forces appeared to be keeping things under control. Several thousand feet below the Port City of Toghazi glided into view but with two disconcerting columns of smoke rising from its centre. Habib shuddered – this looked ominous – but thankfully most of the rest of the city appeared peaceful enough. A linear settlement straddling the coastal road and with a population numbering only 300,000, Toghazi was like any other place – just a typical provincial backwater with no natural defences. Any trouble would easily be dealt with, and if not, then special reinforcements would ensure a speedy resolution. This is how things had always been since the General had seized power forty two years ago. There was no reason that Toghazi would be any different.

All this was in contrast to Martyrbad, lying much further along the coastal road, some 200 miles West of Toghazi. The one million inhabitants had boasted a long tradition of defiance and it was they who'd led the original revolt against Dayria's *'European Colonial Masters'* several decades previously. It got its name from the dozen *'martyrs'* who'd been hung in the city square by these selfsame *'Masters.'* Martyrbad nestled between a couple of narrow peninsulas so any government forces operating against it would find themselves confined to an ever smaller front as they approached the downtown Port from the outlying suburbs. Both peninsulas had well sited fortified positions, providing excellent covering fire for any defending force. The General had ordered them to be built some two decades before when he'd feared an American invasion. Were they ever to fall into rebel hands there could well be problems. Habib reflected that *'Psycho Ali'* had demanded that Martyrbad be left for him to deal with personally should security forces lose control. So far Martyrbads position was ambiguous, was it still in the general's hands or not? No one could yet tell. What couldn't be disputed was that *'Psycho Ali,'* had plenty of scores to settle in the city that had once defied his authority. The General could be certain that his son would *'resolve matters'* in the appropriate manner should disturbances increease. In contrast, Toghazi would be altogether easier to sort out; a few shootings and hangings would do. A succession of bumps confirmed that the plane had successfully touched down without a shot being fired: another good sign that some sort of order was still in place and that the General's forces were in the ascendency.

Once off the plane, Habib walked briskly toward the terminal building which consisted only of a large corrugated shed. Being reserved for military purposes meant that it lacked the facilities of its civilian counterpart lying to the East. Most of those who passed through this military airport were usually on the General's secret business. Like Habib they could stride through it in several minutes without fuss or distraction. But this time, there was a complete lack of staff which was mildly irritating, though hardly surprising given the blockade already imposed upon Toghazi. It was another small inconvenience that the *'General Store'* was closed, so he'd have to wait until he was offered some foul-tasting coffee at the Central Toghazi Military Centre. This was an imposing place which stood in the main square encircled by a thick concrete wall, topped by coiled, razor-sharp barbed wire. More perplexing was the lack of any military escort to greet him. As a VIP he'd expected to have been greeted by a Senior Army Officer and four well armed body guards. But there was no sign of anyone. It was with a growing feeling of anxiety that Habib left the shed and began scanning the taxi rank, but still no escort. What should he do? He could telephone the Military Centre but that had been forbidden for *'security reasons.'* He could wait, but *'Security'* had confirmed the time of the appointment and they always made a point of being punctual for important people like himself. The sound of his plane taking off increased his sense of isolation. As the noise of its engines faded he could hear his own heart beating. He was alone and as each second ticked by he was uneasily more aware that he'd fallen into some sort of trap. But what was that he could see? At the far end of the rank stood a traditional London taxi, painted in the General's favourite colour, Royal Purple. Perhaps it had been laid on for him to ensure a safer and more discreet entrance into the city. Now here was an explanation that made sense, for surely it couldn't be waiting for anyone else? His palpitations slowed as he regained some of his composure. He approached the cab and impatiently tapped on the front window, awakening an unshaven, moustached driver wearing a flat cap. Habib then opened the rear door and with some reluctance took his place on the back seat immediately behind the driver who was only just beginning to rouse himself from what had appeared to be a very deep slumber. It was only after several yawns and some fumbling that he managed to eventually switch on the ignition.

"Take me to the Toghazi Military Security Centre. Hurry up! I've got an urgent appointment at nine-thirty!"

The driver cocked up one eye suspiciously

"The Security Centre?"

"Yes, are you deaf?"

"That will be double fare."

"Don't you know that I am Dr Habib Al Nubbai, Assistant Prosecutor to our beloved General."

The driver cocked up the other eye, registering a suspicion bordering on utter disbelief. Habib responded by slapping a Government IOU into the driver's hand. As the driver well knew, this document meant that no payment would ever be made. But kick up a fuss and you'd end up in prison.

"Can't have that! I need to receive payment in currency."

"Accept this official IOU otherwise I'll have you arrested!" snapped Habib who was not used to any show of defiance – least of all from a minion taxi driver. Where had all the fear and fawning gone?"

"Just let me check with the Centre."

"This is ridiculous, you lazy dog!"

"Hello, I've got a Dr Habib Al Nubbai, Assistant Prosecutor to our beloved General."

Habib noticed the sarcastic tone in these last two words, uttered just before the driver closed the Perspex screen situated behind his seat.

However, he could still hear what the driver was saying as he had a loud, rasping voice.

"You are most <u>certainly</u> to bring him in. We'll pay you double rate as agreed."

"Make it treble for safe delivery."

"You son of a whore, we agreed upon double."

"You <u>do</u> require safe delivery!"

"OK, make it treble, you piece of camel dung," crackled the voice over the radio.

"Don't make a fuss over any IOU. We'll make sure you'll be <u>very</u> <u>generously</u> recompensed. However, you'll have to go through the College District to make sure he reaches the <u>appropriate</u> destination. The most direct routes are blocked by demonstrators."

"OK, understood."

"And <u>do</u> make sure Mr Al Nubbai arrives safely – we can't have anything happening to our distinguished guest now can we?"

As Habib settled uneasily into the back of the cab he thought 'What on earth is our country coming to when impudent taxi drivers dare haggle with esteemed members of the security forces? I'll put him down on the arrest list.' He suppressed a nagging doubt that the cab driver had had some other Centre in mind (rather than the Security Centre) during their conversation. Habib tapped ferociously on the Perspex screen, the driver, nonchalantly wound it down to listen.

"To the Security Centre at the quickest possible speed and along the shortest route."

"As you wish your Excellency" the taxi driver replied, again with more than a hint of sarcasm in his voice.

### S2: An Unwelcome destination

Habib settled himself into the seat and once more turned to his beloved book. 'Ah Dickens, the most satisfying of authors – such a profound understanding of human nature and of the legal system too; such vivid execution scenes! He began reading his well-thumbed copy of 'A Tale of Two Cities,' anticipating the point when the hero is guillotined. Such magnificent drama, so gripping to read and so very helpful in distracting him from the less pleasant aspects of his work. During an interrogation he would often sit to one side whilst the more *'thuggish'* elements of the security forces set about their grisly task of *'working over a guilty one.'* Earplugs firmly in place, he would read Dickens whilst some poor unfortunate was beaten or electrocuted into a quivering wreck several feet away. Only after *'due process'* had been completed would he obtain a signed confession and then give his written assent to yet another set of documents. These would secure his (or more rarely her) exit to a mass grave or to one of the General's dungeons (which amounted to the same thing). Once there'd been a rather unfortunate incident where blood had shot up and smattered his copy of *'Bleak House'* just as he'd been getting to an interesting point about that splendid lawyer Tolkinghorn. Yes, yes, most unfortunate. The other form of persuasion – namely the rape of both male and female prisoners – he'd found most distasteful. It was so dreadful, that he'd arranged a *'gentleman's agreement'* with Security whereby, only <u>after</u> this aspect of their work had been completed would he be called upon to attend. By then, all but the most stubborn of *'the guilty ones'* would be broken and ready to confess.

The drive through the suburbs of Toghazi continued at what seemed an annoyingly slow pace. The radio crackled into life: -
"Is our distinguished guest comfortable?"
"Most comfortable."
"Make sure you keep him that way."
"I will."

Perhaps it was the nuanced irony in their voices that provoked Habib to look up from his book and observe the streets more closely. He noticed flags almost everywhere; hanging out of windows, festooned to lamp posts and draped around the palm trees lining the main route into the city. The problem was that they were <u>not</u> the flags of the General (showing a portrait of him as a young man) but the garish orange striped flags of the old Monarchy. The cab passed a park where a statue of the General had once stood like a colossus. Now only the plinth remained. Especially ominous was the way in which pictures of the General and his heir, Ali, had either been torn down or defaced with obscene graffiti. One showed the General's face painted over with a Star of David and the words *'Zionist Pig'* scrawled across it. Another had two horns drawn on top of the bearded countenance of his son *'Psycho Ali,'* complete with pitchfork in hand. One of the few pictures of Kissem, his debauched younger son was defaced by having a penis drawn against his mouth. A shiver of panic took hold of Habib. For the first time in his life he was tasting some of the fear that had hitherto been the unhappy lot of the hundreds of prisoners he'd helped *'process'* during a lifetime career serving the regime. Here he was, having blundered headlong into enemy territory, knowing he could expect no mercy. No time to observe protocols – he'd <u>have</u> to contact the Security Centre and get them to rescue him. He fumbled for his mobile phone and hurriedly pressed the keys, keeping his voice as low as possible: - "Hello, Al Nubbai speaking, how are things at your end?"

"Habib! Don't come! We're surrounded! Half my men have deserted and bulldozers have broken down the security wall. We're being fired on from all sides and we're holed up in the main complex!" It was the Commander bellowing down the phone. The fact that he'd addressed Habib Al Nubbai by his first name (instead of using the honorific title; *'your Esteemed Excellency'*) betrayed the level of fear. Known as *'the bone cruncher'* the Commander's reputation as a particularly brutal torturer meant that he too could expect no mercy.

"Just remain calm and we'll soon have something sorted out" answered Habib with a total lack of conviction.

"Where the hell are you?"

"In a taxi heading towards 'the College District.'"

"That's where the rebels have their Centre – it's in the College – God help you!"

"Surely there's a way to resolve this situation?" quizzed Habib whilst struggling to lower his voice still further.

"Just get out! Just get out!" the Commander screamed over what appeared to be the noise of gunfire.

"I'll order the driver to take me back to the airport."

"No good – the rebels took it over last night. They allowed the plane you were on to land because some defector had told them you were coming."

Sweat began to pour down Habib's face as he realised that he was stranded hundreds of miles away from home, in a hostile city, being driven to enemy headquarters where all he could expect would be the kind of treatment he'd inflicted on others. His expensive suit would be stained with more than just a smattering of his own blood. 'Get a grip! Use that cunning which has stood you in good stead serving the General's regime. Quick! Think! What to do? First *buy time*' and confuse that treacherous rat of a driver!" Habib deliberately raised his voice as he again spoke into his phone, "Ah, do not worry my darling rose petal. Your willing slave Habib knows it will take more than some little trouble to separate me from your lush green eyes."

At the other end of the line the Commander, (now crouching beneath his desk as a bullet flew above his head) couldn't fathom why a Senior Government Lawyer was blowing kisses down the phone and using endearments, obviously reserved for one of his mistresses. "Goodbye, my ravishing honeysuckle, I cannot wait to kiss your red ruby lips."

Call ended. Think of alternatives. He could ask to be dropped off, but even if that was feasible the driver would be sure to betray his location. Also, he'd run the risk of colliding with an angry mob and you can't negotiate with a mob. Habib gazed mournfully at the column of smoke billowing from the location of the Security Centre. Even within the confines of the taxi he could hear the muffled cracking of what seemed to be gunfire. 'Think Habib! Think! For the first time in your life you're on the losing side! Can't expect mercy! Can't run away! Ah wait, wait – brilliant! It's a desperate remedy but it stands a good chance. Buy time Habib! Buy time! First step – win the confidence of the taxi driver. A bribe will be needed!' He gently coughed and then asked rather loudly.

"Driver?"

A slight turn of the head was the response.

"Are you a man of honour who can be trusted with an extremely delicate matter?"

'Of course he's anything but a man of honour but using that term will flatter him. '

In response, the driver's head leaned slightly back toward the partition.

"As a fellow countryman with many connections to this illustrious city may I humbly make a confession?"

A curt nod of assent followed.

'Remember your Lawyer's training and start to plead your case. The man's uneducated but streetwise. A moderately dramatic approach will be right – but don't overdo the flattery. It might seem fake.'

"I'm really here to escape that wretched infidel the General and his degenerate son, that butt licker Kissem." ('Be careful – don't insult Ali, word may get back.')

"Like you and all the noble people of this illustrious city, he's made my life a misery and now he's sent me on this devilish task of crushing the dear inhabitants of this place. However, fearing the raging fires of Hell..." 'Go on, use religious imagery, and appeal to his sense of piety if he has any.'

"...I've had a change of heart. I've got useful information that will serve the interests of the glorious Council who are tirelessly struggling for the freedom of our long-suffering people. Will you please take me to the rebels – oh, I mean glorious liberators' 'Command Centre' which, I believe lies in the College District. I know you're a good man who will guide me to the noble leaders of this just uprising. If you could please contact them and tell them that I could make myself <u>very</u> useful."

"Funnily enough, we're driving past there in the next few minutes. Dropping you off will be no problem at all your Excellency! However, I wouldn't mind taking your watch as security – I've taken a fancy to it"

"My watch!" exclaimed Habib, knowing that it had been given to him as a personal gift from the General.

"Yes, your watch! It looks a very nice one and I do have a living to make with a wife and six mouths to feed."

'You greedy dog!' thought Habib, desperately trying to conceal his rage under a wan smile.

"Just drop it on my lap – there, thank you. That should fetch a good price on the market. I trust you'll make no fuss about this."

"There won't be any" replied Habib sullenly

"Good, that's what I like to hear" the driver replied, a satisfied smile on his face.

He then switched on the radio

"Our distinguished guest is due to arrive shortly. He says he wants to change sides and make himself useful."

"Tell him we've provided a special guard of honour and some <u>very</u> comfortable accommodation."

Seconds later, the cab drew to a halt near the College steps.

"Just as you wanted sir, safe and sound outside the Council Headquarters. Oh look – there's your Excellency's special guard of honour!" A band of bearded, gesticulating men, armed with AK 47 rifles swarmed around the taxi. 'Forget that dog' thought Habib as he was roughly pulled out of the taxi, a gun barrel prodding his stomach, 'it's time to enter into some serious negotiation with my new comrades.'

The cab sped off as Habib was man-handled up a stairway and pushed through some swing doors. Meanwhile, the driver gazed down fondly at the expensive watch. 'Should fetch a good price or I could use it as part of a dowry for my eldest daughter. 'Even if I don't get paid my treble bonus this trip will have been worthwhile. That stuck-up lawyer had his uses. Stopping at a junction he quickly picked the watch up, slipping it onto his wrist. It was the last thing he would do. A sniper's bullet smashed through the windscreen, embedding itself into his skull. When his relatives eventually re-claimed his body the watch had long since gone. His wife left the morgue wailing, 'What about the dowry?'

# INTERMISSION 3:

## (How to tame a member of the opposite sex)

# HOW TO TAME YOUR MAN

Remember ladies that taming your man is a genteel art, not a science and that when it comes to the finer emotions men just do not *'get it.'* They must be patiently and lovingly coaxed into showing even a modicum of sensitivity. Endless nagging simply won't do and is to be avoided at all costs! To enlist that mode of behaviour is to cause him to curl up into a ball of resentment or even to look for a lady whom he thinks <u>does</u> understand him. Poor sap, he doesn't realize that you perhaps understand him all too well!

The best way to tame a man is to massage his ego. Most men have an enormous ego – after all, it's simply part of being a man. Remember girls if you massage his ego you can have him for life – but if you massage only his body you'll keep him for barely a night, if that.

Now ladies – how can this be done? The short answer is to lavishly praise him for the little things he manages to get right – even if they are few and far between. Should he condescend to help you around the house then you must convey the impression that he's doing you a huge favour. Thank him profusely, even when he fails to tackle a job to your complete satisfaction (which will almost invariably be the case). Correct the job later when he's out of the house – to correct it in his presence is to leave him feeling insulted.

Should you wish to make a suggestion about anything be sure to convey the impression that it's in <u>his</u> best interests. Even better – that it was really his brilliant idea all along! His ego will feel cosseted with such adulation and he will be like putty in your hands.

One practical *'must do'* is to place all of his personal belongings (like keys or wallets) in a safe place. This should lessen the chances of him shouting and trying to pin the blame on you when he's mislaid them. Should such an earth-shattering scenario actually arise then, in as carefree a manner as possible, gently point him toward the aforesaid *'hidey hole.'*

His hobbies are one particular minefield, requiring much negotiation. Any interests <u>you</u> have he will view as trivial or unimportant. But will expect you to make <u>his</u> hobby the centre of your life (even if he excludes you from active participation in it). If he loves football (but you hate it) he'll still expect you to feign a keen interest. In this area men are so contrary and they have the cheek to say that women are illogical! Yet hobbies can have a good spin off – especially when they necessitate him being out of the house. This of course will render you a well-earned break. Indeed, another ploy to get him to exit the house for an evening is to invite your lady-friends around. Try holding a lingerie party or something else the male ego would find utterly embarrassing. Yet who hasn't suffered when a hobby has become an obsession and a greater threat to your relationship than any other woman could ever be? Who doesn't pity the wife whose husband loves to read bus or rail timetables late into the night? Here, it's wise to observe the following three rules: -

**RULE 1:** Should you be fortunate (or otherwise) to marry a man, please remember <u>you also marry his hobby</u>! If you really dislike what you see as his *'strange interest'* then don't marry him because he'll nearly always put his hobby before you.

**RULE 2:** Take care to ensure that his hobby is something you can both share, (perhaps, on your part only on a casual basis). Your showing of even a modicum of interest will create good will on his side.

**RULE 3:** Don't expect him to acknowledge your interests. Your man will expect that <u>he</u> is your one and only interest. The only way he'll be persuaded to change his mind on this point is if he sees your interest as serving <u>his</u> interests. Drop subtle hints that <u>your</u> interests may make some money or help his career and it's amazing how solicitous he can be. In the area of hobbies much discretion and forbearance is needed.

Another minefield to negotiate is illness. If your man is even an incey-wincey bit poorly he'll automatically expect you to drop everything and become his *'Florence Nightingale.'* Calling him a *'baby'* simply won't do and is the surest way to launch him into a mammoth sulk. Accept that when he's poorly he'll feel his whole world is coming to an end. Men are <u>utterly</u> hopeless when it comes to bearing even the slightest ache and you mustn't be surprised when he roundly rebukes you for failing to show him oodles of sympathy. However, should <u>you</u> be poorly, <u>never ever</u> expect any sympathy from his quarter – he'll simply look to you to bravely carry on regardless. However, should you take to your bed don't mistake the look of panic flashing across his face as that of genuine concern for your welfare. In reality he'll be coldly calculating *'who'll do the house work or cook my meals?'* To a man a minor sniffle from his lady spells imminent and utter disaster. Eventually, he may make some attempt at aiding the healing process by making you a cup of tea. Ah, how sweet and caring of him. Yet sadly, it will either be too strong or too weak or will contain too much or too little sugar. Having thankfully recovered from your indisposition the most you can expect is for the dishes <u>not</u> to have been washed properly, the pans burnt and the dusting left undone. He will of course expect you to thank him for *'trying his best'* even if all he did was to have successfully fed the household pet. Remember, the key to a man's heart is to praise him for the little things he <u>does</u> get right.

One thing a man really does hate is a woman who complains about everything. If life really is tough then it's especially helpful to have a couple of close female friends with whom you can share your troubles. Your man will prefer you to unburden yourself to other women than to him. If he has an ounce of intelligence (which isn't always the case) he'll realize that the more you complain to your friends the less you'll complain to him. However, never overdo any complaining to him about other women. All that will do is to convey the impression that most women are psychotic neurotics, especially when they have to work together. A lady rarely gains respect from a man if constantly *'doing down'* other women. He may well just wonder what she might be saying about him behind his back.

Always try to convey the impression (no matter how exaggerated) that he's your Mr Rochester and you're his Jane Eyre (rather than the mad woman who needs locking away in the attic).

Taming a man requires an infinite amount of adaptability and even some low cunning. That's not to mention all the multitasking you have to do. (Unlike women, men can only ever do one thing at a time.) On any one day, you may have to discharge the roles of mother, diplomat, housewife, money earner, seductive temptress as well as confiding friend. In short, what he expects is for you to be *his 'superwoman!'* when discharging the above roles always convey the impression that he's getting his own way when in reality you're getting yours by exercising your womanly wiles. Learn to feign pleasure even if deep down you believe he's a bit incapable. A man who's happy in bed is less likely to stray.

It has to be admitted that taming your man is not always easy and requires a certain plucky resourcefulness. But keep well-practised and you may find yourself with a life-long faithful friend![60]

## HOW TO TAME YOUR WOMAN

The first thing to realize is that taming your woman is a near – impossible task. Her emotional needs are many, varied and complex. Hence, no man can ever expect to make a woman completely happy. All you can do is to lessen her degree of misery and patiently endure her inevitable complaints made against you.[61] After all, is it your fault if she wants a Mr Darcy and you're only a Reverend Collins? Indeed, the acquisition of what may be termed *'womanology'* is a lifelong task. For example – those everyday matters (which to you may be trivial) will to her be of the utmost importance. Also what, in your opinion is just plain common sense will, in her estimation, be something complicated, requiring her utmost attention.

---

[60] This was first written on Wednesday, 22nd September 2011 in response to a light-hearted suggestion from a certain lady at a poetry evening.
[61] This was first written on Wednesday, 22nd September 2011

The first and most necessary step is to go out and *'catch'* the right woman to tame. One good sign is an ability to make a woman laugh during the early stages of courtship. Achieve this and you're half way to winning her heart – fail and you might as well abandon everything with as much dignity as possible. However, never ever fall into the trap of thinking you're funnier or cleverer than you really are. She'll see right through your charade and you'll tumble down in her estimation.

Should your relationship prosper, convey every impression that the lady concerned is the centre of your life. If she's the motherly type she'll be looking for stability and babies – if the careerist she'll be looking for stability and money. In both instances the key thing is to provide stability because almost every woman wants her man to be her rock, her anchor and her emotional support. Don't fall into the trap of assuming that marriage will solve any problems that may have arisen during courtship. An unhappy courtship will produce only an unhappy marriage. Remember that *'to marry in haste is to repent at leisure!'*

Should all be well between you don't endlessly delay the fatal (oops final) day for there's nothing a woman hates more than a lack of commitment. When a lady is reduced to endlessly nagging you about marriage either have the honesty to end the relationship or marry her. Remember, *'he who hesitates is lost.'*

Once you've gained the right woman you really do have one of the greatest blessings in life. Be heartily grateful and show your thankfulness to the lady concerned. Yet take care <u>not</u> to expect her to think in the same way that you do. They don't. This ability to think differently is at once her most endearing and yet most exasperating feature. You don't have to be a Professor Higgins to wonder *'why can't a woman think more like a man?'* This difference in thought processes means that women can be great nitpickers (and I'm not just referring to the nits they may need to pull out of a child's hair). The dishes you think you've done thoroughly she'll throw back into the sink because of some tiny and perhaps imaginary stain. She'll also criticise you for a tiny speck of dust you failed to remove when you condescended to help her with some housework. However, should you happen to be a writer then such attention to detail can be extremely helpful –especially with draft manuscripts, requiring the unstinted devotion of an unpaid proof reader.

Having given this difference in thinking the genuine respect and consideration it deserves you can then turn to those *'tried and trusted'* methods, used to keep your relationship alive and meaningful. Buy her an occasional box of chocolates (but never tell her the cost or that you got it for nothing from a friend). Should you be so generous and kind-hearted as to take her away for a few days you must never moan about how expensive it is (even if you are a Yorkshire man who likes to count every last penny). It's also helpful to complement her on her looks even when she's having a *'bad hair day'* or she's grumpy because it's that *'time of the month.'* Always remind her that she's someone who's loved and who's very special. Above all, express appreciation for her cooking or you may well find yourself living off *'takeaways'.* Remember, a little praise can help tame any woman.

Keep alive any remaining romance in your relationship – even if your woman is convinced that you don't have a romantic bone in your body. This is best done by sharing some common interest or by arranging breaks for you both to spend time together. Calling her silly pet names can help add spice to a relationship even if she does pretend not to like them or says they're childish. Balance this by releasing her to develop her own interests – especially if they're a means of bringing in extra money. Doing this will allow her to be a woman in her own right.

Understanding a woman's emotions is even more difficult than understanding her thought processes. Studying a PHD in *'String Theory'* is easier. Not only do women <u>not</u> think like men – they don't have the same feelings as a man. Sometimes they're happy for no real reason and at others they're miserable – equally for no reason. At their very worst, female emotions can cause commotions that hinder promotions and even lead to demotions! The best way of coping with all of these emotional *'ups and downs,'* is to assume the <u>appearance</u> of listening. (But please take care that the cotton wool you've stuffed into your ears doesn't fall out whilst she's in mid-flow otherwise you'll get the thumping you deserve.) Hardest of all are those times when she begins to complain late at night when you're in bed together. Should you find yourself drifting off to sleep and actually beginning to snore then an angry kicking will soon wake you up. This may be of such violence that you'll find yourself hitting the floor with an almighty thump.

Should all else fail, encourage your lady to share her problems with a couple of trusted female friends. She'll be relieved to unburden herself with them – seeking their mutual understanding and reassurance. Encourage her to invite them around for tea and then vanish from the scene with a one way ticket to Siberia. Perhaps the best excuse for your absence (which she'll be really wanting yet all the while pretending not to) is to claim you're visiting your aged mother. Saying this will create a most favourable impression in front of her lady friends. They're bound to view you as a very caring man. However, never call the woman in your life *'mother'* or *'mum'* nor compare her cooking unfavourably with that of your own mother. To do this is to guarantee that things other than food will come flying in your direction ... watch out – duck!

In terms of relationships your lady's main problem will be around other women. In most employment situations a group of women does not so much work together as *'work'* on each other's nerves! Almost always it's an endless saga of who's not speaking to whom, who's been inconsolably upset and who stormed out of the workplace in tears. Women can harbour petty grievances in ways that are totally inconceivable to most men. Indeed, a good definition of hell is a workplace full of women. When placed in such a situation even the lady you love can turn into a Lucretia Borgia (of gossip) a screaming harridan or a silent assassin whose cold looks may well freeze the hearts of other females. Indeed, there's something about women working together that brings out their most disagreeable traits! Here, a good rule of thumb is to observe that, where men may disagree and remain friends women cannot. Any arguments they have are almost always taken personally.

Should your own good lady get caught up in such turmoil then you must need to remember that she's <u>always</u> right! Nothing is ever her fault and any problem is as a result of that *'awful boss'* or that *'impossible workmate.'* Above all, <u>never</u> suggest that the women she has fallen out with may be right about an issue. Doing that will result in many bruises on your arm! Much patience is required. It's probably best to simply accept that female relationships can be very tangled and any resulting disputes are sometimes incapable of resolution. It's a case of *'bitterness and darkness'* rather than *'sweetness and light.'* Tiresome though it is, men do have value in providing a *'sounding board'* for their woman's feeling of animosity toward other women. However, never dupe yourself into thinking you can resolve her work problem or even understand its causes. Rather than offer advice it's better to allow her to *'sound off'* to you about it all and let this be her *'safety valve.'*

Now for some helpful tips on how to make your woman feel loved and wanted. First of all let's begin with a few *'don'ts.'* <u>Don't</u> look too comatose when she drags you around the shops and <u>don't</u> visibly squirm when you find the dress she tries on makes her look like a psychedelic clown. However, never expect your opinion to be accepted even if you do say she looks very nice. Also, <u>never</u> laugh at her new hairdo or remark that she looks like a cleaning lady. Other irritating habits to avoid are breaking wind or belching during a meal she's cooked ... oh and never click your fingers at her as if she were a downtrodden *'maid of all works.'* The rule here is to avoid making a woman feel like your skivvy even if she <u>is</u> your skivvy! Remember! The more you show appreciation for her work the more work she'll do for you. Cunning eh?

And now we'll proceed to the *'dos.'* <u>Do</u> try to make at least some pretence at maintaining basic bodily hygiene. There's nothing more a lady hates than a dirty man who smells unwashed. Where possible, keep all disgusting bodily noises to the bathroom (for this she will be heartily grateful and praise you for your thoughtfulness.) <u>Do</u> smile at her even if she does mistake it for an idiot's grimace. In addition, do take a hand in the housework. Although your efforts will <u>never</u> be up to her perfect standard, she'll certainly appreciate the gesture. However, when engaged in the said activity always wear a martyr's look and give the impression that she's taming you when, in reality, you're taming her.

Perhaps the most important rule of thumb to remember is that <u>open communication is vitally important to your relationship.</u> Accept that work pressures may well intrude at awkward moments but never allow them to get to the point where they prevent you from spending any quality time with her. Also note that she'll be less than happy should a computer game or the television get in the way of her relationship with you. She'll certainly be quick to show complete and utter *'zero tolerance'* should your alternative interest be another woman. A man is a fool if he thinks he can *'play the field'* <u>and</u> keep his own lady happy. On this matter it's best to heed the warning, *'Get out while you've still got your trousers on!'*

In the end the best way to tame your woman is to let her know that she's very special and not just some *'add on'* to your life. Never forget the point that a team which laughs together stays together. Yet whenever you think you've finally tamed your woman – watch out – she's actually taming you!

# THE WARNINGS

**(How Societies turn evil and the implications this has for the Anglo-Jewish Community)**

# A WARNING TO THE ANGLO-JEWISH COMMUNITY

*This letter was written in response to the visit I made to Auschwitz Birkenau in October 2011. It was originally addressed to an old school friend of the Reformed Jewish Faith. Adapted for wider publication in March 2014, it looks at how the growing madness in Western Society is likely to have a negative impact upon the Jewish people. It does **not** represent an uncritical endorsement of the policies of the Israeli government nor of the behaviour of militant Zionist settlers.*

## Section 1: An Open Letter

**1)** This *'open letter'* is addressed to all responsible members of the Anglo-Jewish Community (and to those non-Jewish parties with a sympathetic interest in its welfare). The points made could equally apply to the Jewish Communities of North America and Continental Europe as well as to Great Britain. It argues that <u>another systematic attempt to destroy the Jewish people could well be in the offing</u>. Within our increasingly corrupt and dangerously insane neo-pagan society a deadly consensus is emerging wherein the eradication of Israel is a development which would at least be tolerated or even welcomed.

**2)** During our lifetime we could see another attempt to implement *'a final solution to the Jewish Question.'* Sadly, I believe that our nation will lend its tacit support to such an attempt, its response being more akin to that of *'Marshall Petain'* (who was the French *'puppet ruler'* of Vichy France) than *'Winston Churchill.'* Obviously, this will have implications for the Jewish Community living in this country – especially those operating in the public domain. At this juncture, I could assume the role of a history lecturer and provide reams of evidence to support this argument. However, time constraints and the realization that the recipients of this letter are often very busy people; oblige me to outline my case in thirteen, closely connected prepositions. Information in support of each point will be found in the Bibliography. For ease of reference numbered paragraphs and sub-headings to individual sections are provided.

## Section 2: A Mental and Moral Derangement

To avoid the same naivety that some of their counterparts displayed in pre-war Germany, responsible members of the Anglo-Jewish Community need to consider the following arguments: -

**1)** The careless abandonment of its Judaic-Christian heritage has caused British Society to suffer from a growing moral and mental derangement, characterized by a spendthrift materialism, a casual amorality and a growing detachment from reality. Any sense of being accountable to an external standard has been lost and having *'cast off restraint'* most people in this country are content *'to do what's right in their own eyes,'* (Proverbs 29:18 & Judges 21:25). Also present is a spiritual vacuum, currently filled by a mixture of militant secularism, fundamentalist Islam and mystical Neo-Paganism – all of which possess an inherent bias against Jewish people.

**2)** One effect of this moral and mental derangement has been a growing reliance upon subjective impressions and impulses rather than upon sound reasoning. Much of the population has become incapable of logical thinking. This has served to increase public susceptibility to even the most slanderous forms of anti-Zionist propaganda found throughout all sectors of the media. The legislation passed in favour of same sex marriage has demonstrated that things not tolerated a few years ago can very rapidly become a *'taken for granted'* feature of *'normal'* life. It has highlighted the speed at which public opinion can change under sustained legal and media pressure. There's every reason to suppose that it could (with equal rapidity) turn against the Jewish community in this country once the circumstances are ripe.

**3)** At every level of British Society a consensus is emerging whereby Israel is viewed as a *'pariah State'* whose destruction would be acceptable – especially if oil supplies could be secured by appeasing Arab-Iranian opinion.

**4)** The support given to Israel by the Anglo-Jewish Community means that they too will be subject to the same process of demonization as Israel itself. Attacks on the Jewish community are likely to increase and take on a more organized form. As the decision by the 2010 Methodist Conference to boycott Israeli goods from the West Bank has shown, most English Churches will adopt the role of *'useful idiots'* to bodies like Hamas and Hezbollah. As the Chief Rabbinate may find to its cost, any reliance upon English Church Leaders will lead only to betrayal and disappointment. The English Churches are like broken reeds, swaying in every direction (2 Kings 18:21 & Isaiah 36:6).

**5)** Britain will no longer be the safe haven it once was for the Jewish people. Their position could deteriorate as rapidly as it did in pre-war Germany. This is particularly likely should Israel be blamed for a Middle Eastern War that causes a disruption in oil supplies and a severe economic depression.

**6)** Inflaming any trend toward anti-Semitism is the anti-Israeli bias present in media bodies like the BBC. This bias reflects a wider anti-Semitism amongst Britain's opinion-forming classes.

**7)** No matter which Party is in power at Westminster, the British Establishment will (with its usual hypocrisy) betray Israel. In part, this will be due to the ethos of appeasement which still lingers like an unquiet ghost from the 1930s. However, the Public School anti-Semitism present in Government Departments like the Foreign Office will also play a role.

**8)** The growing respectability of both old and new forms of anti-Semitism at all levels of British society reflects a wider global trend in which the destruction of Israel (and by implication the Jewish people) is becoming increasingly acceptable – especially by bodies like the UN.

On a balancing note, it has to be stated that the Israelis don't always help their own case and in terms of public relations they can be a disaster. Examples include the appalling behaviour of West Bank Settlers (whose hatred can match anything put forward in the Arab World) and the tactical mistakes made by Israel's political and defence establishment (the fiasco of the 2006 Lebanese campaign is brought to mind here). Also present is the harassment of Messianic Jewish Assemblies by militant Orthodox Communities (this risks alienating Christian Zionists who are about the only genuine friends Israel has left). The effect of such maladroit public relations is to further legitimize the *'elimination agenda'* being pursued by Israel's increasing number of enemies.

**9)** The growing sophistication of ICT has facilitated collusion between anti-Semitic groups who may hate each other but will still collaborate in a future destruction of the Jewish people. A coalition of evil is forming, consisting of: -

**9.1** Militant Islamists – wishing to establish a *'New World Order'* based upon Sharia Law

**9.2** Far Left Secularists – wishing to establish a *'New World Order'* based upon *'The Brotherhood of Man'*

**9.3** Far Right Racists – wishing to establish a *'New World Order'* based upon white supremacy

**9.4** Traditionalist Christians – wishing to establish a *'New World Order'* based upon the imagined glories of a *'Christian Empire'*

**9.5** Neo-Fascist Environmentalists – wishing to establish a *'New World Order'* of ecological communes

**9.6** Bureaucratic elitists – wishing to establish a *'New World Order'* based upon International Organizations

**9.7** Human Rights Lawyers – wishing to establish a *'New World Order'* based upon International Law

**9.8** Ambitious Careerists – wishing to secure a prestigious position within <u>any</u> *'New World Order'*

**9.9** Managerial Administrators – wishing to *'do a good job'* within <u>any</u> *'New World Order'*

**9.10** Media Propagandists – wishing to promote anti-Semitic values in <u>any</u> *'New World Order'*

**9.11** Complicit Supporters – wishing to secure a comfortable position within <u>any</u> *'New World Order'*

**9.12** *'Self-hating Jews'* – wishing to hide their Jewish identity and gain social acceptance within <u>any</u> *'New World Order'*

**9.13** Criminal Opportunists – wishing to find an outlet for their own thieving and murderous inclinations

In most of the above cases, the project to create a *'New World Order'* is used as a vehicle to gain power and a powerful sense of wellbeing – which often results from following a popular cause.

**10)** A common denominator found within most of the above groups is their view that Israel is an obstacle to them imposing their own idea of a perfect world. Israel's presence is viewed as a hindrance to Utopia. It doesn't *'fit in'* with their scheme of things. This means that, despite having different priorities, these groups will (either openly or tacitly) co-operate with one another in order to accomplish the destruction of the Jewish people. This would also suggest that, when it comes to an attempt to eliminate Israel, there will be a *'small minority'* who'll actively pursue it, a *'larger minority'* who'll desire it and a *'vast majority'* who'll casually accept it. This was the pattern followed in Nazi Germany and there's no reason why it shouldn't be repeated again on a global scale. All of the above *'groupings'* can be compared to towering storm clouds, all coalescing to form a hurricane of immense and devastating power.

**11)** A common motive found amongst active members is the desire to gain power and glory through the legitimization of each group's Utopian cause. (This desire can be known as *'The Haman Motive.'*) Just as the ambitious careerist Haman (in Esther 3) wished to gain power in the Royal Court of King Ahasuerus (through the destruction of the Persian Jewish Community) so these groups wish to do the same. Their aim is to gain power in their respective communities by destroying the Jewish people. Despite fluctuating socio-economic and political conditions, self-aggrandisement remains a consistent motive in anti-Semitism. A militant anti-Semite will kill Jews in order to secure a respected or powerful position within society.

**12)** The presence of semi-rational motives (like a desire for power or status) doesn't preclude the fact that, at the deepest level, anti-

Semitism represents an irrational and obsessive hatred, characterised by an insatiable desire to throw off the restraints represented by the moral teaching of the Mosaic Law. In essence, anti-Semitism is a manifestation of human lawlessness. This means that there is something extremely visceral about it, expressed in a deeply felt resentment against the God whom Israel represents. Consequently, any attempt to murder the Jewish people is often an attempt to murder the Deity. It's a case of genocide being used as a means to accomplish a longed-for Deicide.

**13)** The obsessive intensity of this irrational hatred means that it's impossible to argue or reason with militant anti-Semites – some of whom delight in wickedness simply for the sake of it. Any attempt to negotiate with them is usually taken as a sign of weakness. In relation to Israel this means that the so-called *'land for peace process'* is nothing more than a *'surrender to genocide process.'* It's a case of saying *"peace, peace where there is no peace,"* (Jeremiah 6:14 & 8:11).

**14)** Within Britain, the growing intensity of Jew-hatred at every level of society means that the policy of maintaining a dignified silence is no longer appropriate. An active policy of rebuttal must be followed in order to counter the avalanche of lies being told about Israel and the Jewish Community. This will involve clearly stating the dangerous consequences of anti-Semitism and its potential to add to the already dangerous instability in the Middle East. It will also involve exposing the fact that anti-Zionism is best viewed as nothing more than a new brand name for anti-Semitism. Although a proactive stance will not cure this pathological hatred it could serve to: -

**14.1** *'Buy time'* to prepare effective survival strategies
**14.2** Challenge the more thoughtful members of the British Public
**14.3** Expose the hypocrisy of many anti-Zionists
**14.4** Isolate the more active anti-Semites from their supporters
**14.5** Recognize that silence is not always the best way to respond to a militantly aggressive evil

All these points suggest that the growing tide of anti-Israeli hatred in this country could easily impinge upon <u>any</u> member of the Jewish

Community – no matter how *'integrated'* they may be. Such hatred will be encountered from more than one source. Secular members of the Anglo-Jewish community will be no less a target than their ultra-orthodox brethren who make a point of being different.[62]

## Section 3: An Escalating Hatred

**1)** You may wonder where all of this escalating hatred will end? My own view is that we could be heading for a regional Middle Eastern war, involving the use of nuclear weapons and possibly other weapons of mass destruction. Should, as now seems likely, the present upheavals in the Muslim World lead to a situation in which semi-rational thugs like Bashar al-Assad are replaced by totally irrational fanatics then Israel will move from a cold war type *'stand-off'* to a pre-war relationship with its Arab neighbours. This is because the new leadership will not be operating under such semi-rational motives as trying to establish a wealthy ruling dynasty with lucrative property investments in Mayfair. The rise of fanaticism in the aftermath of the Arab Spring indicates that <u>the underlying conflict in the Middle East is neither territorial nor political but is, in essence, religious.</u> In each of their sacred texts Judaism and Islam have mutually exclusive claims to the land. For most religious Jews the land has been given to Israel by God but to the Arabs the presence of Israel is an affront to the honour of Allah. Most so called *'peace moves'* flounder because they fail to consider this religious dimension (which is constantly being inflamed by a revival in fundamentalist forms of both Judaism and Islam.) Such *'peace moves'* are vain expedients, cobbled together by secular men, wholly failing to appreciate the passions that religious faith can arouse. They also seem oblivious to the geographical and demographic realities on the ground. This means that the proposed *'Two State Solution'* is an unworkable piece of nonsense. What could make the next major war so terrible is that <u>it will be a war of religious legitimization.</u> Fundamentalist rulers will feel impelled to try and eradicate Israel in order to legitimise their own

---

[62] My experience of working in the ultra Orthodox community would suggest that they have a far more realistic attitude toward anti-Semitism than their Reformed or Secular Jewish counterparts. Intellectually, I owe them a lot.

Faith and to further bolster their position within it. However, what they don't see is that, if faced with a choice between enduring another Auschwitz and inflicting a nuclear Masada, Israel is likely to take the latter option. The result will be many millions dead, severe disruption to oil supplies and a global economic depression for which the Jews will receive the blame. Played out will be the scenario described in my meditation: *'Memorial Cities.'* Ensuing anti-Semitic riots will force another exodus to Israel – thus compensating for any population losses suffered in the previously-mentioned war. Although she will narrowly survive the latest attempt to destroy her, a weakened Israel will have no choice but to accept the presence of external peacekeepers and she'll become once more an occupied land.[63] Because of the odium incurred Israel will be *"no longer numbered among the nations,"* (Numbers 23:9c). So this aforementioned next major war is likely to have a paradoxical effect – on the one hand it will force many Jewish people to return to the land; but on the other Israel will not be officially recognized as an independent *'Nation State.'* Another result of this situation will be an enormous spiritual vacuum, most likely to be filled by a deviant form of Christianity (which will be more dangerous than anything seen in Islam). Some of its leaders will put across a good pretence at being friendly with Israel but it will be a hollow charade. Strongly reinforced will be any hatred of what's perceived to be a religious fundamentalism. Also receiving a major boost will be any trend toward the formation of a *'One World Government.'* It will be viewed by many as a wonderful development and the correct thing to support.

**2)** Admittedly this scenario is speculative, but given the intractable nature of anti-Semitism, I can't see how the Middle East can go any other way. The suffering on both sides will be horrendous. It's sobering to recall that the last time anti-Jewish hatred reached this level the result was piles of smouldering corpses and they weren't just Jewish corpses either. More than once during the blitz my parents nearly met such a fate.

---

[63] This will possibly be under the *'mandate'* of an international body – either the UN or a successor Organization

## Section 4: Insights from Midrash

**1)** Midrash (Ancient Jewish methods of Bible Interpretation) will confirm that, whilst societies may change in terms of Socio-economic and technological developments, human nature does not. This means that it tends to re-cycle the same prejudices under a variety of (sometimes respectable-sounding) names. Hence, anti-Semitism is an evil that never sleeps; it can assume many different guises whilst preserving its essential nature. Like a virus it can mutate in order to adapt to widely different environments – and also spread like the plague once conditions are right. Yet despite its incredible adaptability the abiding aim of anti-Semitism remains the same – to kill all Jews, preferably in as cruel and degrading a manner as possible. This desire to murder every Jew represents its abiding *'constant.'* Although influenced in its expression by the societies in which it's embedded, anti-Semitism represents a deeply spiritual evil, which can neither be met by appeals to reason nor conscience. By definition, a hardened anti-Semite is irrational and in the matter of the Jews, simply has no conscience.

**2)** Particularly shameful is the anti-Semitism of the *'Left.'* The protest slogan *'We're all Hezbollah now'* during Israel's (admittedly bungled) incursion into South Lebanon during 2006 was especially sickening. Whereas a previous generation of *'Leftists'* had the courage to fight Fascism in places like Spain and Cable Street, London, this present generation all too eagerly embraces it. They are repeating the mistake of the German Communist Party before World War II and the Tudeh Party in Revolutionary Iran, (1979-1989). Like those Parties, present day *'Leftists'* are undermining Democracy at the price of reinforcing a burgeoning Totalitarianism. Such irresponsibility would suggest that the German Communist and Iranian Tudah Party members were amongst the more deserving victims of the Totalitarian regimes their own folly had helped to install. Any sympathy for their plight must be qualified by the fact that, if they <u>had</u> gained power, they too would have resorted to mass torture and murder. Present-day *'leftists'* have simply failed to learn from their own history. Neither can they see that those who ride a tiger usually end-up falling off and being eaten by it. Genuine socialists within the Anglo-Jewish Community can only be heartbroken by such a development.

**3)** Equally reprehensible has been the revival of anti-Semitism in many Churches. One can recall the resolution to boycott West Bank goods accepted by the 2010 Methodist Conference. The following meditation, *'The Sleep of Reason'* aptly sums up the moral and spiritual state of the United Kingdom (UK): -

*True faith has departed*
*Morality has collapsed*
*Decency has been abandoned*
*Reason has fallen into a restless sleep*
*Intellectuals display a pernicious hatred*
*Whilst the masses succumb to a dull apathy*
*Britain connives in a shameless evil and*
*Once more the Jews are deemed fit for elimination*
*Behold the old gods are back*
*And they greedily demand*
*A mass human sacrifice*

In this country, anti-Israeli forms of hatred could quickly reach psychotic levels and this means that any Jewish person or pro-Israeli sympathiser could be made subject to its malice. As the example of the Second World War has demonstrated, it's a hatred that's well able to spread to affect individuals and groups not previously linked to the Jewish community. As mentioned earlier, my parents were nearly bombed out of existence because a certain German Chancellor had been permitted to get away with his inflammatory Jew-hating stance. Their near death confirms that, when anti-Semitism is allowed to thrive *'we are all targets now.'* This grim reality would suggest that an active response is needed. The point is being reached when to be silent is to lend complicit support to Jew-hating lies. Also, if (in March 2014) the UK governing class was willing to abandon the Ukraine to Russian invaders because the British Economy needed commercial and financial links with Russia how much more would it be willing to abandon Israel because of even stronger links with the Arab world? For Israel, the Ukraine crisis sets an ominous precedent.

## Section 5: Recommended Action

**1)** Within Britain there is an emerging consensus desirous of (or at least willing to tolerate) the destruction of Israel. This consensus has profound implications for members of the Anglo-Jewish Community who currently hold a public position. A programme of action is needed based upon the assumption that being in a public position provides opportunities unavailable to others. Such action should contain the following steps, are applicable to members if the Jewish Community living in the UK: -

**Step 1:** Return to the roots of your faith because you're going to need all the spiritual resources you can get. Adhering to Judaism as an ethical system is one thing, employing it as a means to interpret the events around you is another. To do this effectively you'll need to read (and re-read) the sacred writings of Judaism and utilise Midrashic methods of interpreting them. I would, however, caution against any dabbling in the Kabbalah – not only can it be psychologically damaging, it also represents the importation of Eastern Pantheist thought-forms into Judaism and has as much to do with true Judaism as Baal Worship. It came into Judaism from Hinduism via Sufi Islam and Muslim Spain.

**Step 2:** Consider employing (either singularly or in combination) the following strategies: -

**Strategy 1:** Exercise a discreet *'behind the scenes'* influence to reinforce an already existing network of pro-Israel sympathisers, both inside and outside Parliament. This is important because the Jewish Community in this country will need all the friends it can get. In a Parliamentary context, it may well be necessary to privately point out to ministers that their stance on certain Middle Eastern issues is rather naive. The real challenge we face as a Nation is not to secure a lasting peace deal (one isn't possible) but to avoid being complicit in another attempt to destroy the Jewish people. Continuous attempts to impose a peace settlement will lead only to further destabilisation in an already volatile situation. What can best be hoped for is a continuation of the present *'cold'* peace. It displays a lack of realism to presume otherwise.

**Strategy 2:** Open confrontation in Parliament and/or the media. One line of argument that could be pursued is that, if it becomes acceptable to kill Jews then why isn't it acceptable to kill anybody? Clearly present here are echoes of the often used Palestinian Slogan *"First the Saturday people, then the Sunday people."* However, this approach is *'high risk'* and could provoke unpleasant opposition (it's easy to imagine the hate-mail that would be generated).

**Strategy 3:** Have, as a final back-up, the alternative of making a return to Israel. However, to do this it would be wise to have relevant resources in place – especially given the speed at which supposedly civilized societies can collapse into a *'Dark Age'* of barbarity, once conditions are right. The violent riots and mass looting which took place from Saturday 6th to Wednesday 10th August 2011 confirms that the veneer of civilization in our society has now worn extremely thin. Imagine the damage such rioters (with a little more organisation) could inflict upon unpopular minorities.

**2)** Whatever strategy (or combination of strategies) may be employed, it will be necessary to constantly recall that the main aim is the welfare of Israel and the Anglo-Jewish Community. The intention is to *'buy time'* and at least temporarily weaken the forces arrayed against Israel. Hopefully the *'media savvy'* American Jewish Community could provide some idea of the right tactics needed to best put forward the case for Israel before the British people. A greater number of sympathetic advocates are needed.

**3)** What would be most unwise is to repeat the mistake made by secular members of the early Twentieth Century German Jewish Community. They thought that safety lay in growing Kaiser Bill moustaches and being good patriotic citizens. It didn't! They were so comfortable being *'honouree gentiles'* that they failed to see that anti-Semitism is a hatred which can't be *'bought off.'* To an anti-Semite a Jew is a Jew no matter whether they wear the funny hats and side curls of the Orthodox Community or the neat suit of a high class member of society. In the case of many German Jews the road to annihilation lay through assimilation. I almost weep at the sufferings I see coming but I'm also profoundly disgusted at the way our Nation (and its useless, cowardly churches) is turning against the Jewish people. As a result I don't see things going at all well for our neo-pagan country. Britain's days of glory are over and what freedoms we once enjoyed are now fast being whittled away. We have to adapt to this grim reality.

## Section 6: Concluding Points

**1)** Although latent at present I believe that the growing anti-Semitism within British culture will force all members of the Anglo-Jewish Community (especially those in a public position) to choose between a policy of silence and one involving some form of firm stance. As previous contents have shown I don't believe that silence is a credible option to follow. As my visit to Auschwitz Birkenau amply demonstrated, ignoring an evil won't make it go away. After all, silence was a policy followed by the German Jewish Community just before Hitler rose to power and we all know where that led to. To quote an old saying, *"All that's needed for evil to thrive is for good men to remain silent."* In today's growing anti-Jewish climate such silence is tantamount to suicide.

**2)** The programme of action assumes that it's better to do something rather than nothing, even if the effect of that *'something'* is only temporary in holding back the tidal wave of hatred threatening to engulf Israel and the Global Jewish Community. I foresee that this cancerous hatred will have utterly tragic consequences (of the kind described in *'Memorial Cities.'*) The whole world will have to re-learn (the hard way) that anti-Semitism is one of the most pernicious and destructive hatreds known to Mankind. On a more positive note, I believe that the Jewish people will survive this next attempt to destroy them and that unexpected good will come out of this tragedy. Yet this doesn't preclude me from the obligation to do my part in alleviating its consequences. Present is a responsibility to facilitate such a preservation and this is precisely what I've tried to do. To paraphrase a quote from the Talmud (Mishnah Sanhedrin 4:5; Babylonian Talmud Tractate Sanhedrin 37a), *'To save a life is to save an entire world.'*

# WHEN EVIL COMES

## (A look at how evil can take over whole societies)

*This article looks at how the growing madness in Western Society is likely to have a negative impact upon vulnerable groups like the disabled. It followed from a personal reflection delivered to an audience attending an evening cultural event on Wednesday, 19th January 2013. The theme explored was 'disability' and such was the impact that three requests were made for paper copies and for greater clarification of some of the points. There were 13 (7 men and 6 women) at the original meeting, some of whom were suffering from disabilities themselves. They were well aware of how it felt to be on the 'sharp end' of bureaucratic oppression.*

## Section 1: A Warning from Auschwitz

**1)** Great evil rarely emerges bearing sharp fanged teeth or wearing a sinister black cape. Instead it can, (especially in its early stages) creep in almost imperceptibly, in the form of the anodyne ministerial statement, the secret decision taken behind closed doors or the attractive media personality. Evil can be compared to a colourless, odourless gas which slowly poisons its victims without them even being aware. It may assume many subtle (and even attractive) guises.

**2)** Great evils – like The Nazis' attempt to destroy Europe's Jewish population or the terror of the Soviet Gulags – need to be traced back to their origins. Such horrific evils as these began very slowly, gradually building up to reach a critical point where society (or significant sections within that society) willingly accepted them. Such evils were endorsed by either active perpetrators or (at the very least) by complicit sympathisers. If my visit to Auschwitz-Birkenau (in October 2011) had taught me one thing – it was this – that by the time *factories of death*' become established it's usually far too late to do anything. Evil will have gained such an iron grip that its removal could only be achieved through external forces (as happened with the Nazis) or by internal collapse because of its own corruption (as happened with Soviet Communism). Either way, millions will have perished in the most degrading of circumstances. Also, untold harm will have been inflicted upon the short and long-term socio-economic and psychological health of a given society. In Germany some scientific disciplines like physics never recovered from the persecution of the Jews.

**3)** Evil, if it's to be tackled at all, <u>must be challenged at an early stage before an *'Auschwitz Birkenau'* happens.</u> Should certain dehumanising trends within our own society be left unchallenged, then we may well see the systematic murder of millions. Auschwitz itself is a warning that the veneer of civilization only ever runs skin deep. A collapse into a degrading psychotic, mass barbarism can be all too easy.

## Section 2: Collective Desensitization

**1)** It's sobering to recall that the self-same *'collective desensitization'* (a necessary precursor for a major crime against humanity) is rapidly gaining a sinister momentum within so-called *'civilised'* nations. Already both the UK government and the media are labelling the disabled as *'shirkers'* or *'slackers'* or a *'burden on society.'* For years we've already had the term *'unwanted pregnancy'* and now we're appearing to be having *'unwanted elderly,'* *'unwanted disabled'* and *'unwanted whoever next is to be disposed of.'* Already present is a systematic misuse of language – another necessary precursor for a great evil to take place. In March 2012, an influential Oxford University Journal of Medical Ethics published an article advocating *'after birth abortions'* which involved giving lethal injections to healthy (as well as unhealthy) infants who were not wanted by their mother at birth. The clinical detachment in which this argument was presented was absolutely chilling. That same measure of detachment is also present in the Swiss-based euthanasia group, Dignitas which is willing to facilitate the administration of fatal poison to those *'suffering from a general weariness of life.'* Such a term could be widened to mean absolutely anything. Truly, we're dwelling in the world of George Orwell's *'Newspeak.'* In his novel entitled *'1984'* *'nice'* words like *'love'* and *'truth'* were used to disguise *'nasty'* realities whilst *'negative labelling'* was attached to potential target, groups – one being the term *'unperson,'* referring to someone who'd been killed by the state.

**2)** In the near-future we could well have a scenario in which the lives of the disabled will be made unbearable through *'Benefit'* cuts and general stigmatization. Having been *'forced into a corner'* they will then be pressurised into accepting a lethal injection – offered free on the NHS! Such a scenario makes the term *'cutback'* take on a fresh and sinister meaning. There were the scandals associated with the *'Liverpool Care Pathway'* (c.1999-2014) which involved depriving vital nutrients to those deemed incurably ill (which doesn't always turn out to be the case) – often without the consent of the patient or their relatives. Already, we're living in a society where hospital patients are being starved to death and they call it *'death with dignity!'* The Report into the abuses at the Stafford Hospital (February 2013) further underlines the extent to which this *'collective desensitization'* has taken place. Especially chilling has been the lack of accountability laid at the door of those desk-bound *'professionals'* who appear to have presided over the corporate manslaughter of hundreds of patients. These people are still holding high positions within the Health Service years after this appalling situation became public knowledge. Justice has been denied to the most vulnerable members of the community. Truly we appear to live in a society that's gone mad.

## Section 3: Downward Steps

**1)** To understand how *'collective desensitization'* can become a reality on a wide scale it may be helpful to know that a society undergoes a number of fairly distinctive *'downward steps'* before committing some great iniquity. The first step consists of a slow build up, lasting years or decades. A stigmatized *'out group'* is selected *e.g.* the Jews in pre-war Germany, the Kulaks (rich peasantry) in Stalin's Russia or the disabled in our own time. The next step is to create unpleasant associations with the *'out group'* by labelling them as *'exploiters,'* *'bloodsuckers'* or *'shirkers.'* This creates negative stereotypes of them in the public mind. Here a sinister *'Goebbels' law'* comes into play, which states; *"if you tell a big lie for long enough most people will end up believing it."* Over time, this produces the *'collective desensitization'* needed to move into the next phase; to inflict harm upon the stigmatized *'out group.'* At this point, things may escalate rapidly, moving from boycotts, legal restrictions and the severe curtailment of benefits to death in a gas van, mass executions in a remote forest and compulsory euthanasia. By this latter stage a vast bureaucratic apparatus of oppression will have been constructed. Its *'senior functionaries'* will wish to promote their own careerist interests, so keeping the *'wheels of terror'* in motion. These people will have become complicit in mass murder – their consciences steadily dulled as they blindly follow orders or simply, *'do what everyone else is doing.'* Once this dreadful point is reached, everyone can become a target. Amply vindicated here is the observation of the Soviet writer and poet Boris Pasternak (1890-1960)[64] regarding *'the inhuman power of the lie.'*

**2)** Represented here is an increasingly rapid *'movement of goalposts.'* What was unacceptable yesterday has become today's politically correct orthodoxy, soon to be enforced by the Law. Any *'rights'* and *'exemptions'* remain in place only so long as it's convenient to those tolerating them. An aggravating factor in Western Society has been the influence of Post Modern Relativism which allows for no *'fixed positions.'* *'Truth'* is viewed as being a matter of socially constructed opinion. Society (or more often the ruling powers within Society) may well decide that one *'truth'* should be replaced by another *'newer truth'* with *'special measures'* taken to eliminate the *'out group'* who had originally championed the *'old truth.'* When this happens a lethal consensus is created wherein the mass murder of a particular group becomes socially acceptable. This replacement of one *'truth'* by another can, with the help of social media, happen very rapidly. Already this process has occurred with regard to the redefinition of marriage that accompanied the passing of Same Sex Marriage Legislation in July 2013. (The first same sex marriage ceremonies were conducted on Saturday, 29th March 2014.)

### Section 4: A Toxic Mixture

**1)** How can a well-developed society take these dreadful steps to committing a great evil? Why has there been this growing *'collective*

---

[64] He was the author of the famous novel, Dr Zhivago

*desensitization'* within our Western Culture? Perhaps a starting point can be made by noting that a whole generation reared on violent computer games will have little compunction about casually tolerating the killing of others, so as long as their *'amusements'* remain untouched. Conceivably, such killings could well become a source of entertainment – just as they did throughout the Roman Empire. This latter example would confirm that evil is at its most powerful when it's been *'normalised.'* Arguably, there are already telling similarities between Western Culture and Ancient Greece and Rome, (Ferdinand Mount, 2010).

**2)** A current symptom of such *'normalisation'* has been the recent bland amorality of many senior political and media figures as exemplified by the *'cover up'* of the predatory antics of Jimmy Savile for over half a century. In the full glare of publicity, Savile was honoured as a *'Saint'* by Church and State alike. However, it was the BBC who gave him the sea to swim in. Without the opportunities provided for him by that Organization his behaviour, although still devastating to those involved, would have been greatly curtailed. He would have remained in obscurity as the disreputable Manager of a provincial Dance Hall.

**3)** More generally, there now exists the same *'toxic mix'* of cultural decadence, psychological disorientation, economic volatility, discredited politico-religious leadership and linguistic manipulation as was present in 1930's Weimar Germany (shortly before Hitler's rise to power in January 1933). Also in place is an external threat posed by a militant, terror-based ideology; Communism in pre-war Germany and militant Islam today. With regard to class structure Western Society boasts a combination of an arrogant (and out of touch) ruling class, an insecure middle class and a working class blighted by mass unemployment. Again, this mirrors pre-war Germany before Hitler's meteoric rise to power. The Weimar Republic was bankrupt and rapidly developed a moral-spiritual vacuum which could be exploited by anyone with the determination and opportunity to do so. It seems that now, in the West (as with Weimar Germany) a perfect storm is brewing. The West is only *'one* *great economic depression'* away from a complete socio-economic breakdown, so often the pre-cursor for the legitimization of crimes against humanity. (Some countries like Greece, Cyprus and Spain are already into *'great depression'* territory.) The West as a whole hovered on the edge of such a scenario following the banking crash of September 2008.

## Section 5: A Dark Energy

**1)** The Savile affair exposed the foul well of corruption present within our society, examples of which have come to light in the financial, political and media sectors. It also demonstrated that evil can acquire *a 'dark energy'* all of its own – akin to that which drove some of the worst atrocities in human history. As a Social Scientist and History Teacher I believe that, within the Western World, this *'energy'* is reaching a *'critical mass'* where it could spread like a wild fire. Consequently, it seems highly likely that <u>we could be in serious danger of seeing the rise of a mass extermination society which will have the potential to devastate the lives of millions.</u> As has already been demonstrated, significant indicators suggest that this is the case. The warning lights are flashing amber, if not red.

**2)** Already Britain's financial, political and media elites appear to be suffering from a growing mental and moral derangement. They are becoming increasingly detached from reality, presuming that they can abolish all moral constraints without there being any unpleasant consequences in terms of public disorder and a serious rise in social problems (*e.g.* alcohol abuse). Successive governments in the Western World are <u>also</u> adopting the same destructive policies in the vain hope of a different and more positive outcome; their capacity for delusion knows no bounds. One noticeable example of this trend is the current obsessive attempt to advocate greater European integration, in spite of the fact that previous attempts have already turned countries like Greece into an economic wasteland.

**3)** Sadly, modern communication has served only to further accelerate and amplify this whole process of derangement, ensuring a greater possibility of whole societies going insane very rapidly. It's not simply a case of shifting the goal posts, but of blasting them out of the way altogether! The West is comprised of a decadent civilization, held together by a fragile prosperity; and should that collapse then anything becomes possible.

### Section 6: A Realistic Stance

**1)** So what of those who are intuitively discerning a *'downward shift'* in the West's moral compass? Perhaps one useful and realistic stance would be to view evil as being something wholly mutable and beguiling, with all manner of appealing and seductive qualities. Evil can be slickly presented by many plausible advocates with a capacity to dupe whole swathes of people. Indeed, evil is never more dangerous than when it masquerades as a form of *'enlightenment,'* (which, in revolutionary France led to many receiving a *'close shave'* from Madame de la Guillotine). When this happens whole nation states can fall into a collective psychosis which is characterised by extreme violence and a growing detachment from reality. This leads to the assumption that every moral barrier can be torn down and flung away without producing painful consequences. If euthanasia is legalised with the same speed and determination as Same Sex Marriages then we could quickly find ourselves in a mass extermination society. This was a point that appears to have gone unnoticed amidst the furore of the Same Sex Marriage debate. Present is a grim logic which says, *'first Same Sex Marriages and then mass Euthanasia.'* This already appears to have been the path trodden by countries like Belgium which in February 2014 legalised the euthanasia of children (just a decade after it had legalised same sex marriages). Arguably, both pieces of legislation are symptoms of a growing mass psychosis which has the potential to consume the lives of millions. Personally, I believe that within a generation the Western World could produce horrors to rival those I saw in Auschwitz. Such a development I'd find horrifying but I wouldn't be surprised by it.

**2)** One needn't be an Adolf Hitler, a Joseph Stalin, or a Jimmy Savile to become a member of the evil *'Hall of Fame.'* Evil can quietly build up through a succession of petty misdemeanours or just a plain and callous indifference to the needs of others. Also, evil lies in an unquestioning acceptance and conformity to the values and dictates of an increasingly brutalized society. Petty careerism and a desire to *'get on'* in life (again with little care paid to the needs of others) can be just as devastating. Contributing to the formation of a great evil will be one of the easiest things to do in this life. <u>Not</u> to ask questions and to passively accept everything the media portrays is a sure way to allow evil to have its way. It's such apparently *'little'* shortcomings which provide the bedrock upon which a mass extermination society may develop. Unwillingness to counter requests made by those in positions of authority is clearly seen in the *'conformity'* experiments of Stanley Milgram (1963) and Philip Zimbardo (1971). They provided quantifiable evidence, showing that the majority of psychologically normal people could commit acts of torture and murder, once the conditions were right. To become either an actual or a *'desk'* murderer is very easy. We must never lose sight of our own personal vulnerability to the fatal enticements of evil.

## Section 7: Upward Steps

**1)** Once a realistic stance has been adopted and we <u>do</u> become aware of our fatal attraction to evil we need to react in a way that will be constructive and helpful to others. We are not to give way to suicidal despair, nor to seek solace in some tawdry TV *'soap opera'* (or a Jane Austin costume drama should one's tastes be more refined). A far better way is <u>to use what freedoms remain to us and to take a definite and firm stand.</u> After all if we are going to be earmarked for destruction we might as well go down fighting.

**2)** The first thing to do is <u>to emancipate ourselves from a blind conformity</u> by not unquestionably imbibing everything the media (or others with a predetermined agenda) gives us. We're to use our minds and the wonderful faculty of *'common sense'* in order to <u>question everything</u>. We should be especially aware of any attempt to *'single out'* a particular group for vilification, in either a subtle or an overt manner. We're to emancipate ourselves from *'the inhuman power of the* *lie*[65] and to take encouragement from others who did the same when confronted with totalitarian propaganda. One example of such defiance was provided by the Russian Writer Alexander Solzhenitsyn (1918-2008) who endured eight years in Soviet labour camps (1945-1953). During his 1970 Nobel Prize speech, he chose to quote a Russian Proverb which read *'one drop of truth can outweigh an ocean of lies.'*

**3)** Secondly, we must find and remain true to a *'value system'* that offers a healthy alternative to the one currently operating within our society. It's not for me to advocate one particular value system – as mature adults we need to make our own choice. However, a salutary note of caution needs to be sounded – <u>never accept a value system based solely upon the word of some authority figure like a Priest, a professor or a Guru.</u> The best policy is to trace the system to its original source <u>and only then</u> to decide whether it represents a valid means of navigating the storms of life. It needs to be rationally thought-through, because in stressful times it's all too easy to *'latch onto'* something for reasons of emotional security. Millions of people in pre-war Germany did just this (when they gave their allegiance to Hitler) only later to reap devastating results. When a charismatic leader gives a nodding assent to the extermination of those deemed not fit to live, it's rather too late to consider that they may not always have been what they originally appeared. In Hitler's case, the charismatic power he displayed had an uncanny ability to make people feel very good about taking a fatally misguided and criminal direction, (Rees 2012). When it suited him Hitler could be very charming and persuasive. His case confirms the earlier point that evil is never more dangerous than when it masquerades as some form of enlightenment and/or emancipation. A psychopath knows how to be persuasive and smile in a friendly and winsome way; having a talent to *'ape'* an emotion without necessarily feeling it.

**4)** Thirdly, when and wherever possible, be a voice of dissent. State your point but be tactful – don't alienate people unnecessarily. Ensure you know your facts lest you expose yourself to ridicule.

---

[65] A phrase attributed to the Russian writer Boris Pasternak (1890-1960)

However, should you fulfil this role you will have done much to *'chip away'* at this blind conformity which allows evil so much free reign. Get people to think, appeal to their conscience (or common sense), and know when to be diplomatic, but also when to be confrontational. As the studies of Zimbardo have shown, <u>dissent is one of the best ways to limit abuse.</u>

**5)** Remember to take *'time out'* and rest by doing something creative and/or relaxing. Not only will this prevent *'burn out,'* but will give the needed strength to challenge apathetic conformity to evil. Beware of focussing exclusively on the negative – especially on the Internet. If already depressed, then spending wasteful hours trawling through a web site showing (in great detail) how the *'Worshipful Guild of Pork Butchers in Harrogate'* is planning to take over the world through nefarious means would really not be helpful.[66] Yes – all of this may well be *'tongue in cheek'* but anything that continuously fills our minds with a hate-filled paranoia is to be avoided, especially if we have issues regarding our own physical or mental health. We need to be informed – but not so well-informed that it destroys our sense of wellbeing. There is a definite need for balance.

## *Section 8: A Reason for Living*

**1)** As our society spirals downward it will be necessary to think of a good reason for living. What this reason is will vary from one person to the next. It may be the desire to spite the *'powers that be'* just by going on living, or it could be because of some personal relationship or creative interest. Whatever the reason <u>use it to carry on living on a day-by-day basis.</u> Also, remember that to give up in despair is to give the negative elements of society exactly what they wanted, a DIY euthanasia. Where possible, avoid isolation and get out amongst people whose company you enjoy. Being alone for a protracted period of time can allow all sorts of things to prey on the mind.

---

[66] Note how *'pork'* is a symbol of *'unclean influences,'* *'butchery'* a symbol of *'death'* and *'Harrogate'* a symbol of *'the arrogance produced by wealth gained through living on a Ley Line.'* The title *'worshipful'* must mean something especially sinister, perhaps implying a link with the Freemasons or even the Pope! As can be seen in this *'overplayed'* and ridiculous example, the whole thing can so easily get out of hand.

**2)** Should you have a creative bent then seriously consider exploring some of the themes mentioned here. Put into effect (in whatever art or literary form you'd care to use) the theme of a civilization's collapse into a mindless barbarity. This weighty subject really is something to stir the emotions and get the creative juices going. Here is a *'grand'* theme, worthy of a Dickens, a Tolstoy or a Solzhenitsyn. Should you have the stamina, skills and opportunity to do so then consider developing such a legacy to pass on to future generations. Let them know exactly what sort of social mindset led to a whole civilization's collapse. A related theme (that's also worth exploring) is the immense shift in perspective currently taking place within contemporary society. Despite a great deal of exaggeration and plain silliness those who are involved in what may be loosely termed the *'New Age Movement,'* are not altogether wrong in pointing out that some sort of *'paradigm shift'* really is taking place. The outcome of this fascinating process remains to be seen but it's certainly one with the potential to stir the *'muse.'* The presence of such far-reaching issues means that we devalue our own craft as artist, writer or poet if, at a mature age, we've managed nothing more than to write about sexual frustration, suicide and the local pub. The times we live in demand a widening of our horizons and a willingness to pass on what we've learnt to future generations.

**3)** In the end, whilst we're unlikely ever to be in a position to change the whole of society we can at least influence those around us; we can contribute to small-scale changes (which may well lead to more significant ones.) Although we cannot do everything, *'to do something'* is still far better than *'doing nothing.'* After all – if we who see there's a problem don't speak out or act, then who will?

### Section 9: Summary

In summary, it's reasonable to conclude that: -

**1)** A great evil may develop slowly and insidiously within a society. It's often too late to deal with such an evil when it's got to the stage of producing an *'Auschwitz.'* Consequently, evil is best tackled in its earlier, emergent stage(s).

**2)** A growing indifference to the needs of others (often associated with a systematic misuse of language) is a precursor for a greater evil to take hold on a society.

**3)** Before committing a great crime against humanity a society often follows a process characterised by: -

**3.1** The selection of an already unpopular *'out-group'*

**3.2** Vilification of the selected *'out-group'* (in order to make their persecution acceptable)

**3.3** Harming the selected *'out-group'* who may be specifically targeted for extermination

**3.4** Constructing a self-perpetuating bureaucracy which may eventually target anyone it deems as *'unfit for existence.'*

**4)** A mass extermination society may emanate from a combination of factors, including: -

**4.1** Cultural decadence

**4.2** Widespread psychological disorientation

**4.3** Economic volatility and insecurity

**4.4** A failure in political and religious leadership

**4.5** Growing class division

**4.6** Mass unemployment

**4.7** An external threat posed by a terror-based ideology

**4.8** A spiritual vacuum with a growing demand for authoritative answers

**4.9** The presence of an unpopular *'out-group'* to vilify and put forward as a convenient scapegoat

**5)** Evil possesses its own *'dark energy'* which: -

**5.1** Assumes different guises to attract all sorts of people

**5.2** Often masquerades as an acceptable form of *'enlightenment'* and/emancipation

**5.3** Is amplified and speedily propagated by the use of modern technology

**5.4** Constantly moves (or totally eliminates) the boundaries between what is and (and what is not) morally acceptable
**5.5** Has a highly seductive power
**5.6** Orchestrates major crimes against humanity
**5.7** Can t reach a *'critical point'* when it's capable of taking over whole societies

**6)** In response to negative cultural developments it's necessary to adopt a stance of stoic realism, knowing that: -
**6.1** Evil is never more dangerous than when it assumes the guise of enlightenment and/or emancipation
**6.2** Evil is built up through the petty misdemeanours of which we're all capable
**6.3** No one is immune from the attractions of evil

**7)** Positive steps to counter evil are to: -
**7.1** Avoid blind conformity
**7.2** Adopt an alternative *'value system'*
**7.3** Be a *'voice of dissent'* whenever and wherever possible
**7.4** Avoid filling one's mind with negative influences

**8)** It's also helpful to: -
**8.1** Find a positive reason for living
**8.2** Accept that *'to do something'* is better than *'doing nothing'*

# POSTSCRIPT: ENDPOINT

Mission accomplished
Aims fulfilled
Warnings delivered
Work done
Targets met
Tasks completed


The endpoint has been reached
The blood of an unruly people is no longer on my hands[67]
Today I rest
Tomorrow, I'll write some more poetry[68]

---

[67] Ezekiel 3:18 & 33:6
[68] This was written on Friday, 6th July 2012 during a time of torrential rain which caused flash-flooding throughout the United Kingdom

# FURTHER READING

# B1) Booklist

## B1.1: On World Views

Mount Ferdinand (2010)
*Full Circle:*
*How the Classical World Came Back To Us*
Simon and Schuster
ISBN: 978-1-84737-798-2

Overmann Christian (1996)
*Assumptions That Affect Our Lives*
Published by Micah 6:8
ISBN: 1883035-50-6

Sire W. James (1997)
*The Universe Next Door*
*A Guide to World Views*
IVP
ISBN: 0-85111-188-2

Wolters M. Albert (1985)
*Creation Regained:*
*A Transforming View of the World*
IVP
ISBN: 85110-757-5

## B1.2: On the Collapse of Western Christianity

Brierley Peter Dr (2000)
*The Tide Is Running Out*
Christian Research
ISBN: 1-85321-137-0

Brierley Peter Dr (2006)
*Pulling Out Of the Nosedive:*
*A Contemporary Picture of Churchgoing:*
*What the 2005 English Church Census Reveals*
Christian Research
ISBN: 1-85321-168-3

Brown G. Callum (2001)
*The Death of Christian Britain*
Routledge
ISBN: 0-415-284-7

Bruce Steve (2002)
*God Is Dead:*
*Secularisation in the West*
Blackwell Publishing
ISBN: 0-631-23275-3

Campbell Colin (2007)
*The Easternisation of the West:*
*A Thematic Cultural Change in the Modern Age*
Paradigm Publishers
ISBN: 978-1-59451-224-7

Galbraith Kenneth John (1953- Penguin Edition 1992)
*The Great Crash of 1929*
Penguin
ISBN: 978-0-14-013609-8

Hitchens Peter (2009)
*The Broken Compass:*
*How British Politics Lost its Way*
Continuum
ISBN: 978-1-84706-405-9

Moreton Cole (2010)
*Is God Still An Englishman?*
*How We Lost Our Faith (But Found New Soul)*
Little Brown
ISBN: 978-1-4087-0180-5

Mount Ferdinand (2010)
*Full Circle:*
*How the Classical World Came Back To Us*
Simon and Schuster
ISBN: 978-1-84737-798-2

Phillips Melanie (2010)
*The World Turned Upside Down:*
*The Global Battle over God, truth, and power*
Encounter Books
ISBN: 978-1-59403-375-9 486

Whitehouse Mary (1977)
*Whatever Happened to Sex?*
Wayland Publishers Ltd

Zimbardo Philip (2007)
*The Lucifer Effect:*
*How Good People Turn Evil*
Rider ISBN: 978-1-84-413577-6

## B1.3: On World Wars, Weimar Germany and Nazism

Bosteridge Mark (2014)
*The Fateful Year:*
*England 1914*
Viking
ISBN: 978-0-670-91921-5

Bonhoeffer Dietrich (1978)
*Life together*
SCM
ISBN: 334-00904-9

Evans E. Suzanne (2007)
*Hitler's Forgotten Victims:*
*The Holocaust and the Disabled*
Tempus Publishing Ltd
ISBN: 978-0-7524-4175-7

Hersh Arek (1998)
*A Detail of History*
Beth Shalom
ISBN: 1-900381-06-0

Heschel Susannah (2008)
*The Aryan Jesus:*
*Christian Theologians and the Bible in Nazi Germany*
Princeton University Press
ISBN13: 978-0-691-12531-2

Rees Laurence (1997)
*The Nazis:*
*A Warning from History*
BBC
ISBN: 0-563-38704

Rees Laurence (2012)
*The Dark Charisma of Adolf Hitler*
*Leading Millions into the Abyss*
Edbury Press
ISBN: 978-0-09191-763-0

Robertson Edwin (1987)
*The Shame and the Sacrifice:*
*The Life and Preaching of Dietrich Bonhoeffer*
Hodder and Stoughton
ISBN: 0-340-41063-9

Sturmer Michael (1999)
*The German Century*
Weidenfeld & Nicolson
ISBN: 0-2978-2524-0

## B2) Articles & Lectures

Cook Michael (2011)
*Where is the worst place in the world to be a doctor?*
MercatorNet

Connolly Kate (2012)
*Dutch mobile euthanasia units to make house calls:*
*New scheme called 'Life End' will respond to sick people whose own doctors have*
*refused to help them end their lives at home*
Guardian.co.uk Thursday, 1st March 2012

Giubilini Alberto and Minerva Francesca (2012)
*After-birth abortion: why should the baby live?*
JME Online First, published on Friday, 2nd March 2012 as
10.1136/medethics-2011-10041

Kelly Tom and Fagge Nick (2011)
*Dr Death suicide film being shown in schools: Euthanasia fanatic gives workshop*
*on how to kill yourself in educational video for 14-year-olds*
Daily Mail, Saturday, 16th April 2011

Muggeridge Malcolm (1966)
*The Great Liberal Death Wish*
New Statesman, 11th March 1966
(For replies to Muggeridge's article please refer to the Letters Column of the New Statesman 18th March 1966)

Thomas Liz (2011)
*BBC accused of being 'cheerleader for assisted suicide' after filming man killing himself in Terry Pratchett documentary*
Daily Mail, Friday 15th April 2011

Reicher Stephen, Haslam Alexander S. and Rath Rakshi (2008)
*Making a Virtue of Evil:*
*A Five-Step Social Identity Model of the Development of Collective Hate*
Social and Personality Psychology Compass 2/3 (2008): 1313–1344, 10.1111/j.1751-9004.2008.00113.x
http://bbcprisonstudy.org/pdfs/SPPC%20%282008%29%20Evil%20and%20hate.pdf (Retrieved Thursday 21/2/2013)

Solzhenitsyn Alexander (1970)
*Nobel Lecture*
http://www.nobelprize.org/nobel_prizes/literature/laureates/1970/solzhenitsyn-lecture.html (Accessed Monday, 11/2/2013)

Unattributed (2014)
*Belgium's parliament votes through child euthanasia*
BBC News Thursday, 13/2/2014
http://www.bbc.co.uk/news/world-europe-26181615 (Accessed Thursday, 27/3/2014)

Unattributed (2014)
*Children's euthanasia bill signed by Belgium king*
Reuters News Agency Monday, 3/3/2014
http://rt.com/news/belgium-king-sign-euthanasia-bill-566/
(Accessed Thursday, 27/3/2014)

Unattributed (2014)
*UK storms leave thousands without power and destroys railway line*
BBC News Wednesday, 5/2/2014
http://www.bbc.co.uk/news/uk-26044073
(Accessed Thursday, 27/3/2014)

Woolf Marie (2014)
*Companies Refusing to cater for Gay Weddings Face Prosecution*
The Sunday Times Sunday, 31st March 2014

## B3) Web Sites

http://en.wikipedia.org/wiki/Eugenics
http://blogs.bmj.com/medical-ethics/2012/02/28/liberals-are-disgusting-in-defence-of-the-publication-of-after-birth-abortion/
(Retrieved Wednesday, 7/3/2012)

http://en.wikipedia.org/wiki/Eugenics
(Retrieved, Thursday, 19/5/2011)

http://en.wikipedia.org/wiki/Julian_Savulescu
(Retrieved Wednesday, 7/3/2012)

http://jme.bmj.com/content/early/2012/03/01/medethics-2011-100411.abstract#aff-1
(Retrieved Wednesday, 7/3/2012)

http://jme.bmj.com/content/early/2012/03/01/medethics-2011-100411.full.pdf+html
(Retrieved Wednesday, 7/3/2012)

http://www.dailymail.co.uk/news/article-1377062/BBC-accused-cheerleader-assisted-suicide-Terry-Pratchett-documentary.html#ixzz1ZCF2fNTq
(Retrieved Monday, 18/4/2011)

http://www.dailymail.co.uk/news/article-1377412/Dr-Philip-Nitschke-gives-euthanasia-workshop-video-14-year-olds.html#ixzz1ZCDAQOua
(Retrieved Monday, 18/4/2011)

http://www.dailymail.co.uk/news/article-2108433/Doctors-right-kill-unwanted-disabled-babies-birth-real-person-claims-Oxford-academic.html?printingPage=true
(Retrieved Wednesday, 7/3/2012)

http://www.guardian.co.uk/world/2012/mar/01/dutch-mobile-euthanasia-units
(Retrieved Thursday, 22/3/2012)

http://www.mercatornet.com/articles/view/where_is_the_worst_place_in_the_world_to_be_a_doctor
(Retrieved Wednesday, 21/9/2011)

http://www.telegraph.co.uk/health/healthnews/9113394/Killing-babies-no-different-from-abortion-experts-say.html
(Retrieved Wednesday, 7/3/2012)

http://www.theblaze.com/stories/yes-we-are-serious-ethicists-defend-after-birth-abortion-argument-in-raucous-radio-interview/
(Retrieved Thursday, 22/3/2012)

## B4) Television Programmes

Prachett Terry
*Choosing To Die'*
BBC2 Broadcast on Monday, 13th June 2011 from 9.00-10.00 pm

*Choosing to Die Debate'*
BBC2 Broadcast on Monday, 13th June 2011 from 10.00-10.30 pm

# Notes

www.ingramcontent.com/pod-product-compliance
Lightning Source LLC
Chambersburg PA
CBHW032137270626

47172CB00008B/167